Praise for *Kat*

'This is an amazing book for more than (50-plus years it is still incredibly readabl Taylor's writing, conveying a message ~~that is~~
– Dries Brunt, *The Citizen*

'Kathie is a far ranging and moving novel.'
– Shirley Kossick, *Cape Times*

'This gem from Taylor is being heralded as a genuine literary find. A must-read.'
– *City Press*

'The story of Kathie is a remarkable one.'
– Rebekah Kendal

'Affecting and striking'
– Shirley Kossick, *People's Post*

'Kathie is a remarkable novel.'
– Meneesha Govender, *The Daily News*

Praise for *Don't Tread On My Dreams*:

'Through her impressive ability to evocatively describe the people and places in such beautiful detail, Taylor manages to transport the reader back to a South Africa that meant different things to each of us who lived through the old regime.'
– *City Press*

'While the overall tenor of these stories is sad and often tragic, there are many moments of ironic wit and humour.'
– Shirley Kossick, *People's Post*

RAGE OF LIFE

DORA TAYLOR

Edited by Sheila Belshaw

PENGUIN BOOKS

PENGUIN BOOKS

Published by the Penguin Group
Penguin Books (South Africa) (Pty) Ltd, 24 Sturdee Avenue, Rosebank,
Johannesburg 2196, South Africa
Penguin Group (USA) Inc, 375 Hudson Street, New York, New York 10014, USA
Penguin Group (Canada), 90 Eglinton Avenue East, Suite 700, Toronto, Ontario,
Canada M4P 2Y3 (a division of Pearson Penguin Canada Inc)
Penguin Books Ltd, 80 Strand, London WC2R 0RL, England
Penguin Ireland, 25 St Stephen's Green, Dublin 2, Ireland (a division of
Penguin Books Ltd)
Penguin Group (Australia), 250 Camberwell Road, Camberwell, Victoria 3124,
Australia (a division of Pearson Australia Group Pty Ltd)
Penguin Books India Pvt Ltd, 11 Community Centre, Panchsheel Park, New
Delhi – 110 017, India
Penguin Group (NZ), 67 Apollo Drive, Mairangi Bay, Auckland 1310, New
Zealand (a division of Pearson New Zealand Ltd)

Penguin Books (South Africa) (Pty) Ltd, Registered Offices:
24 Sturdee Avenue, Rosebank, Johannesburg 2196, South Africa

www.penguinbooks.co.za

First published by Penguin Books (South Africa) (Pty) Ltd 2009

ISBN 9780143025610

Typeset by Nix Design
Cover design: Marius Roux
Front cover photograph: Gavin Furlonger / PAPA Collection
Printed and bound by CTP Printers, Cape Town

Throughout her life Dora Taylor worked passionately to
gain human rights for the people of
South Africa – a dream she never gave up

Quoting from her diary, Dora dedicated all her writing:

'To and for the people'

Oft have I pondered in the night's silence
Dry-eyed,
Wide-eyed in the whirling dark
Of all that man suffers between waking
and sleep,
Between the hour of innocent birth
And stark death,
Vanishing, empty-handed,
Strengthless as a shadow,
Alone in his going, as he came,
Alone.

Wakeful in the cold dawn,
Hugging thought in my bones
To keep them warm,
I have found strength in weakness,
In all that man dreams and endures;
Man born of woman,
So ardent of living,
Sap-rich as earth
And hungry as the sea;
So full of trust,
So full of despairing,
A creature compounded
Of weakness and strength,
Of dust and fire.

An old tale of forgotten times,
Old and eternally new,
As long as the human heart beats
And is always young,
Loving a tale of love and sorrow,
Its own youth remembering.

'Tristan and Iseult', Dora Taylor

One

Linda Malindi was born and bred in Sophiatown. Every bone and tissue of her, every manner, every thought, every idea and every expectation was fashioned in that urban township, that seething pot of humanity, that compost heap flung outside the city confines and left to stew with the hot stinking manure of poverty and vice, violent, full of death, yet heaving with the ferment of an irrepressible vitality.

To be sure, Sophiatown claimed the status of urban township, and as such prided itself on certain freedoms, more especially to go to the devil faster than all the rest of the vast litter of locations and townships spawned by the mother-body, Johannesburg; she who had sprung up on the Witwatersrand: fabulous Ridge of White Waters of the High Veld – the City of Gold. Or Goli, as the Africans call it.

It wasn't one of your black townships proper, those conglomerations of dwellings barricaded with barbed wire fences and uniformed officials who night and day keep a check on all who enter within its gates. Still less was it one of the newer whitewashed variety made up of row upon row of concrete boxes. Nor was it one of your shanty towns of sacking and scrap iron, monstrous mushroom growths shooting up overnight on the bare veld.

No, Linda Malindi's Sophiatown had a contemptuous disregard for uniformity. Africans from many parts of southern Africa, Indians from the Natal Province, coloured folk from the Cape Province at the southernmost tip of the continent, together with an odd sprinkling of Chinese and even a few white bohemians eager to sample the eccentricities of the infamous New York of South Africa, existed perforce cheek by jowl in dwellings as varied as their occupants.

The respectable poor, the destitute and the desperate made up a turbulent assortment: the sober-coated black minister and the tsotsi flaunting his tight trousers and his flashy girlfriend; the sleek-oiled Indian shopkeeper, hated by the blacks because he sucked their last penny out of them for the bare necessities of their diet; the illicit liquor-seller and the humble washerwoman; the teacher armed with his leather briefcase and the devil of a taxi-driver throwing up a rain of filthy dust and blasting on his horn as he passes; the writer, the artist, the jazz musician keeping the pulse of Sophiatown beating to his effervescent rhythm; the gangster with his gun and his Cadillac – a vibrant multicultural cauldron of humanity.

Solid brick houses with gaudily painted pillars stood out amid a confusion of tumbledown shacks. Something less than builders' refuse did duty for many dwellings, which had spread like a measle rash obliterating a child's healthy skin. Rusty corrugated iron was all-pervading, in roofs, walls, doorways and dustbins. Slum-yards – nothing more than human warrens with waterless, foul-smelling latrines lined up opposite one another as for some obscene dance in scrap iron.

A house ordinarily suggests shelter and security, a place to relax with family and friends after the day's work – in a word, home. But this region of desperate makeshift suggested more of exposure than protection, of denudation rather than shelter, a dismal denial of privacy and peace.

Dingy garments flapped against windowless iron walls; starve-ling dogs, tails drooping, competed with the children and the flies scavenging in the refuse dump; spindle-legged, pot-bellied, snotty-nosed toddlers played in pockets of winter-dry dust, where in summer the torrential rains carved out miniature dongas; at a street corner squatted a group of gambling young tsotsis, their expressions daredevil, yet secretive, watchful, while at the opposite corner rose the foreshortened steeple of a church – easily the best building in the vicinity.

This was Sophiatown, a place dear to Linda Malindi. For she knew no other. Sometimes known as Kofifi, it had sprung from the same ferocious needs of a modern industrial city that had thrust its non-white workers to live outside the City of Gold itself, but near enough to minister to its insatiable demands. While the machines consumed human life, men and women consumed one another in the township jungle. The empty dead body found sprawling in an alleyway in the early morning was swept up with the refuse spilling over the bursting dustbins.

Linda's real name was Lindeka, though everyone called her Linda and that's how she thought of herself too. Besides, you didn't go around telling your real name when you were looking for a job as nursemaid in Goli. They called her Fanny, and it was all the same to her what they called her. It was all the same, too, to the white mistresses who employed her. Fanny or Lena or Clara or Sara, they took their choice and she didn't bother to correct them. Afterwards she always wanted to laugh when she thought of herself as the prim nursemaid in uniform. Nanny, or was it Fanny? That had been the year before her mother died, when she was only fifteen and didn't know any better. In fact it had all been her mother's fault; she wanted her daughter to be a nursemaid because she fancied it was a respectable way of earning a living. Not like charring. She herself had been a char cleaning offices in the city ever since she had come up from a reserve in the Eastern Transvaal, a bewildered country girl. Charring was back-breaking. It was soul-killing, said Linda's mother. She would never wish a daughter of hers to be a char. Never. But was being a nursemaid any better? A nursemaid's job – respectable? Her mother must be kidding herself. The golden-haired brats you had to look after learned to spit 'kaffir' at you while they were still dirtying their pants and you had to wash the dirt out. They kicked your shins when their mother wasn't looking and bawled murder when you gave them a good kick back.

Her mother didn't know what she was talking about. She had no pride. That was her trouble. She was still living in what some folks called the good old days – good, like hell – and she didn't know times had changed. Linda used to fight her mother like a cat, until she started crying and that made her madder than ever. No more of the nursemaid business. She flatly refused. Of course she would have to look round for some way to make money. A girl wanted decent clothes, and lots of other things, things you could never get on a nursemaid's miserable wages. Linda Malindi loved nice clothes.

But the following year her mother died. It was just as well the sixteen-year-old Linda was a bright girl and had learned early to fight back whenever anybody tried to play her a dirty trick. Her father vanished into jail only a week before her mother died, the devil knew what for, because he'd always been one who went out of his way to avoid trouble with the police. It was then that her mother gave up. She turned her face to the wall – where Linda had stuck the pictures of film stars to hide the cracks – and gave up her breath without any fuss. Linda got a fright in the morning, putting her hand out to shake her mother – she had never known her to lie so late – and encountering an ice-cold hand. She ran to the jail with the news, but was told that her father had been taken off in a lorry-load of prisoners to a farm-jail in the country. Nobody could tell her where. She hadn't seen or heard of him since.

She'd once had a big brother, too. Joel was his name, but not his real name. His real name was Sipho, though even Linda got into the way of calling him Joel. That was what everybody called him in the yard where they lived and in the streets where he'd played as a kid. Linda thought he was a great guy. She loved him. He was her hero. He would often bring her presents. Maybe it was a bit of jewellery or a gay bit of cloth for a skirt. He'd come into the room at supper time and tell her to shut her eyes and open her mouth. Then he'd roar with laughter at his sister standing gaping there like a ninny, while their mother looked on, smiling. Of course Linda would risk shutting her eyes for him. He was the only one she did trust, anywhere. She remembered one night feeling a cold hard thing in her hand, opening her eyes and gasping at the trinket glittering in her palm, a big red stone gleaming in the centre of polished metal with a chain to go round her neck. She had rushed at him, hugging and nearly choking him; and he had laughed at first and then pushed her roughly from him. For some reason her mother spoiled everything by starting to tell him off, saying she was an honest woman trying to bring up her children the way they ought to be. But neither of them would listen to her, and nor would their father. This had made her brother screaming mad. Could you blame him?

'Honesty!' he shouted. 'That's a mug's game. Who are dishonest? Us? Because we steal sixpence? Jeez, Ma, you'd lie down and let them rob the very skin off your back.' He was about twenty years old then.

He had yelled some more at their mother and Linda was ashamed to see her starting to cry again. Her brother stalked out, banging the door behind him. Her mother looked up anxiously as the lamp on the table flickered and the flimsy walls shook. She shouted after him. 'You'll come to a bad end. You'll see!' Then he flung the door open again.

'So what!' he yelled. 'At least I'll live while I'm alive and not stew in this dirty hole like you and Pa.'

With that he swaggered through the doorway in his short leather jacket and his tight jeans – with a sensuous, rhythmic movement of his shoulders that made Linda want to run and hug him. As her mother sat down and started weeping afresh, saying she couldn't go on, life was too hard, Linda slipped on to the bed, her back to her mother, and secretly opened her hand to look at the trinket glistening in the cushion of her palm. She slid it over her head. Then hand on hip she walked over to the cracked mirror and gazed at her elfin face and the bauble on her neck. The crack distorted her reflection and she put out her tongue at it.

That was not the end of events that night. Her father came back late from his work on the railway and he had no sooner sat down when her mother shrilled at him for not looking after his son. He did absolutely nothing to help her with the upbringing of their children. He just left his son to roam the streets. The boy didn't even have a job. And now look at him. He had fallen in with some dreadful tsotsi gang where they would teach him to rob and kill. She was sure of it . . .

As Linda listened to her mother's voice becoming shriller and shriller she put her hands over her ears. Without a word her father took up the knife her mother had been using to split some kindling. Linda ran and crouched behind the bed and the next moment the knife flew through the air into the wall. Luckily the wall was only made of wood and so it didn't break the knife; it just quivered there as if it was stuck in the flesh of a bull Linda had once seen in an exciting Western at the Odin bioscope. It shut her mother up all right. She began to tremble and put her hand over her face. Linda didn't feel sorry for her when she saw the tears trickling through her fingers; she herself was determined never to cry. Her father stood there glowering at her mother.

'What are you whining for? Nobody has touched you. Give me some food, woman, I'm hungry.'

Linda had felt easier after that. Nevertheless, while he was eating, she kept her hand closed tightly over the trinket. She was glad her mother had forgotten about it. She didn't care how Joel had laid hands on it. It gave her a thrill to feel the metal cutting into her flesh. She would never give it up, not even if her mother was mean enough to tell her father about it and beat her for accepting something she knew had been stolen.

Linda could not remember how long it was after this that a dreadful thing happened. Something so dreadful that it would change her life for ever.

One night two men came lurching in through the door carrying a body covered in blood and with the side of its head battered in.

6

She had rushed into a corner and started shrieking and crying. It was her brother Joel! She recognised his shiny coat, remembering the day he had first put it on, swaggering up to his mother so that she might admire him in it. Now it was muddied with his blood.

Her brother was dead.

Her father shouted at her: 'Stop bawling, child!' And as she held her breath, one of the men told her father and mother that there had been a fight between them and the Tsomi gang. One of the Tsomis had also been killed. The police were out on a pass raid, they said, and searching houses for dagga and illegal liquor. There were plenty of the gang on both sides who could be seized for lack of a *dompas*, so they just had to scatter.

The two men laid her brother's body on the bed and moved off in a great hurry, slamming the door behind them and leaving an empty silence laden with shock and fear.

Linda crept over to the bed where her mother and father usually slept, her gaze trapped by the gory thing that had been her brother. Clamping her hands over her face she ran blindly to the corner of the room. She wanted to cry and shriek, but no sound came out. She felt icy cold and her whole body began to tremble.

Gradually the trembling ceased. She peered through her fingers. Her father was standing like a stone-cold corpse himself, standing and staring upwards. Her mother? No, she wasn't crying either. She was sitting on the bed close up to the body, her fingers wandering over its face. Her fingers were bloody. Linda didn't want to go near the thing again. It wasn't her brother Joel any more. Finally her mother drew a piece of cloth over the body, mercifully covering that horrendously mangled face.

A sudden banging on the door shook the walls. Linda wrapped her arms around her body in terror, making deep indentations in her skin with the ends of her fingers.

Four policemen entered. The two white ones carried guns. The others flourished their knobkerries. One shouted at her father in Afrikaans, demanding to know if he wasn't hiding somebody in the house. Hadn't two of the Tsomi gang come running this way? Her father said no, he didn't know anybody belonging to the Tsomi gang. The policeman struck him, calling him a liar. Her father staggered, crashing into a chair and breaking it. But he quickly righted himself, standing stiff and silent, his head held high.

'Who have you got here?' The policeman pounced at the thing on the bed, whipping off the bloody cloth. Linda's mother and father never said a word. Linda wanted to shout out that one of the Tsomi gang had killed her brother, but something about the way her father stood looking at the policeman kept her silent.

'So they got the young tsotsi,' remarked the policeman laconically to his mate.

The other laughed. 'Ja, man. That's one kaffir less.'

One of the black policemen meantime was nosing round the room and poked his stick under the bed where some boxes were kept because there was no room for them anywhere else. The way he emptied out all the bits and pieces of household paraphernalia her mother kept in the boxes you'd have thought it was something precious, like dagga, but she knew her father didn't go in for smuggling dagga. He was too scared for that kind of thing. When the policeman found nothing he moved right round the room turning everything else over.

The first policeman's face was tense with rage, his body poised like a boxer ready to attack his opponent. He glared at Linda but she vowed to herself he'd not be able to drag anything out of her. She'd keep her mouth shut, like her father.

At last the four of them trooped out, knocking over her mother's treasured vase of artificial flowers and leaving the room looking like a rubbish tip. Linda heard them banging on a door close by in the yard. That must be at Mrs Beta's house. Linda hoped Mrs Beta had time to hide the illicit beer she'd seen her making two days ago.

Her father shuffled over to the door of their room, closed it and bolted it. Her mother carefully covered up her son's body again, tucking it in at the corners as if to keep out the cold.

'They can't touch him now,' she said, her hand lingering on the raised bit that had been his head.

After that Linda lay awake for hours. She couldn't remember falling asleep. All she could remember was waking up with a start, hearing the wailing and looking fearfully towards the bed. She couldn't see anything because the room was full of people, mostly wailing women. Some were sitting on the floor leaning against the wall, others hovering around the body. She wished they would stop, but she knew that was what her mother often did at other people's houses. There was always trouble somewhere, always someone dead.

One of the mourners broke into a hymn. She had a soft, clear, plaintive voice that sounded as though it was coming from far away. Gradually the others joined in, a man, too, with a deep bass voice that vibrated right through Linda's body. She remembered having heard the hymn once at the mission Sunday School at the corner of their street, where her brother Joel had taken her when they'd had nothing else to do, and they'd joined in joyously in the singing.

Now a feeling of resentment came over her. She was sure these women had never known her brother. What were they all making such a noise for? She looked over to where her father was sitting by himself. He was not crying. She looked at her mother. There she was, shedding tears, and yet she almost seemed to be enjoying herself with all those people around her. She could never understand her mother.

Linda herself would never show anybody what she was feeling.

They would never trick her into it again.

Two

After her mother's death Linda went to live with Elias Khumani, a distant cousin of her father's who also lived in Sophiatown. The house he rented was a cut above her parents' backyard shack. Its iron roof, its solid though peeling walls, the two uneven but polished steps leading to a narrow stoep betokened an unequal battle on the part of countless tenants between respectability and poverty. Its present occupant, Elias, had the hollowed look of the dreaded TB. His clothes didn't look properly filled up and he kept a grey scarf round his neck in broiling summer as well as biting winter. Linda hated that scarf.

On Sunday mornings Elias had a fondness for sitting on the open stoep and smoking his pipe, except when Maria Ndeba – the woman he lived with – nagged him so much that he went off down the street to a neighbour's house. He usually came back in an hour or two, smelling of his pipe but quite sober. He wasn't one to souse himself in a beer hall and he never set foot in a shebeen.

He'd once had a job in a factory lifting heavy cases, but now had to be content operating a goods-lift and of course there was no sick pay. Maria complained she had to work herself to the bone to keep things going. Bred in Sophiatown herself, she emphatically averred that you cannot get anything for nothing in this world and she needed every penny she could scrape together to keep her son Yivani at school. Education was something you had to make sacrifices for. So what with the TB and the high rent, she was more than willing for Elias to take in his cousin's daughter. She counted on Linda Malindi helping them out by paying for her lodging, and agreed to let Linda share a small room with her daughter Titi and her twelve-year-old son Yivani, both by a previous husband, as well as her two younger sons by Elias Khumani. The children all slept in the one room, with a curtain that the teenage Titi had demanded to partition off her part of the room.

Titi embraced Linda Malindi with an eagerness that her thin arms could not well express. Nature had been kind to Linda, but somehow it had left Titi's limbs and bosom as sapless as a grasshopper's. Being a year older, Titi was by way of taking the younger girl under her wing – not that Linda fancied the role of fledgling – and suggested she should try for a job at a garment factory where she herself worked, in one of the Reef towns adjacent to Goli. For lack of anything better, Linda agreed.

So together with Elias, Maria, Titi and thousands of others, Linda Malindi joined the throng of the city's workers; the morning exodus – on foot through the dirty township streets, by bus to the city and then by train to its tributary towns.

For township dwellers, getting to work on time means rising in the dark most of the year round. In winter it is worse, and it is a High Veld winter right now, as biting as anyone could wish for; anyone, that is, who can stay under a snug pile of blankets until the cloudless midday sun spreads its benison over Goli. But then not many around here have the blankets. Or the chance to stay abed. Except perhaps the tsotsis, who are animals of the night.

In Linda Malindi's Sophiatown it is still in the small sharp hours. Workers have already shaken off their uneasy sleep.

Hands trembling with cold fumble for matches to light the candle and one by one windows open bleary eyes to the dark. On small paraffin stoves a feeble flame boils some water with maddening slowness. Men and women scramble into their clothes and gulp their tea if they're lucky, or depart with empty bellies. Children whimper and are hastily comforted – or cuffed. Mother hands them over to an older child, who will put out the candle, shut the door and creep into her empty place when she is gone.

In the greying dark, shadowy shabby figures emerge from one doorway after another, huddling into themselves against the cold that is as keen as a knife-blade concealed in a tsotsi's fist. Young and old join the throng stumbling down the dry rivers of the roads to join the main highways all leading to Goli. They must hurry. For it is they who keep the wheels of the great city turning.

There is a stampede for the buses, which are always too few, and the battle goes to the strongest. The unfortunate ones left behind wait close together in the queue, while the breath of their lungs steams palely into the chill air. Curses are deep but for the most part silent.

Other workers, Titi and Linda among them, trek on to the railway station to wait for the trains taking them to the Reef towns further on. With a clanking of metal and wood, ramshackle trains hurtle along with their human loads hanging on to windows and doors. Wheels screech, brakes grind to a halt and the seething cargo tumbles helter-skelter on to the platforms, thence by exits for blacks only, into the highway to footslog it once more.

Hurry! Hurry! Factory workers, office cleaners, messengers, washerwomen, domestic servants, they must all be on time when the robot-clocks of Goli swing into motion and set the desperate pace of the day's activity.

They walk so urgently, their bodies awry with haste, that they have no time to look about them as the landscape begins to glow in the crisp-dry air of this winter's morning. In the near distance rises the powerful concrete headgear of one of the Reef gold mines, its tall rigging, its spars and girders like a multiple scaffold, or the skeleton of some antediluvian giant, unfleshed in a grim and elemental contest. Black smoke from unseen furnaces belches out of a high, narrow chimney. Ant-like figures, pouring out from their stone bunks in the mine compound, hurry to enter the skips that will carry them underground, for the hungry machines beneath the City of Gold must be fed night and day. In the background stands one of the many ashen-pale slag dumps, the gigantic excrement of the gold mines, petrified monsters shrouded in the morning mist.

Though the factory pay was higher than that of a nursemaid, Linda had to sweat for it, and too much of it went into Maria Ndeba's pocket. Linda felt sick every morning as soon as she entered the barrack-like room in the warehouse, breathing in the musty fumes given off by the rolls of material they worked with, the machines whirring like a thousand devils in her ears. The factory supervisor didn't give you a chance to slacken for a second. She had a razor tongue in her head when she wanted her regiment of women to get a move on. And by five o'clock Linda felt as if somebody had stuck a knife between her shoulder blades.

This wasn't her idea of a life, not by a long way. But what else could she do? Thanks to her mother's strenuous efforts, she had received four years' education at a Sophiatown school reserved for non-white children. Four years should have been enough to equip her for something better, but it was no more than a modicum of literacy, with Xhosa enforced as the chief medium under what was called Bantu Education. Her English was sparse and redolent more of the township compost heap where tsotsitaal, the lingua franca that evolved from the need for people from such diverse origins to communicate, was widely spoken. She also knew some Afrikaans, the compulsory coin of exchange between the black servant and the white baas, and more especially the baas in uniform – the police. But it was language divorced from the rich soil of its original European culture which signified an ordered way of life and human relationship. Two or three times a week she idled away her time in the crackling darkness of the Odin cinema in Good Street, or if money was shorter than usual, in that low-class flea-pit, the Balansky, watching the latest American movie and necking with her boyfriend of the moment. Or more often just roaming the streets, beating it up with a gang of youngsters as determined as herself to have a good time.

Youth with its vague hungers and desires had other and quite innocent ways of imbibing the new society, besides the bleak days spent amid the frenzied factory machines. Outside working hours the City of Gold was a prohibited area for people like Titi and Linda – a forbidden city. But commerce is a powerful solvent of barriers and it is the business of shop windows to seduce all eyes. On their way to the train station, Linda and Titi liked to indulge in window-shopping. Standing close together, noses pressed towards the magically invisible glass, they gazed at wax models bedecked in the latest European fashions. Sometimes they stole glances at a well-dressed white woman, staring with a sharply critical eye at a figure as remote as those behind glass. With her quick hands, Linda, not to be outdone, would run up a scrap of material after supper and drape it round herself with a boldness that outshone both the white woman and the fashion model. Titi enviously admired Linda's flair for dress. But it was more than a flair. It was a passion. For a skirt in the newest shade and style, shoes and nylon tights for her trim legs, she frequently put up with an empty stomach.

Titi had a boyfriend, Max Takane. He was rather older than the youths Linda had played around with when her mother was still alive, and she thought Titi was a lucky girl. So did Titi.

Linda thought Max wasn't bad looking, though he wasn't a patch on her brother Joel. He wasn't his style. He had some job in town though he never mentioned what it was. At the weekends he dressed up fit to kill, swaggering around with his brown and white shoes, new baggy trousers and even a dandy fedora. Nearly every evening he travelled home on the train with Titi, so when Linda started working in the city the three of them travelled together. Max fought for a seat on one of the wooden benches and had the satisfaction of sitting between the two girls, each one squeezed close up against him. As the train had a habit of rocking round corners at high speed – the drivers always seemed to be in a hurry – there was much giggling when Linda was flung across his lap.

Then one Friday night a young tsotsi terrorised the compartment when he stabbed a man, robbed him of his pay-packet and leapt off the train as it was slowing down. It all happened so quickly. The conductor, as usual at such times, was nowhere to be seen and nobody had dared to interfere with the tsotsi. His knife was at the ready, gleaming in the dim light of the coach. There were screams from some of the women, while Titi and Linda clung hard to Max. The older girl was crying, but Linda made no sound. Max slipped his arm round her waist.

That night when Titi and Linda were going to bed, the atmosphere was tense. Finding her companion unwilling to chat, Linda tossed her head, jumped first into the bed, pulled the blankets around her and fell asleep almost immediately. They hadn't mentioned the name of Max Takane. Titi stayed sitting on the chair till she was shivering, but when she finally climbed into bed and tried to tug the blankets to her side, Linda held on to them even in her sleep. At last Titi slept, wriggling her body disconsolately under her scanty covering.

After the incident on the train events began to move fast. Linda had occasionally joined Max and Titi on their visits to the Odin and now it seemed that she was always with them. One evening Titi had to stay in bed because of a sore throat and a high temperature. Linda did say she thought she would stay at home too, but Titi for some reason quarrelled with her and said she wanted to be left alone.

'Well, if that's how you feel, I'll make myself scarce,' said Linda. And she did.

She and Max did not go straight home that night after the film.

Next day Titi wanted to get up and go to work. Linda told her not to be a fool. Why risk getting pneumonia for a firm that squeezes the last ounce out of you anyway? And for once Titi's mother, who had never liked this distant cousin of Elias Khumani, backed her up. Elias was a sick man, sick in the chest; she couldn't afford to see her daughter going the same way. Then where would they be? If Titi wasn't earning, she'd have to take her eldest son away from school. He was a bright boy and loved his school. Titi must stay in bed and get well, and no nonsense.

All that week Linda was thrown together with Max and when Titi rose from her sickbed she flung the word 'man-snatcher' at her, whereupon Linda retorted that it wasn't her fault that Titi had been sick. This made Titi mad. She didn't put it past her dear friend having 'fixed' her with the flu for her own wicked ends.

'Jee-ssus!' exclaimed Linda. 'Your mother's been putting silly ideas into your head. That's what comes of going to that witch doctor nearly every week. Why the hell should I go out of my way to fix you – or anybody?'

To Titi this sounded like blasphemy. Her mother had great faith in what the witch doctor could do and it was she who had persuaded Elias always to wear that dirty grey scarf round his neck, on the witch doctor's advice.

The quarrels between the two young women increased. But Linda found it a very different matter from quarrelling with her mother. With Titi it wasn't a walkover. The two were well matched in a battle of tongues; between them no quarter was given and there were no tears on either side.

The fates, however, played Linda a rotten trick. She had still a lot to learn after all. Before long she began to be sick every morning at the factory. It was that devil Max Takane's doing. She told herself she'd been a fool to let him mess around with her.

She had little hope of concealing her condition from Titi, yet she wasn't much bothered about Titi's feelings in the matter; she had a serious problem of her own to solve – how to get rid of the child she was carrying. The only person she could think of confiding in was Max himself.

For a month she kept her mouth shut, while anxiety, shooting out of her in bad temper, increased the tension between them. Clinging to the hope that she might be mistaken, she waited another month. Then she began to get scared.

One night she and Max were coming home from a dance at the house of one of Max's affluent cronies, where illegal liquor had flowed freely. (You paid for it, of course, and paid through the neck.) Max started being fresh.

'Aw, keep your paws off me!' Linda twisted her body away from him.

'What's up, man? Having the sulks?' His drunken breath was foul on her cheek. She couldn't stand the sickly smell of it. On an angry impulse she blurted out her news.

His reaction taught her something more about men, something she chalked up against them, something she would remember. She was learning the hard way.

First of all, he didn't believe her. 'Think you can pull a fast one over me?' he said, grinning. 'I know your woman's tricks.'

'A trick, is it? And who pulled a fast one on me? You dirty swine. You've got me into this mess and you'll bloody well get me out of it.'

'Why me, eh?' Max pulled at his cigarette.

Linda stopped right in the middle of the road.

'Say that again. Say it!'

'Come off it, man! I know what I'm talking about. You needn't try and play the innocent with me. Just get this straight. You won't get away with palming the brat off on me. Nothing doing. See?'

Speechless with rage, Linda struck him in the face. The lights of an approaching car flung their figures into grotesque relief. The car hooted impatiently but Linda didn't budge.

'Hey, man!' said Max, pulling her violently aside. 'Don't get run over.'

'Why not? A lot you'd care. It'd help you out.'

'Hell! There's no need to talk that way. Go and ask Ma-jaze. Maybe she'll tell you what to do.'

'Ma-jaze? Who runs Angels One – the shebeen with the best jazz band in Kofifi?' Linda swayed her hips.

'The one and only Ma-jaze, my dear. All two hundred pounds of her.'

'You can laugh.'

'What's wrong?'

'I've never seen the woman, but I've heard tales about her and her shebeen. I'm scared, man, and that's flat.'

'She's not bad, Ma-jaze isn't. I'm trying to help.'

'Thanks for nothing,' she said.

'Then get out of your mess your own bloody way. I'm off!'

'I will too, I will!' she screamed. 'And if anything happens to me, maybe you'll do me a favour.'

'Christ, what are you up to now, you and your threats?'

'Call in the cops! They'll know what to do, to you and all.'

'Man, I know you better than that. Nothing that happens to us is any business of the cops,' he said soberly.

Torn between rage, fear and frustration, Linda ran off down the street and it was this rather than her threat of what she might do to herself that penetrated his hide.

'Hey, Linda, come back!' he yelled.

But all he could hear was the click-clack of her heels in the darkness.

He shrugged and went on slowly to his own abode where he stepped gingerly over several sleeping bodies. The flashing light of a police van pierced the privacy of the crowded room as it swept past, stopping dead the drunken singing outside the window. His younger brother grunted crossly as he pushed in beside him and pulled his thin blanket over his face.

Linda had uttered her threat with a vague but violent desire for revenge. If the thought of self-destruction seized her for a mad moment, the bitter vitality of her spirit could not possibly turn against itself. She knew herself frustrated by the sheer imperviousness of the man to her attack, his stolid indifference to her fate. It was true, what he said, she would get out of her mess somehow. With that self-knowledge the iron entered her soul and in her own perverse way she felt the better for it. But she was not ready to put herself in the hands of Ma-jaze, a woman with a formidable reputation in the district. The very fact that the man who repudiated the fathering of her child could put her at the mercy of such a woman increased her suspicion. She would find some other way.

Throughout the following weeks with dogged persistence she tried every possible means of extinguishing the vital seed she carried within her. Gin. Quinine tablets. A syringe filled with Sunlight soap. Jumping into deep ditches. But with a stubbornness exceeding her own it clung to her unwilling body, steadily drawing nourishment from it, increasing and multiplying with the fearful complexity of the human foetus.

And then, one day at the factory, she felt a faint fluttering in her belly.

What was that?

Quickly excusing herself she fled to the relative privacy of the latrine. And there it was; another flutter and before her widening eyes an almost imperceptible rippling of the taut skin.

Her baby!

Gazing with wonder at her body, she began to have a peculiar feeling of possession towards the unborn child, and with it a fierce determination to go through with the ordeal facing her.

It was *her* child.

For a long time she concealed her condition so as to be able to carry on with her job, while brazening it out in the house of Elias Khumani. After all, it was she who paid for that extra room, not Titi. They needed her money all the more because Titi had increasingly to stay away from work. What Maria Ndeba had dreaded had come to pass. Her daughter Titi was sick like Elias, only with a more virulent form of TB. The bout of flu she had at the beginning of winter had left her weak and spring brought on another attack. Now it was early summer and the days were growing warmer. Too warm for Linda in her present state. Too late for Titi, who irritated her at night, lying beside her trying to suppress her cough.

'Cough, Titi. Let it go. Get it over with and let's get some sleep.'

Linda shifted restlessly in the narrow bed. She felt the unborn child pressing against her side. She felt that gentle flutter of limbs that so excited her. In the darkness she imagined the child already in her arms.

Maria Ndeba was storing up her wrath against this girl that Elias had given shelter to. She didn't need to be told who the father of the child was, and for some inexplicable reason she blamed Titi's condition on her. What was more, Maria's son Yivani had been pushed out to sleep on the stoep. Not a place for anybody when the dust comes swirling in from the street, or a torrent of rain turns your bed to ice.

As the months passed, bringing Linda nearer to her time, it became evident that the disease was eating away at Titi's vitality. While grudging the heavy fee, Maria at last called in the doctor, who recommended complete rest, fresh air and sunshine, a holiday from work – no more bending over the machines that constricted the chest – and good food, such as eggs, milk and fresh fruit.

'How in heaven's name does the doctor think I can buy all those luxuries?' said Maria to Elias. 'Does he expect me to steal them?'

So Titi stayed on in the sunless, airless room, eating the same monotonous diet of mealie-pap and whatever fresh vegetable relish Maria could afford. When Linda came back from work she was aware of Titi's large, slightly protruding eyes hungrily following her every movement. They seemed to bore into the very womb where each day her child sprouted new human shoots.

'For Christ's sake, what's going on inside that head of yours? Don't stare at me,' exclaimed Linda. 'Go to sleep. I'm tired out.'

Titi seldom said anything on these occasions. She had ceased to make any reference to Max Takane and as far as Linda was concerned he had simply dropped out of both their lives.

The full tide of summer brought the thunderstorms with it. More than once Linda was drenched to the skin waiting in the queue for a bus back to Sophiatown. It was now the seventh month and she felt the burden of her child. She dreaded the thought of having to give up her job.

One Friday night – it was pay-night and always the worst on the trains and the buses – she waited longer than usual. Nearing the house, she was conscious of an intense fatigue through her back and all her limbs. Bed was the best place for her. She couldn't disguise it from herself: she was feeling terrible.

On entering Titi's room she saw at once that something was amiss.

Titi was not alone.

Her mother and Elias were sitting on her bed, one on each side of her. At the sight of Linda, Titi started up, then threw her head into her mother's shoulder and clutched her round the neck.

'Ma! Ma! Don't let her come in. It's she has done it to me. Don't let her come near me!'

Maria did her best to soothe her daughter.

Elias had a sheepish air.

'Something came over Titi this afternoon. I had to get Elias to come and help me to quieten her.' Maria looked at Linda accusingly. 'What trick have you been up to, to make her like this?'

'I don't know what you mean.'

'She's been crying out about something you've done to her. She's a very sick girl, thanks to you.'

'Why should I do anything to hurt Titi?'

'Don't listen to her! Don't listen to her! Tell her not to look at me with those eyes of hers. She's doing it on purpose!'

The distraught girl covered her face with her emaciated hands and buried herself in her mother's embrace.

'Will somebody please tell me what all this is about?'

Elias at last spoke up: 'Titi is sick, Linda. She keeps on saying you have been plotting with somebody to fix her.'

'Me?' Linda suppressed an impulse to laugh. 'Fix her? But that's utter nonsense!'

'She says you've been to see some witch doctor and he has given you the power to do her harm.'

'Witch doctor indeed! You surely don't believe that non-sense?'

Elias was silent.

'Whatever you've been up to, it's your fault Titi's in this state,' said Maria.

'Mrs Ndeba, how can you say that to me? True's God, I'd never hurt Titi. I wish I could help her get well.'

'She's telling lies! Don't listen to her. Don't let her turn you against me, too!'

'But, Titi, how can you believe . . .' Linda took a step towards the bed.

Titi shrank back. 'Don't let her come near me! Don't look at me!'

'You see? That's what you've done to her,' said her mother.

Linda felt the woman's hatred surge through her body like a poison. Involuntarily she placed her hand against her heavy womb.

Elias made a half-hearted move towards Linda. 'You must understand, Linda. It's very difficult for us. What are we to do?' He bowed his head.

Maria turned on him. 'Yes, you stand there helpless. What are we to do? There's one thing at least we can do. It was you who brought her here in the first place!'

Through Linda's whole being a wave of anger succeeded the first shock. Maria was still speaking.

'I should never have let her darken our door!'

Elias had a guilty air.

'Linda, it's Titi we have to think of. You must understand that. Her mother and I must do everything to make her well . . .'

Linda controlled herself with an effort. 'And so?'

But he could not continue.

Exasperated, Maria goaded him again: 'What's the matter with you? You agreed with me a minute ago. Don't leave it all to me!'

'You see, Linda – ' began Elias again.

'You're kicking me out. You don't need to say it.'

'We're sorry this had to happen, Linda. But what can we do? Titi is sick – '

'You're all sick!'

Linda seized her suitcase from the top of the wardrobe, flung it on the floor and began throwing her clothes into it, running to and fro, her breath coming hard. Her head felt as if it would burst.

Maria and Elias looked on, while on Titi's face came an

expression of pitiful triumph as she watched her every move. But she shrank into herself as Linda stepped up to her bed.

'What now?' said her mother, leaping in front of Linda. 'What are you up to now?'

'If I'm to sleep in the road, I'll need my blanket,' she answered, ripping it from the rail at the end of the bed where it had been folded.

She took up her suitcase and hurried to the door. Then she stopped and put it down. 'Oh, I forgot. Here's the money for the rent.'

She flung some coins on the bed, seized her suitcase again and without looking back she left the room.

Titi's mother got up and slammed the door shut.

From the street Linda heard the bang, with all its finality.

She stopped dead. Until this moment anger had sustained her.

Suddenly pain, immediate and imperative, shot through her body.

Oh God, her time had come!

Where could she go? Whom did she know? Who was her friend? She had acquaintances, youths and girls in the district, in plenty. But who could help her in her extremity?

She moved on. She mustn't linger here outside the house where they had thrown her out. She must put as great a distance between them and herself as possible. The suitcase she carried dragged her shoulder down. The pain in her body had mercifully passed and she moved fast. It was late and it was dark. Where? Where was she going? There was no older woman she could turn to. Her acquaintances were all desperately seeking their pleasures in the dance hall, the shebeen or the bioscope. They didn't go to one another's homes. Did they have any homes? Weren't they all like herself? Women like Maria threw them out. They didn't care if your baby died.

Could she go to Max Takane?

Suddenly she stopped. She dropped her suitcase. She laughed. She didn't even know where he lived. Hell! If she went to the bioscope she might find him there. And speak to him in front of all those people? Never. He'd kick her sooner than help her. But she must find somebody. She must.

She picked up her suitcase again. If only she could think properly. Her mind was in a fog. She'd never been like this before.

Jeessus! The pain again!

She dropped the suitcase. Gripped her distended stomach. Felt a sticky wetness between her thighs. For a moment panic overcame her.

She looked up at the houses lining the street. Most were in darkness but there was one on the opposite side with signs of life. Its small, narrow window was curtained and a mottled light came through. She'd go up to the door and ask the people to take her in.

As she was crossing the street she heard a child wailing and sharp sounds of an altercation rose shrilly. The door burst open and a man lurched out. Pulling his hat over his eyes he hurried off into the darkness. He had not noticed her. The door banged. The wailing of the child continued.

Linda moved on. Quickening her pace she looked at all the windows as she passed along the street. Houses without light were shadows that shut you out. Those with pale windows, pale with candlelight – they were like white faces without features . . .

Hau! She must think of something sensible to do. This pain that strangled your insides, it was worse than a human hand striking you. When her father had dealt her a blow, well, it was over, and you were quickly friends again. But this pain lay in wait for you, ready to strike. She'd have to seek out Max Takane after all. There was nothing else. How far was it to the bioscope? But supposing he'd gone somewhere else tonight?

Then a mad thought darted through her mind.

Ma-jaze!

Max had said she knew what to do when a woman was in trouble. She had been scared of her then. Even at the thought of her. But it was different now. There wasn't anything this Ma-jaze wouldn't know. She was a woman after all. Sure, she'd help her through. For her it would be simple.

But how to get to her place? How far? She must hurry.
Hurry!

Tixo! The pain was coming on again. And with it a sudden
gush between her legs and a strange metallic smell. She must not
let herself lie down in the street. No!

From a distance she saw the lights of a car approaching.
Would she be able to attract the attention of the driver?

She waved and shouted. She could just make out two figures
close up to each other. A woman beside the driver, all dressed up,
and they were laughing together. And then the car was gone.

'Don't lie down in the street,' she repeated to herself out loud,
over and over again. 'Do not lie down – '

She knew what would happen. She'd get left there. In her
own pool of blood. Often in Sophiatown somebody was clubbed
or stabbed in the night and nobody dared come out to help. They
were too scared.

She must move on.

Linda never knew how she reached Ma-jaze's shebeen. Ken
Madoda told her afterwards what had happened. He was the tall
talkative fellow who liked to hold an audience while he spun a
yarn and you didn't know what was true and what he'd made
up.

Yes, if Linda Malindi – he liked to call her by her full name
– wanted to make a sensation, she had certainly managed to pull
it off. She'd scared the living daylights out of them. Everything
had been going on merrily inside Angels One, as usual. The
Sophiatown Dixies in full blast, the folks footing it as crazy as you
like, the liquor nicely tucked away in the back premises – at least
what wasn't already tucked away somewhere better. Glasses
newly refilled and stomachs tingling with illegal hooch . . .

And suddenly there was a bang – or was it a thud? – against the
door. Eyes popped and somebody said: 'The cops!' And, oh boy,
were those glasses emptied at the double! You couldn't afford to
throw away good liquor, no matter what happened afterwards.
As Ma-jaze herself had gone to unlatch the door, bottles were
hustled out of sight. She wasn't in any hurry. The cops could

go on knocking, as far as she was concerned. And besides, you couldn't hurry a good two hundred pounds of female flesh.

When Ma-jaze opened the door, the young woman standing there just fell inside, flat on her face. Had she been murdered? The band stopped. Ma-jaze at once took charge of the situation. There's nobody like Ma-jaze for keeping her head. It needs more than a body, alive or dead, to upset her equanimity. She signed to the band to resume.

Linda was carried through to the back premises, a good place, too, among all the liquor. Folks crowded round. Was the woman dead? Had she been knifed? But Ma-jaze shooed them all away, telling them to get on with the dance – and the booze, or she'd have some complaints to make about their poor consumption. Ken Madoda had managed to stay by, together with his girlfriend Edith Sonke, since Ma-jaze didn't mind Ken. He had his uses – yeah.

Well, Ma-jaze soon found out what was what. There wasn't a white doctor to beat the way those strong hands of hers felt the young woman's body. The rest of Ma-jaze had its fat in the wrong places, but those probing fingers were sensitive and quick.

'She's alive all right. But if you don't move fast, Kenny-boy, it's maybe a corpse we'll have on our hands. And you know we can't afford that here.'

Ma-jaze turned again to examine Linda.

'I wonder what made her tumble into my place. Ever seen her before?'

'Never set eyes on her,' said Ken.

'Not a bad-looking slut, eh?' remarked Ma-jaze.

Ken was looking hard at Linda when Ma-jaze's voice made him jump to attention.

'What the hell are you waiting for?' she said.

So Ken had rushed off to old Pakati's store to ring for a taxi to take Linda straight to Bridgeman Maternity Hospital. It would be quicker than waiting for an ambulance to come all the way to Sophiatown. Ma-jaze had the foresight to make a quick pass-round of the hat amongst her clientele, since the taxi man would demand his money on the spot – or no ride. His was no charity bus, no matter how urgent the case was. A black man was too easily squeezed out of business by no end of pirate taxi men, the devils.

'Well, it's cheaper than paying for a funeral hearse, isn't it?'

So Ma-jaze had remarked, and to please her everybody pulled the bits and pieces out of their pockets. They had a holy fear of Ma-jaze.

Linda spent ten days in hospital. The premature baby was stillborn. No life had stirred in the womb for some time before birth, though she had not understood this. She had lost a lot of blood before she reached the hospital. And the surgical instruments had not been kind to her body.

As her senses came back to normality she enjoyed just lying and looking about her, watching what went on in the ward, at first numb to what had happened to her. What a busy ward it was! The nurses were run off their feet and complained with gusto about the place always being short-staffed. They were young women just like her, all about the same age, except the staff nurse, who was so bossy, fussy and eager to find fault, with the airs of one newly promoted above her equals. The other nurses mimicked her behind her back, causing Linda to laugh when she didn't want to laugh. She was still very tender inside and the stitches hurt. With the night sister in charge it was different. She had such a quiet, yet authoritative voice and she spoke very little. As she went from bed to bed Linda thought to herself she would like to wear flowing headgear like hers. It was so pretty and feminine.

Nurse Shiloane was her name. Linda forced herself to stay awake so that she would come over and talk to her. With a small torch in hand she would bend over Linda, whispering a scolding at finding her wide awake, and lay her cool, soft hand on her forehead. Never before had Linda seen such a kindly face. And such warm, bright, glowing eyes. She felt a pang of disappointment when a new nurse came on duty. Stiffening up as soon as the woman came near her, she didn't try to hide her dislike. And it seemed to be mutual. The new nurse's touch was hard against her body.

The young white doctors who breezed in and out in untidy white overalls seemed just as busy as the nurses. They had hardly a minute to spare to talk to the patients, at least not those who were progressing according to schedule. After all, mothers with babies were routine work – even mothers without their babies. The bossy staff nurse brightened up as soon as a young doctor appeared. With what smiles she trotted after him! But he didn't seem to notice.

Linda tried not to let her thoughts dwell on the baby she had lost. What was the use? She told herself she hadn't wanted it in the first place, even though once she had felt the flutter of life inside her she had stopped being afraid and had begun to feel the glow of possession. It wasn't easy when the nurses brought the babies into the ward so that their mothers could give them the breast. Linda wanted to block her ears as she lay there listening to the sucking, smacking sounds the babies made with their lips. She wanted to cover her face with the sheet when a mother snuggled her baby's head into her neck; she screwed her eyes up tight when she saw the soft, self-satisfied smile on a mother's face.

Curse these women with their babies! Curse them!

One of the nurses had told her it was a little boy. She had pushed aside the momentary pang of loss. She could not afford to wallow in sadness. He was dead. A good thing, too, when you came to think about it. It solved a hell of a lot of problems. Maybe she should count herself lucky . . . Yes, she had begun to feel almost happy.

During visiting hours she knew she needn't expect anybody. Imagine her surprise one evening when a complete stranger, a lanky fellow, stopped beside her bed, with a young woman just behind him. They must be making a mistake. She had never set eyes on either of them before. However, the man spoke her name and then introduced himself and his companion. He was Ken, he said. Ken Madoda, and his girlfriend was Edith, Edith Sonke. Linda noted that she looked very light in colour for an African, and she had on a stylish dress that must have cost quite a bit. She spoke very little, in fact she looked rather bored, but Ken Madoda made up for it. Hau! He liked to hear his own voice.

He explained all that had happened that night when she had passed out and told her she had to thank Ma-jaze for saving her life. How did Linda know Ma-jaze? He hadn't seen her around at Angels One. She didn't know her, Linda said. Then how come . . .? Oh, well, it didn't matter. As it turned out, Linda couldn't have picked a better person. Folks told some hair-raising tales about Ma-jaze, and he didn't say they were all garbage, but at any rate he reckoned Linda had struck it lucky with her that night . . .

Ken's voice went on and on and she was sorry when the nurse rang the bell for closing-up time. In fact the nurse eventually had to give him a telling off. Edith Sonke was already going out the door when Ken called out that he hoped they'd see Linda around some time when she was better.

Her visitors didn't come again and two days later she was discharged from hospital.

Three

Unencumbered, but with a desperate weariness in her body, Linda walked away from the hospital. Her first necessity was to find somewhere to sleep that night and, equally pressing, to find a job. She did not want to return to the garment factory, not that daily grind to the rattling rhythm of the machines.

Her thoughts turned to Ken Madoda. He had seemed a good-natured fellow, and friendly. What she could do was wait till the evening and look for him at Angels One. After all, Ma-jaze had done her a good turn, even if she had a reputation for toughness that made Linda feel as inexperienced as a newborn puppy. She knew she couldn't expect soft treatment a second time; Ma-jaze wasn't one to dole out charity for nothing.

Coming near to Angels One at about midday, she hesitated to knock for admittance. Though the sun was shining, the window was closely curtained. She had no memory of the time when she had stumbled up to this shabby side entrance. Her memory was not of sight but of a blind physical agony that had driven her to this lair for shelter – something that was best forgotten.

She sauntered past, her ears alert for any sign of life within, but it was too early in the day for Ma-jaze's familiars to have put in an appearance. She might be concocting her potent brew in her backyard; she might even be pronouncing over it those incantations that would bring release to the pent-up spirits of her customers. But of this the blank exterior, like a shuttered face, gave no sign. There was as yet no sound of the frenzied saxophone or the delirious drumbeat, those powerful exorcisers of the depressions of bleak living.

At the corner of the street she noticed a store with the inscription: 'N. PAKATI. General Dealer'. It was a fair-sized shop with windows less fly-marked than was usual in a Sophiatown store; the owner had made some attempt to show his goods more attractively than his rivals did. Feeling hungry, Linda decided to treat herself rather better than she could afford. A youth, with wrist bones much in evidence, served her and she devoured her meagre fare. With time to burn, she looked idly round and approached a rail of dresses not far from the food counter. There was no other customer on this side of the shop.

Like every woman who has endured the ungainly bulges of pregnancy, she longed to celebrate her newly recovered slenderness by sheathing it in a seductive wisp of cloth, the more contour-catching the better. The problem was to find the money. But at least looking at and fingering the luscious textures, and holding them up against her, didn't cost anything. Engrossed in these tantalising pleasures, she was startled when a man spoke to her, almost at her elbow.

'Looking for a dress to fit that pretty figure of yours, eh?'

Linda saw before her a squat body with a heavy face balanced on top of it, the head having but a short stump of neck to support it. The eyes, with their half-moon of unhealthy flesh underneath them, held her in sharp focus. She stared back coolly. He might have been about fifty, but it was not easy to say.

'It's a smart outfit I'm looking for, but I haven't seen it yet.'

'Look again.' He swept a proprietary hand across the rail.

'What colour do you fancy?'

'I don't see my colour.'

'You're hard to please, eh? Have a look at this other rail.'

He waved her forward, measuring her with a hungry eye.

'What about this nifty little suit? It looks just right for you.'

'I'll say not!' Stepping away from him she extracted a vivid green nylon number.

'Hau! You have good taste. It's the best I've got in the shop.'

'How much?'

'Wouldn't you like to try it on first?'

'How much?'

'Six pounds nineteen eleven, and cheap for the quality.'

Linda didn't flicker an eyelid.

She passed her hand over the silken texture.

'If you like it all that much, maybe we can come to some arrangement. You go over there, my dear, and try it on. Just to please me.'

'Why should I please you?'

'The right dress, the right woman. It doesn't happen every day.'

Linda assumed a pout of reluctance and went into a makeshift cubicle between boxes, where she quickly removed the cheap cotton wrap-around she was wearing and slipped the deliciously unattainable dress over her shoulders. The soft-sharp coolness tingled against her skin. With a frown of annoyance she found there was no mirror.

'If you want to have a look at yourself, there's a mirror on the hardware side,' the man called from the other side of the curtain.

Linda hesitated, knowing very well she could not afford the dress.

She stepped out. The man's eyes narrowed in approval; the youth at the grocery counter goggled and grinned; a woman turned and stared and a nipper gave the whistle. No further salesmanship was required.

Her eyes lingered on her reflection. To buy, or rather – how to buy? Behind her own bright image loomed the storekeeper's beady-eyed shadow.

'You can't refuse yourself that pleasure,' he said.

'How much deposit?' she asked.

'For you, I'll make it two pounds.'

'Too much. I'll give you one.'

'See here, young woman. I've a proposition to make to you. Would you like to take on a job?'

'What kind of a job?'

'I'm enlarging this side of the business. Ladies' dresses, underwear and suchlike. You're just the saleswoman I've been looking for. What about it?'

'How much do I get?'

'Let me see now. You'll get a rise if sales go up – '

Here the man interrupted himself to shout at the grocery assistant. 'Hey! Get a move on there. Don't keep the customers waiting.'

Then to Linda: 'Just step into my office and we'll talk things over.'

What Pakati called his office was as makeshift as the cubicle; only boxes screened it from the prying eyes of customers. Linda couldn't get out quickly enough, but when she finally went back to the box cubicle to change, she had landed both the job and the new dress – to the storekeeper's satisfaction. She told herself the job would be sufficient to mark time with till she looked round for better. The pay wasn't good, but she reckoned it wasn't nearly such hard work as at the factory.

The chief complication was her boss himself. If she could make use of him in the way of some perquisites, she was prepared to put up with the repellent hunger oozing out of him whenever he came near her, but she'd have her work cut out keeping him in his place. From now on she meant to be boss as far as men were concerned. Max Takane had taught her that much. If there was any taking to be done, she would be in charge of that department.

Before she'd left the shop, Pakati discovered she was looking for lodgings. He wished he could put her up in his own house – he had the biggest in that corner of Sophiatown – and the only thing that stopped him was the necessity to allay the suspicions of his wife, Buyiswa. She had a venomous eye for all possible – and impossible – usurpers of her legal bed. So he had to fall back on his assistant, Ned Ngonoko, who lived close by. With adolescent enthusiasm Ned was only too ready to enjoy the ecstasy of being a doormat for Linda's sharp little heels and assured her and Pakati that his mother, the mother of six, would find a place for Linda in her three-roomed house. He himself would give up his bed for her. Not that he had a whole one to give. But he'd jolly well make his small brother yield up his portion, or he'd know the reason why. Linda graciously accepted the sacrifice and by six o'clock it was all fixed up. Ned's mother was secretly relieved at the extra money her lodger would bring in.

Hardly waiting for evening, Linda went to Angels One, wearing her new dress. This was unknown territory. In answer to her tentative knock a toughly built young man in jeans opened the door. Ma-jaze wasn't in sight and Linda was relieved to hear the familiar voice of Ken Madoda hailing her across the comparatively empty room. He drew her towards a cigarette-stained table where Edith Sonke sat poised over her glass with conscious sophistication, and two tsotsi youths slouched head to head. Turning a lazy eye on the newcomer, the youths expressed their appreciation in a simultaneous waggle of the cigarettes stubs hanging from their lips.

'Ma-jaze!' called Ken, going towards the curtain that served as a door to the back premises. 'Come and see who's here!'

The brightly coarse-grained pattern of the curtain material crumpled up and Ma-jaze filled the entrance.

Linda felt herself being sized up while she in turn was aware, not of the large body in its tight black dress, but of the strongly featured face whose massive chiselled planes suggested the character that had impressed itself on the district as something to inspire fear. The woman's brows relaxed with a slightly quizzical gesture of recognition.

'Turn that radiogram down,' Ma-jaze shouted to nobody in particular. Then she turned back to Linda. 'So this is the young woman who gave us a fright on her first visit. You look good,

Linda Malindi.'

'I'm all right, thanks to you, Ma-jaze.'

'Forget it. You should have seen the way they all downed their liquor that night when you – er – banged on my door, eh, Ken?'

'Sure, Ma-jaze, it was a great night.'

'Good for business it was, my dear. It made them thirsty.'

Ma-jaze's shoulders shook a little.

'What about something to drink now, to celebrate?' said Ken.

'A soft drink.' It was Ma-jaze who answered.

Ken stared.

'Ma-jaze's gone all motherly,' mocked Edith Sonke.

'Easy does it, my child. There's time enough,' said Ma-jaze, ignoring Edith and answering the glint of resentment she noted in Linda's pinched face.

'Okay, Boss,' said Ken.

At that moment some other customers arrived and Ma-jaze busied herself in the back room.

As she sipped her sickly looking drink, Linda had a feeling of flatness in her surroundings. She'd been keyed up to venture into this unknown territory, even to encounter Ma-jaze, about whom she had heard such sinister tales – and all the woman had done was to bully her into drinking this insipid green stuff.

The shebeen had an air of drabness, like an empty circus-ground with shrouded roundabouts and swings, with nothing but sawdust and silence where before had passed the clamorous pageantry of elephants, acrobats and clowns, and the lights had blared as raucous as the trumpet blast of the circus band.

In Edith Sonke she sensed a keen hostility. Her glances burnt up the green nylon – a sensation that would ordinarily have given Linda pleasure, if her experience with the jealous Titi had not been so raw in her mind. It had cost her dear.

'I wouldn't stand for being treated like a baby,' said Edith, looking down her nose at Linda. 'Have a gin on me.'

'Thanks, I will.'

Ken laughed.

'What's so funny?' Edith asked.

'I like to see you enjoying yourself.'

'Like hell I am,' she retorted. Ken shrugged while Linda looked demure.

The drinks were brought by a leggy slip of a girl of about thirteen, who looked as if she needed to make up a long lack of sleep. Somebody said she was Ma-jaze's daughter, but another contradicted this, remarking that she took good care to keep her own filly in the country. Through her hard work she could afford to send her daughter to a mission boarding school.

Ken kept up a running conversation now with this one and now with that, with the air of a privileged regular, though it was heavy going.

Suddenly he rushed to the door to usher in three newcomers.

'The renowned Sophiatown Dixies!' he announced.

There were shouts of greeting as the trio of players entered, each one as different in shape and size as were the instruments they carried. As they tuned up, Ken made comments for Linda's benefit. There was the guitar player, Toni Ngusa, no more than twenty, with a rubbery face as pliant as the strings of his instrument, which he held against him as soulfully as an outsize heart. 'And that's Sonny Matyolo, a helluva performer on the sax – the best in all Sophiatown. Watch him, Linda Malindi. He uses his limbs like one of those wire mascots you see dangling in the rear window of a car. He's the master of his instrument, or more properly its slave, for he woos it with his very life-breath, coaxing out of it its strident soul. Just listen to those notes!'

Linda agreed it was a sound the likes of which she'd never heard before.

'And don't be deceived by Stan Zondeka, with that deadpan mug of his,' whispered Ken flashily. 'He can shake you into a wild war dance once those drumsticks get kissing the cow's hide fast enough. He swears the spirits of his fathers are in that old drum. And not only that. He's also a wizard on the xylophone.'

Ma-jaze hailed her musicians as if they were conjurors, as indeed they soon proved to be. More people began to arrive and in no time the jiving bodies were sweating out the boredoms, the insults, the fears and anxieties of the week.

After a preliminary skirmish with Edith, Ken pulled Linda

to her feet and in spite of herself she became as madly gay as the best of them. When the Sophiatown Dixies stopped to wet their whistles, the jivers collapsed like puppets with slack strings at the end of a show. This was the interlude when Ma-jaze was at her busiest, her strong, solid body seeming to glide as though on wheels back and forth, trays laden with glasses, without any sign of bustle or hustle, a formidable Ganymede to her thirsty clientele.

Leaning back in her chair, pleasantly exhausted, Linda found herself being accosted by a tsotsi of small dimensions and a large amount of bounce. Sprucely careless in his long wide trousers and his fashionable two-tone shoes, the latest garb of the more affluent gangster, he looked the complete tsotsi – to the gaps in his teeth.

'Say, beautiful, where've I seen you before? Say, where you been hiding yourself?' he said.

This wasn't even original.

'Diz Dinake, at your service,' he added.

But Linda did not unbend to his overtures that night. In this unknown territory, the good-natured Ken was the safer bet, all the more because he was already hooked by the possessive Edith. Linda was in no mood for the excitements of a cat fight. Not tonight.

A peremptory rat-tat on the door jerked everybody alert.

'The cops!' someone muttered. And with a mechanical repetition of gestures familiar on such occasions, glasses were emptied at the gulp and with remarkable speed removed out of sight.

'Ma-jaze, you handle this,' said Ken.

Taking her time as usual Ma-jaze went to open the door. A square-shouldered figure of a man, with a shadowy figure behind him, stood on the threshold.

'Ag, man, Jo! You and your tricks!' said Ma-jaze, turning on her heel and disappearing into the back premises.

'There goes Jo Bula, with henchman number one,' whispered Ken to Linda.

'Not Jo Bula, the leader of the Tsomis?'

'The very chief himself, knife-scar and all. Until last week, that is, when he broke away and left them all in the lurch to form a new gang. He'd found some of his men had been doing the dirty on him and you can't do that to Jo Bula – say, what's up? You look as if a ghost tickled your spine.'

Linda said nothing. It was a Tsomi who had killed her brother.

Jo Bula was a gangster whose style owed not a little to the celluloid heroes beloved of Sophiatown – Humphrey Bogart, Richard Widmark, James Cagney. It was difficult to say where his natural character ended and the mythical began. Nature had made him compact of build, wide in the shoulders, square in the jaw and broad cheek-boned. To this he had added a thrust of the head that suggested pugnacity, while the scar of a long knife wound above the left eye provided his authentic trademark. His stare as he passed Linda was black, hard and peculiarly empty.

Jo Bula had been greeted with mingled curses and groans of relief, a general cry like a balloon deflating, followed by a clatter of glasses that demanded refuelling.

'One day, Jo Bula, you'll cry wolf once too often,' exclaimed Diz Dinake.

'How come, little shrimp?'

'Some of your pals that I know of might be scared, and leave you high and dry on the job – one fine, dark night.'

'Diz Dinake, you'd make a good-looking corpse.' It was Jo Bula's companion who spoke.

With a jerk of his wiry body, Diz flung back: 'That's more than you'll ever make!'

'Stinking's more like it.'

'Who's that with the silly face and the swagger?' Linda asked under her breath.

'He's Nick Noboza. He's got the slickest knife around here.'

Diz had skipped nimbly aside to avoid Nick's thrust. Everyone was watching, knowing that Nick's pretty-boy face belied his vicious nature. But at that moment Stan Zondeka provided a diversion by flourishing his drumsticks and performing a drum dance with such bravura that the mercurial Diz turned his provocative stance to capering instead. Then as Toni Ngusa twanged in with the tenor notes of his guitar, the magic yeast of music was visibly at work among those still sitting around. Faces relaxed, lips parted, the black and the white of eyes gleamed and limbs and shoulders jigged in a preliminary canter. Now Sonny Matyolo came in with a long wail on his saxophone. Hau! The joy of it! That did the trick. Men seized their partners and the crowd soon had the blissfully bemused expressions of those for whom, for the moment, boredom, strife and danger did not exist.

Linda, left out of the swing, stared at Jo Bula, beside whom Nick Noboza sat sipping his drink, an expression of moroseness mixing incongruously with the habitually conceited leer on his narrow face. Neither of the men paid any attention to her. She observed Ma-jaze signal to Jo Bula, who rose and followed her through the curtain. Nick stayed where he was, but he was not long left alone. From the other side of the room a woman slithered over into the empty chair beside him. Swathed in red satin, she was as shapeless as a chameleon. Her colour was a shade lighter and her features were sharper than is usual with an African. Her slanting eyes reminded Linda uncomfortably of Titi's. But this woman consciously overused them, gesturing as she spoke. Her make-up, intended to glamorise, merely made her emaciation grotesque. The lips were wetly smudged with lipstick; the dusky cheeks, artificially beflowered, had a sickly tinge. Whatever she said to Nick, his glance shrivelled any further word on her tongue. Smiling a desperate smile, she spotted Linda and sidled over to her. Almost at once she began to speak.

'Hullo, Kleintjie, I haven't seen you here before. It's a great life. You know, Kleintjie, from the day I was born I started suffering.'

Somebody laughed.

'I can't remember my mother. They say I have her looks. She came from the Cape, you know, and she died here in Kofifi. It's a great life. I wish I'd never seen my father. He's a black swine. When I see him coming, I vamoose, vanish.' She laughed, staring ahead of her, asking no more of Linda than her indifferent presence.

'I was six when I knew about sex. I didn't understand a thing.

Then somebody at the mission church told me I was illeg-it-imit. So what? Everything's illegal for us in this bloody world. It's our fate. You've got to keep your end up, eh? Or get washed down the drain.' Suddenly she picked up the rhythm from the players, half-singing, half-croaking.

> 'You've got to keep your end up, eh?
> Or get washed down the drain.
> Snatch your loving where you can . . .
> You've got it on the brain!'

She laughed again, her shoulder strap slipping with pathetic provocativeness.

> 'Love in dark alleys, like the cats.
> Oh, why should we complain?
> Or in foul privies, drown the brat.
> It's you that feels the pain.
> You've got to keep your end up, eh?
> Or get washed down the drain.'

'Come on, fellows, sing up!' a few onlookers mockingly chimed in. The players, laughing, accommodated themselves to her, the dancers halted and she continued.

> 'You've got to keep your end up, eh?
> Or get washed down the drain.
> Grab your woman. She'll grab your –
> (You've got it on the brain!)
> You'll smash her face in for the fun.
> O, why should she complain?
> The night is murky; she won't tell.
> There's blood mixed with the rain.
> You've got to keep your end up, eh?
> Or get washed down the drain.'

Linda was on the point of moving off when Ma-jaze reappeared with Jo Bula and came up to her table.

'Now then, Emily Vermeulen, just you leave her alone. Remember what I said about you coming here.'

'Okay, Ma-jaze. Okay! Mum's the word,' replied the woman, her manner half placating, half resentful.

'I'll have another drink,' she added, but drifted off to another seat.

'Quite a character, eh?' Ken spoke at Linda's shoulder. 'I split my sides when I saw her trying to hook on to Nick Noboza. He has eyes only for Jo Bula. She reckoned you didn't know who she was.'

'And who is she?'

'It's Emily Vermeulen's misfortune not to know which world she belongs to. She has ambitions. That's the snag. But the coloureds throw her out of their parties. She's too dark-skinned for them. So she falls back on us.'

At this Edith Sonke chimed in: 'She's the wrong colour for the kind of name she's got. So she tries to worm her way in here.'

Linda flashed a look at Ken, who had assumed a poker face. It struck her that the kettle was sneering at the pot for not being black enough.

Linda began to feel bored. Jo Bula and Nick Noboza had been joined by two women who filled her with envy. They were dressed in such style that it made her feel her own dress was a rag; one sheathed in white as though her shapely body had been poured into the dress, the other in a froth of red chiffon. She had made a mistake falling for old Pakati's offer, and now she'd be tied to the job till she could pay off her ill-considered purchase.

She did not know how she felt towards Jo Bula. It surely could not be anything but hatred. He took the two women's flattery with the maddening air of being cock-of-the-walk, while Nick Noboza gazed into his liquor with contemptuous indifference. She watched the cool sophistication of the woman in white as she accepted Jo Bula's offer to dance with her.

The rest of the evening petered out. When she took her departure, nobody asked her if or where she had found a place to sleep. Nobody cared.

Pakati's wife, Buyiswa, believed in hellfire.

One morning Linda was busy making the dress department of Pakati's store look like something for the first time in its life, when she became aware of someone poking a finger into her back. Sure enough, there stood the woman – her two little eyes blinking at her. She guessed at once from what young Ned had told her that it was Mrs Pakati. There wasn't much of her, as if she was all burnt up already with the thoughts inside her. Her hands were clasped tight on her flat bosom. She didn't change her position when Linda looked round, but stood in a rigid posture, shoulders slightly askew. The posture itself bespoke humility, though Linda was not deceived. Those little black eyes – rather like her husband's when you came to think of it; only the setting was so different – were mean, greedy, calculating, and something more. They were sharp with suspicion, positively shooting with it.

Linda turned back to her work, ignoring her. She was doing her job properly, and that was all that Pakati, or his wife, could demand of her.

'So you're the new girl,' the voice behind her said, with heavy emphasis on the 'new'. 'You might say good morning, girl.'

Checking a retort, Linda half mumbled a response.

'New brooms sweep clean, I see. I wonder how long it will last. Where are you staying?'

Linda explained how kind Ned's mother had been in putting her up.

'Very kind, I must say, considering the sort of people who frequent Mrs Ngonoko's house at all hours of the night. But, of course, it is conveniently near. Very near,' she added.

Linda wondered what lay behind the remark.

'I suppose you have plenty of boyfriends. Young girls these days have no sense of what is proper. All they want is a good time. They don't know the hellfire that awaits them, or they would think twice. Any children?'

The question took Linda unawares. 'Oh, no. I – ' She stopped.

'Well, what are you hiding?'

'Oh, nothing, Mrs Pakati. I have no children. I – I'm not

married.'

'That's no guarantee these days. Babies are born more often in sin than in holy wedlock. It's a wicked world. A wicked world. And it's not only the young who have fallen into the ways of sin. There are those who ought to know better, lusting after the pleasures of the flesh. I pray for them. Every night on my knees I pray for them. I pray that God will save them from the clutches of the devil, before it is too late. Too late.'

The last words seemed to Linda to be spoken with a peculiar relish.

'Every night I think and pray, think and pray.'

'What do you think about?' Linda asked. She was aware that her question was on the borderline of insolence, but it had escaped before she could stop herself.

Mrs Pakati looked startled at the direct question.

'Ah. My thoughts are between my maker and myself.'

'Or the devil,' said Linda under her breath.

'What did you say, my dear?'

'Oh, nothing. I was just listening.'

'Well, you had better get on with your work. We can't have idle hands at this time of the morning.'

Mrs Pakati took herself off to the grocery section, where Linda had no doubt that Ned was in for his share of admonition. And yes, there he was looking down with an ill-concealed smirk on his face, saying from time to time: 'Yes, Mrs Pakati. No, Mrs Pakati.' And when she had departed he winked broadly in the direction of Linda, who winked back.

As a devotee of the Anglican religion, Mrs Pakati spoke an almost foreign language to Linda, to whom the words God and devil were familiar as swear words. Her brief contact with the mission Sunday school had left the vaguest of impressions on her mind and indeed was remembered only because of its association with her brother Joel. She had no key to the hungers, the greeds, the needs of Mrs Pakati and others like her that had driven her to seek help from a Christian God whom the foreign missionaries had brought to her people. Not for her the invocations of the powers and terrors of the witch doctor, which could still hang over the life of Titi and her mother. Mrs Pakati would have considered herself superior to such primitives with their attenuated contacts with a dying tribalism. Yet in Sophiatown they shared the same violent pressures of existence. In its teeming jungle, the cunning, the craft, the trickery or the grasping avarice engendered by the dire necessity to climb on top of their fellows, had turned the hunger of the spirit into a travesty of itself. Mrs Pakati's very religion partook of those deformities of character.

Linda could not follow the devious paths of Mrs Pakati's thoughts, with their sanctimonious trappings, but she recognised the physical manifestations of meanness when she saw it. She resolved to steer clear of the woman as much as she could. It was not easy to steer clear of the attentions of her boss, however. His hungers expressed themselves more grossly, without the same need for self-deception. Under the pretext of getting Linda to help him with the stocktaking, he kept her after hours. When she protested, he granted her overtime pay, and she didn't hide her disgust at the amount. Sometimes at Ma-jaze's she retailed for Ken's amusement the man's garrulous confessions. Yet his dreams did in a way make sense to her.

'I want to make enough money to buy a fleet of buses,' he confided one afternoon when the shop was shut. 'I don't see why that rogue Ndababini should have the monopoly. He must be worth a fortune.'

'And how do you think you can get the better of Ndababini?'

'That's the rub. He can hire a half-dozen thugs to do his dirty work. Do you know, he began simply as a houseboy? Then he and his wife saved enough between them to buy a cart and sell vegetables. Then from a cart it was a taxi, and from a taxi to six taxis; and from the taxis to a bus, and from one bus, damn it, to the whole lot. He must have paid a pretty penny to wangle that deal. That takes some doing, eh, my girl?

'Now take this place,' he went on, sidling closer to Linda. 'There isn't a fortune to be made out of selling food. The people are stingy when it comes to buying food. Of course I never give them credit. Then only the devil would make the profit. Whatever

I've made I've done it the hard way, and there are a half a dozen robbers ready to snatch it out of my hand before it even reaches my pocket. Black thieves as well as white thieves. Life's hard, Linda. Tooth and claw it is, my girl.'

One night when they were coming back in his car from a Boer farm where he had gone to collect a windfall of apples cheap, he said: 'You can be top dog when you've got money. There's no kicking you around when you've got a lot of money in your pockets. Do you know why the cops leave Ma-jaze alone? Just ask yourself why she isn't raided for selling illegal liquor, when her rival, Ma Rosie, found herself in court last week? I leave you to figure it out, Linda. You're no fool.'

'Thank you,' she mocked him. 'I notice that the cops leave you alone, too, though you do add on a penny or more to the price when you shouldn't.'

'It's hard work. Hard work, I'm telling you. I'm a very tired man, Linda. A man can't let up for a minute, a second, or he gets pushed to the wall. You've no idea of the worries I have, from all around. I'm a tired man.'

'What are you stopping the car for?' said Linda.

'It's early still, Linda. We don't need to get back yet.'

'I'm asking you, what are you stopping for? This isn't a place to stop. It isn't safe!'

'Linda, I want to talk to you,' he pleaded. 'We never get a chance.'

'You talk plenty, and I listen.'

'I need somebody to talk to. I need it bad. There's no one I can talk to.'

'I listen, don't I? I listen till I'm sick.'

'Linda, don't be so hard on a man. Look, Linda – I've been wanting to ask you – Linda, Linda – '

'I didn't give you the right to slobber all over my name.'

'See here, my girl, you like to play tough. And I admire you for it. But can't you have a little bit of – pity on a man?'

'Pity! How much is pity?'

'Linda, if you'll stay with me, I swear to you I'll be good to you. You'll want for nothing. You'll see what a fine lady you'll be.

You'll dress like the Queen of Sheba herself. Linda, just you be a little good to me, and I'll be good to you.'

'You men are all the same, young or old,' she shouted. 'If a girl is fool enough to believe you, she lands in a mess. Then she can go drown herself in a privy – if she can find one with water. And a fat lot you'd care.'

'Linda, my dear Linda . . .'

'Listen to him! Step on that gas, will you, or I'll scream blue murder. God, man, I mean it. Step on it. I want to get out of here!'

'There, there, no need to get so het up. I didn't mean any harm. We'll have a little talk another time – about money, eh, my dear?'

There was one thing Pakati didn't confess to Linda and that was his mortal fear of the gangster Jo Bula. He suspected him of being in the pay of an Indian storekeeper who had always resented the fact that the African had been granted the right to trade in Sophiatown. Whether or not his suspicions about the Indian were justified, Pakati held a precarious footing between the upper and the nether millstones. He tried to bribe off Jo Bula, who played his own game by cynically offering him protection against interference from a rival gang. Gangsters, themselves living on the razor edge of illegality, while waging war amongst one another, demonstrated the terrible logic of a cut-throat system based on the profit motive. They took their blind revenge against society by menacing the weakest in their own community. In this jungle the storekeeper faced yet another threat, from the police – a manifold and constant threat where Africans were concerned. At any moment one or other enemy could strike out at Pakati and thus disrupt the dung-beetle industry consuming his days in order to amass the pennies that were to procure him the freedoms he dreamed of. He bled every time he was compelled to part with his money to one gangster or another. He got as far as procuring a gun, though he knew it was illegal for an African to possess one. His wife, Buyiswa, went in terror of it going off, or of the police pouncing on him for having it. But all her lamentations that it was a weapon devised by the devil would not make him part with it.

One night, when everyone but himself and Linda had left the shop, and he had gone to the back door to make doubly sure it was padlocked, she looked up to find Nick Noboza standing on the threshold. Surprised rather than alarmed, she was about to speak when he signed to her to keep her mouth shut, and noiselessly closed the front door of the shop.

'You stay out of this,' he said, keeping his voice low. 'You'll see nothing, you understand?'

'What . . .?' she began.

'Are you there, Linda,' called the storekeeper. 'I thought I heard something.'

Again Nick signed to Linda to keep silent. Pakati hurried from behind the boxes, stopping dead at sight of Nick.

'Good evening, Mr Pakati,' greeted Nick with mock civility.

'None of that nonsense, Nick Noboza.'

Pakati edged furtively towards his office. What a fool he'd been not to keep his gun on him.

'You don't look too pleased to see me. That's too bad, when we've been looking after you so well. What are you fidgeting for, eh? No monkey tricks, you bastard, unless you want a knife in your guts.'

The storekeeper tried to bluster. 'Look here, I've no time to stand talking to you. I've had just about enough from you and Jo Bula.'

'Now don't get excited, Mr Pakati. It's bad for your heart. I don't want you to be careless about your health.'

The storekeeper was moving slowly backwards to his office. If only he could reach the drawer where he kept his gun, he could pretend to stumble and get it open. Nick was following close, a grin on his face. The fellow was too cocksure of himself. He'd like to blast that grin into space. 'If you think you'll get any more blood money out of me, you're mistaken. Just you tell Jo Bula . . .'

'What'll I tell Jo Bula?'

'Just you tell him – '

Pakati stumbled with a clatter, hanging on to the drawer

handle.

Linda wasn't sure what happened next. She had seen Jo Bula come stealthily in and had stood rigid as he passed her. He had actually smiled at her. She had seen him take out his gun in a flash just as Pakati stumbled, wrenching the drawer open, and Nick had lunged forward, knife in hand. For a split second she shut her eyes as the shot went off and the old man gave a cry, slumping to the ground. When she looked again, Pakati was groaning and clutching his right arm, from which the blood was streaming. Jo Bula lifted a black object out of the drawer. It must be Pakati's gun.

'So this was the great idea. I thought as much. You're getting rash, eh, old skinflint? Put that knife away, Nick . . . Ungrateful old bastard, wanting to shoot the hand that protects you. Don't you know the cops could nab you for keeping this little toy? I've a good mind to report you, man. Linda, fetch a cloth from somewhere and wipe up the mess. It can only be a scratch, though the old bastard's got a lot of blood in him.'

Linda snatched new cloths from the hardware counter, helped Pakati on to a chair and tended his wound. Finding the cloths soon bloody, she looked round at Jo Bula.

'Nick, your knife,' he said, and going up to a shelf, he ripped a piece of material from a roll and handed it to Linda.

'Don't look so damned sorry for yourself, man,' he continued. 'Next time I'll get Nick to do his stuff. So if you love your precious skin – I'm sure you do – get ready to play ball.'

'I've already handed you a packet,' groaned Pakati. 'At this rate I'll be left without a penny. I can't manage it, man!'

'Tell us another. You can count yourself lucky you've been left with your bloody carcass. Hand over the day's takings.'

'Have some mercy on a man, Jo Bula. Have some mercy.'

'Mercy? In this world!'

Nick Noboza kicked down some boxes out of sheer good spirits. 'Where's the dough?'

Pakati squirmed between rage, fear and greed. 'Aren't you afraid you'll have it come to you, you devil?' he said. 'It'll be your turn one day, man. You'll see!'

'Shut up! On that day I'll know how to behave. Don't you worry.'

As Nick made to strike, Pakati fumbled for the money bag.

Nick snatched it and handed it to Jo Bula.

'Peanuts,' snarled Jo Bula. 'Where's the rest?'

'Jo Bula, man, give me till tomorrow. I'll have to go to the bank.'

'I believe you there. You wouldn't leave a penny lying around, even for a mouse to lick the dust off it. But no double-cross, mind. It won't be a scratch on the arm next time. I'm warning you.'

Nick laughed gleefully, planting his face close to Pakati's as Jo Bula spoke.

Pakati recoiled.

'Okay, Nick. Let's go. See you some more, Mr Pakati!'

As he passed, Jo Bula flicked Linda's chin.

'Why are you wasting your talents in this pigsty, eh, Linda?'

Left alone with Pakati, Linda couldn't bring herself to speak. With Jo Bula's departure she experienced a painful collapse of excitement.

'Help me to the house, Linda,' groaned Pakati. 'I'm all done in.'

At that moment Mrs Pakati burst into the shop.

'Oh, Sol, are you hurt? I heard the shot, but I was scared . . .'

'They've got me in the arm. But, worse than that – '

'So I knelt on the stones and prayed and God heard my prayer.'

'Then he ought to have struck Jo Bula dead. It's going to cost a packet to keep these devils off.'

'More money! You give in to their threats too easily. You're a coward!'

'Blast you, woman! Now just tell me what you think I could have done, with Jo Bula on one side of me, ready to blow my guts out, and Nick Noboza, the knifeman, on the other?'

Linda could take no more. 'I'm going home,' she said.

'So you had the girl here – ' Mrs Pakati began.

'Don't *you* start on that,' he retorted.

'Good night,' said Linda.

'Hey, what's the hurry?'

But she was gone.

He sighed, letting the air escape as though there was no reason to take another breath. 'I'm sick, woman. Help me to my bed. And if you've anything to say, let it keep, for God's sake.'

'Don't you blaspheme to my face. I've been watching you and that girl. I know her kind all right, the slut. How do you know she isn't in with Jo Bula and that lot?'

'Nonsense, woman, she's too young.'

'Young! The younger the better. Look at you making a fool of yourself over her.'

'You hate her, don't you? You hate every woman who's young. You never rest until you drive them out of the shop.'

'Because I know what you're up to. That's why.'

'Look, Buyiswa. I'm sick. Let it be. Can't you just help me to the house?'

'You're in the clutches of the devil. That's what's got into you. I'll lock up the shop.'

Pakati struggled to his feet and put out his hand to pick up the gun Jo Bula had flung on the office table.

'Leave the gun alone. You should have used it earlier,' she said.

But he wouldn't give up his gun.

His wife shrugged, shut up the shop and took him home.

It was true, Pakati's wife wouldn't rest until she had driven Linda out. What she did not know was that her most willing accomplice would be the girl herself; Linda didn't see herself as an ageing man's mistress, no matter what perquisites he had pledged. And Mrs Pakati's obsessions with the handiwork of the devil had no meaning for her.

Mrs Pakati's chance came a few days after Jo Bula had succeeded in turning the screw on her husband; ever anxious about his health, he had gone to the hospital, leaving the girl in charge. Ordinarily, Pakati's wife kept a lynx eye on the business, but for the moment she had an urgent matter to settle, and she didn't know when her husband might return. When she called

Linda to the house, she tried to get out of accepting, under the pretext that things were too busy at the shop. Unbending her stiff features in a smile, Mrs Pakati was insistent, saying she had long promised herself to have the young woman to tea.

'I wonder what the old hag is up to this time,' muttered Ned. 'Watch out she doesn't put poison in your tea.'

Linda laughed. 'I'll look after myself,' she said.

Linda looked round the Pakati sitting room with curiosity. It was as crowded as a pawnshop. The furniture was grander than anything she had been accustomed to, cheaply ornamented furniture that bespoke superiority in Sophiatown. The chairs regimented round the table, unwarmed by use, held themselves as stiffly as Mrs Pakati herself. The closed window was shuttered and there was a musty odour about the place.

Linda was calculating in her mind if she could possibly afford a coat she had seen in an uptown window on her afternoon off, when she became aware that her hostess was speaking. Yes, she took a spoonful of sugar and a little milk; no, she didn't want anything to eat, thank you. She smiled as she sipped her tea, remembering Ned's warning.

'What are you smiling at, my dear?'

'Oh, nothing.' Linda pulled a straight face, wondering what the woman wanted of her.

'You know,' began Mrs Pakati, 'God has never blessed me with any children of my own. It was His will that I should be childless. But I have found a merciful compensation. All his life my husband has been a big baby. Just a big baby. You've no idea.'

'Really?' said Linda, to show she was listening.

'You know his health has never been good. He's always been worried about his health. But I look after him. He's all right, as long as he is careful. You see, he has a weak heart. If he exerts himself, or gets overexcited about anything, then his heart plays up. You can imagine how anxious it makes me all the time when he is out of my sight. And he simply doesn't know how to look after himself. People are always taking advantage of him.' Here she looked hard at Linda.

'My dear, it's a wicked world. From time to time, I'm sorry to say, the devil gets into him – '

'You mean, he's been fixed?' asked Linda with an innocent stare.

'Fixed?' echoed Mrs Pakati, halted in mid-flow.

'Yes, fixed. Mrs Ndeba – that's my friend Titi's mother – thinks the witch doctor fixed her husband, and Titi too, and that's why they're sick. Maybe it was a witch doctor – '

Mrs Pakati looked shocked.

'I'm not talking about the witch doctor, I'm talking about the devil, who puts evil thoughts into people's minds.'

'Oh,' said Linda. 'I'm sorry.'

'You may well be sorry, my girl. I have been on my knees night and morning praying that my husband shall be saved.'

'Saved?'

'Saved from the temptations of the devil. And I want you to help me.'

'Me help you? How? What can I do?'

'I'm sure you wouldn't do anything to harm my old man – my big baby.'

Big baby indeed! Linda's comment was inaudible.

'Now, my girl, I'm going to ask you a very special favour. You have a certain effect on men. Perfectly innocent maybe – and maybe not so innocent. We won't go into that. But one thing I do know – it's not good for my old man, with his weak heart and all. I'm going to be quite frank with you. I'm sure you'll understand.'

'I don't know what you're talking about.'

'In that case, I'll just ask you, my girl, to find another job. There, it's quite simple.'

'I'd say it's damned simple.'

'There's no need to use swear words. I'm simply appealing to your good heart.'

'Appeal my foot! Who wants your big baby? He's quite safe as far as I'm concerned. You've got it the wrong way round. I could tell you a thing or two about your helpless baby! Mrs Ndeba blamed it on the witch doctor. You blame it on the devil. It's all the same to me. I was getting out anyway. Just you pay me what's owing me. That's all I want.'

'You're an evil-mouthed girl. I'll pray for your salvation.'

'You can keep your prayers for your own dirty soul.'

That night at Angels One Linda retailed the scene amid much hilarity, mimicking first Pakati's wife and then her own responses.

Ma-jaze was the only one who did not laugh. Watching Linda, she wondered at the resilience of the girl, who didn't seem to mind that once more she was homeless and out of a job. Or did she? How was anyone to know?

Calling her over on the pretext of needing her help in the back room, she told her where to look for another room to sleep.

Four

Ma-jaze had an ambivalent attitude towards Linda. The very lack of close human relationship, or rather the avoidance of it, common to both, provided a kind of link between them. Ma-jaze had been a woman of strong affections, whom life had hardened and coarsened. Having one daughter, whom she was determined to protect from the hazards of Sophiatown and whom she had meantime left in a school in the country, she had condemned herself to be a childless mother, concerned only with making enough money for her purpose. After her rescue of Linda – little as she had allowed her feelings to be involved – Ken had once teased her by referring to 'that daughter of yours'. She had given him a look for his impertinence, a look that might have quelled a less irrepressible young man. Not that she revealed any softness towards Linda. For her spiritual diet she gave her some of the hard stones of wisdom that she herself had broken her teeth on in the course of bitter experience.

Linda for her part, while she had cast off her original fear of

Ma-jaze, kept her feelings on guard, lest the older woman should take advantage of the fact that she was indebted to her in no small measure. At the same time she conceived an admiration for Ma-jaze that had a profound effect on her own development. The woman had cultivated a ruthless placidity to meet the precarious turmoil of her existence. To an exceptional degree she had the gift of self-preservation acquired in the quicksands of Sophiatown life. Not indeed a gift, for it was derived from an indomitable will, combined with a basic sanity that was unshakeable amid the derangements, the insanities of the society to which they were condemned. Linda observed her toughness, her shrewdness, her coolness in handling those situations that commonly arose among the medley of characters frequenting her shebeen; those explosions bursting out of the tensely hilarious atmosphere into violence. She dominated the scene with a control that had itself something of violence in it, and was a match for the unscrupulous. If any legends of dark doings had gathered about her, she did not go out of her way to puncture them. Myths could be useful.

Finding her alone one day, Linda confessed her anxiety about her next course of action since she'd thrown up her job. Ma-jaze didn't answer her directly on this matter of extreme urgency. If she wanted to eat, Goli had jobs to offer – of a kind. No, the girl was concerned with something else. Something deeper – was it?

'Learn to know your own worth, Linda. And see that you get full price for it. You'd be surprised how few people in this world know their own worth . . . But remember, you get nothing for nothing. For everything a price has to be paid. Everything.'

Linda told herself she wasn't hearing anything new. Advice of this kind didn't put bread in your mouth. Ma-jaze walked away.

One night for some reason Ma-jaze was furious with Jo Bula. Linda was not inclined to pry into what went on between those two. But when he'd gone, Ma-jaze burst out: 'Never let them drink your blood, my girl. These men, they are cannibals! Their hearts have been plucked out, so that they are worse than the beasts.'

And the following night, as if some thought were still eating her, she looked sternly at the young woman. 'I see you giving Jo Bula the glad eye. Look out, my child. I'm telling you, men like him are rotten inside, though you mightn't guess it when you see them strutting and blustering their way roughshod over people's lives, no better than the white man's dog who bursts in our door and demands our *dompas*, tearing off our bedclothes to gloat over the flesh he pretends to despise. Every man is crazy for power in this filthy city. Crazy to see himself as the big shot, standing on top. Every small bum angles to be a big shot, even if it's on top of a dung heap. It's bloody underneath, so he must scramble up somehow on the backs of his fellows. And to be a big boss in this little hell, you have to pay for it. To get a star role in this jungle show, you have to kill for it. Slit somebody's throat on a dark night. Bump off a big shot, before you can be a big noise yourself. But they're all rotten inside, the little bums and the big bums. They've got the yellow streak. I'm telling you, they're cannibals – '

Linda did not rightly comprehend the passion that moved Ma-jaze to such rare speech, and as is the way of youth, she paid little heed to such warnings, lacking that soil of experience from which the words could draw their sap. It is thus that the hard-won wisdom of age must always fall on barren soil, failing in its warm impulse of protection, and youth is doomed to learn its own bitter lessons.

What Linda did imbibe, however, was the quality of the woman's character, which touched an answering chord in herself. The propensity to ruthless self-preservation was there in embryo.

If she did not come nearer to Jo Bula, it was not because of any strictures from Ma-jaze, but because he was in her eyes so far above her, and apparently unaware of her existence.

Of the motley crowd frequenting Angels One, Linda naturally gravitated towards her own age group. These included the tsotsis, that special breed of lawless township youngsters.

They were a mixed bunch, but they had one thing in common. To them, the white man's laws were something to be outwitted. In a climate where you could be scooped up by the police pickup vans as readily for lack of a pass as for a crime, there was no shame attached to having been in jail and, correspondingly, an utter contempt for the law. Morality had become a dirty word.

In this the tsotsi practised a simple logic. Indeed, a novitiate in crime could win his spurs by having served a sentence in jail and graduate to the older ranks of lawbreakers, like Jo Bula; to the ranks of safe-breakers or hold-up men. Where conditions imposed ceaseless humiliation, there was some pride attached to outwitting the laws; a young man could thereby exercise his wits and practise skills that would otherwise rot from disuse. The career of a young tsotsi was his antisocial challenge to injustice; violence, his answer to the deadly boredom imposed by his manifold deprivations, denied respect, education, opportunity. In a word, it was his answer to the violation of his human rights.

Where there had been one vast social dishonesty, one huge theft, of which he was the victim, individual dishonesty seemed the sanest response. Since the laws had outlawed him from society, he answered in kind with his own brand of lawlessness.

It was into this maelstrom that Linda, with her many hungers, was drawn.

The genus tsotsi had its different orders. He might be a drab messenger 'boy' in the city and would effect a neat piece of lifting from a warehouse while on the job. Nonchalantly, from among the other workers, he might deposit a bale of goods on the back of his bicycle and ride off. Cycling through the streets of Goli, he was as good as a disembodied ghost; for the eyes of white folks were conditioned not to see him. His black skin and his khaki dust coat rendered him pretty well anonymous. Then there was your well-behaved, well-dressed 'native', by day a docile handyman in an office, where nobody thought of asking himself how the youth contrived to be so decently dressed on a pittance. But in the dead of night a new being emerged into enemy streets, cool, cunning, agile, daring in his exploits.

The lesser breeds included the parasites, those who lived on the earnings of their womenfolk, sleeping or gambling by day, thugs and robbers by night, especially vicious in terrorising their own people. Their existence swung between torpor and violence. Violence was for them a way of life. They both peddled and themselves fed their craving on the deadly dagga weed that turned a man's blood to a raging fire, capable only of assuaging its fury in destruction, knowing only the bestial joy of the knife-thrust and the crunch of splintering bone under the clenched fist.

The sexual life of the tsotsi partook of the same violence. Vanity dictated possession and theft naturally extended itself to the realm of female flesh. The young women, subjected to the same pressures and barrenness of existence, were ready to attach themselves to such youths. If anyone wanted to flaunt her boyfriend in the cheaper shebeens and dance halls, attired in the full regalia of his tough tsotsidom, with tight narrow pants, short jacket, gaudy scarf – the lot, then she had to be a jolly good partner to him in the job of taking. Her full-flaring skirts and her nimble fingers were useful adjuncts in the delicate operation of lifting from a department store.

Backdoor business was a speciality of the young tsotsis and their female accomplices. It was damned risky but it was good business and the townships went in for it in a big way. Dresses, coats, and various feminine accessories; gents' suiting, shirts, underwear, fountain pens, even gramophones and suchlike necessities were coolly pilfered from city shops and warehouses. Others were at the distributing end of the business and sold goods cheaply in the townships. You bought – and no questions asked. The people wouldn't be palmed off with inferior stuff, mind you. The township have-nots were connoisseurs in quality, demanding the best.

Yes, it was into this maelstrom that Linda was drawn. Diz Dinake had a girlfriend by the name of Hilda Noyali, a pert petite who was as nimble of foot and finger as her celebrated accomplice. They made an eye-catching pair, whether it was on the dance floor, swept into a frenzy of motion by the Dixies' pulsating rhythms, or working out a piece of slick backdoor business. Together Diz and Hilda initiated Linda into their profitable game.

Of course you didn't talk about stealing. It wasn't proper.

It was Diz especially who inspired Linda with confidence. Small and agile in his movements, he had acquired a legendary notoriety for his sleight of hand in making a whole rail of dresses vanish from a shop floor.

Linda carried out her first assignment in a big department store in a quake of fear tempered by excitement, and a very special sense of exultation in her successfully completed task. This sense of achievement was reinforced by the praises of Diz and Hilda who, for all their youth, were hardened old-timers in this short-lived career; while Ken Madoda applauded as it were from the wings. He was preoccupied with his own secret undertakings, which it was not the business of the youngsters to pry into. But for some reason he kept his inquisitive eye on her. Linda proceeded to carry out several successful takings, which brought her some coveted additions to her wardrobe; one of them a dress every bit as stylish as the white dream of a garment she had seen Jo Bula's girlfriend wearing, a dress that made Linda feel like Lena Horne in that much-watched favourite of hers – *Stormy Weather*.

Even more important for Linda's ego, she began to acquire poise and with it greater popularity – at least among the young men. With the women it was another matter entirely. So this illegal business was not only a means of keeping yourself alive, but of clothing the body and feeding the hungry spirit. Through it, however precariously, you climbed a little way above the long-suffering, timid, squalid mass, so docile in their misery.

She was becoming hardened and almost forgetful of the hazards of her job, when a mishap to Hilda jolted her out of her complacency. Compelled to do some hard thinking, she had to shed some of her peacock feathers, at least for the time being. The news came one day when Diz Dinake appeared before her with a face as long as a thief's jemmy.

'What's up, Diz?' she said.

'It's Hilda.'

'What's happened?' Alarm sharpened her voice.

'She's been nabbed on the job.'

'Oh, the fool! I didn't think that could happen to her.'

'Who are you to talk?' he snapped. 'There's nobody cleverer at the game than Hilda. They tricked her! Blast them! Damn bad luck. That's all.'

'So you call it bad luck?'

'What else? It happens to nearly everybody sooner or later.'

'Oh!' Linda chewed on this. As far as she was concerned she had always thought she was indestructible.

'And what'll they do to her?'

'She'll get six months.'

'Jeessus! Six months?'

'Six months, because she's been had up before.'

'You never told me that.'

'Why should we? You don't go blabbing about it when things let up on you. It's just damn bad luck.'

'Have they ever nabbed you?'

'Now that you mention it, they have.'

'How often?'

'Oh, once or twice. And here I am alive and kicking. Hey, Linda, you don't look too happy.'

'I'm thinking.'

'Oh, you're thinking, are you? Is it about Hilda, by any chance?'

'No.'

'Well, that's honest, at least.'

'I'm thinking about myself.'

'What about yourself, eh, kid?'

'I don't want to be run in and shut up in jail for six months. Not me!'

'Bloody cold feet, eh? You want to rat on us?'

'Cold feet. Ja! If you like to call it that. But what the hell do you mean – ratting on you?'

'Not ratting? So what do you call it?'

'I'm looking after Number One, as Ma-jaze would say.'

'Looking after Number One, eh?'

'Ja. I'm looking after Number One. Any objections?'

'Okay. Okay. As long as you don't interfere with my Number One. See?'

'Why should I, Diz Dinake?'

'I'm glad you see the point. And how do you figure you're going to look after Number One? Eh?'

'I'm looking to you to tell me, Big Boy.'

'You expect Big Boy to look after you, eh, Linda?'

'Look after me? Like hell! I can look after myself. I want none of that crap.'

'Okay. All the same, two's better than one, eh, kid?'

'Say, what are you getting at?'

'Hilda isn't here. I need company. I'm lonely.'

And he laughed.

'What are you laughing at?'

'Because I'm lonely.'

'I don't see anything to laugh at in being lonely.'

'I'm dead sober. What about it, Linda?'

'If you expect me to risk my neck on another job, you can have another think. I'm damned if I will.'

'You'd lie on a bloody bed of roses, you would, and let me do the dirty work, eh?'

'My neck, it's precious to me. Diz, feel it!'

'Hau! To hell, Linda!' Seizing her, he kissed her violently and she did not push him away.

'We two, we could pull off some good tricks together. What about it? We've both got brains, eh, Linda?'

'Mmm,' she agreed. 'But just put me on a different pitch. No more taking for me. I'll help you at the other end. You're tops at your end of the game. There's nobody to beat you.'

'I do believe you're right there,' he purred with self-satisfied vanity.

'Let me handle the distributing of the stuff. I'll get rid of it fast. You'll see, Diz.'

'You're right. We'll team up, just us two, eh, kid? We'll make our fortune. Wish we had a posh American car like Jo Bula.'

'One day we will. Don't you worry! A Cadillac!' she said.

And so Linda threw in her fortunes with Diz Dinake. The hazards of the game had removed Hilda for the time being, but there was always another to step into dead shoes. No sentiment was lost between the two of them; each considered the new tie-up as a profitable proposition, and before long Linda was surprised to discover in herself an unexplored talent as a backdoor saleswoman. It made all the difference not having a boss like old Pakati over your head.

Her steadily increasing opinion of herself even came near to upsetting the precarious balance between their mutual business dependence and the sex game. In Dinake, it was at once ruthless, timid of emotion, and inarticulate. In both the man and the woman their very senses were impoverished. The breakthrough to deeper feeling came only in those moments of physical abandon inspired by the magic of Ma-jaze's musicians; in the drumbeats and wild rhythms of the jazz tunes thrummed by the Sophiatown Dixies.

Linda liked to think she had the upper hand of Diz Dinake. When she was stingy with her favours, fights ensued. No man, she averred, was going to take advantage of her at any level. Then Diz would storm at her. Hadn't he made her what she was? Never, she shouted. She had made herself. And she had done him a favour by stepping into the breach when Hilda had been swept off by the arm of the law. Diz could go to the devil and she'd still be okay. Just let him try it out!

Yet at the same time she had a jealous nature and was possessive of Diz. When other women came nosing around they were left in no doubt that Diz was her man. And so was Diz.

This possessiveness was as natural to her as her will to survive. It was a part of it.

A year passed by.

Hilda had come out of jail and found herself another man. Diz stuck to Linda. When the two women met, the air around was charged enough to light a dynamite fuse, as Ken Madoda remarked in his flippant way. But Ma-jaze's customers were denied the treat of an actual explosion.

At this time Linda considered herself a match for whatever a lousy world might try to do to her. She never gave anything away, least of all her feelings. She hardly remembered her mother and rarely speculated on the fate of her father. The image of her brother Joel, the memory of whose rebellious nature was a wellspring nourishing her own, was safely locked away, brought vividly to life whenever she fingered the now tarnished trinket he had once given her. The only time she ever allowed a tear to cloud her eyes.

She enjoyed life in her way. Sophiatown was her world, with all its noise and excitement, its smells, its hardship, its ruthlessness and its violence. Here men and women would vanish overnight; for death had multiple ways of snuffing them out in the townships. If it wasn't sickness, TB, starvation, or the living death of madness, it was the knife or the gun; if it wasn't the lethal weapon, it was the police. It was remarkable how the minions of law and order added to the agitations, uncertainties and perils of existence. What with liquor raids, pass raids, political raids, routine raids, the world of the white man impinged on the black, not in any human contact, but rather as a hydra-headed threat – and so in truth did the unknown black world impinge on the white. On neither side of the line did individuals allow themselves to see one another face to face, but walked in a terrible blindness; as if an acid thrower had stalked the streets, shrivelling the vision of a whole population.

But if death was busy in Sophiatown, so was life. Night and day it burned fiercely, indomitable and unquenchable. If it took on a terrible aspect, that was the measure of the immensity of the battle between them.

And there was no doubt which would be the victor.

Five

It was one Saturday on a hot summer's night that Linda Malindi met Simon Manzana.

By the time she arrived at Angels One the usual crowd was there and they greeted her with that gruff camaraderie they accorded a woman with her looks and a certain air of independence they had grudgingly learned to respect. Most of the women liked to think she was no beauty. Maybe. But the men knew better. What was beauty anyway? You had only to watch the men as she came into the room to find the answer.

In the corner Stan Zondeka with his xylophone and Toni Ngusa with his guitar drew from their instruments a crescendo of sound as if to say: 'Hi, Linda Malindi! Here's to you!'

But it was not such a brave burst of music as it might have been; for the familiar figure of Sonny Matyolo with his powerful saxophone was missing.

Linda sang out in surprise. 'What has happened to Sonny and his sax?'

'That's what we'd like to know,' called back Zondeka.

'I hope it's nothing serious?'

'You hope!' Stan struck an ominous beat on his drum to express his feelings of foreboding.

Linda made her way past swirling skirts and thrusting posteriors to a special table where Ken and Diz and some others were drinking. The fug of smoke, the tang of liquor pricking the nostrils, the hubbub of voices and laughter exploding now and again like small gunshot above the jazz-clang, acted on her snapping nerves like a tranquilliser.

The door curtain lifted and Ma-jaze emerged from the murky interior; the sweat beading her temples betokened brisk weekend business. The two women greeted each other laconically, with understanding.

'Isn't it queer about Sonny Matyolo being so late?' remarked Linda.

'I'll give that guy a piece of my mind when he turns up,' said Ma-jaze. 'It's not the first time he has come late. But I can't be angry with him. He's too much in demand. He'll go far, that boy.'

Linda hadn't yet addressed Diz Dinake. She leaned over to Ken.

'You don't look so merry and bright, Ken. Where's Edith?'

'She walked out on me yesterday.'

'Walked out? No, man, you don't mean it!'

'True's God. And she took the bed and bedding with her – the lot.'

'You're kidding.'

'Do I look like I'm kidding?' He pulled a melancholy face.

'You always do.'

'No kidding. I shivered last night. I furnished the place on the never-never.'

Linda laughed aloud. She glanced coldly at Diz who, glass in hand, was already rather glazed of eye. She looked beyond him with an air of boredom, and caught sight of the stranger standing up against the wall.

The cheek of him!

He was looking her up and down, his eyes shooting their lights at what he saw. She knew how to shoot her own, too.

He wasn't bad looking. Thinking about it afterwards, she told herself they had met like two jets in mid-air. Hau! That had been the day, the hour, the split second! Just like fate.

She saw him hesitate, then boldly decide to come over and jostle his way beside her. The battle was on. It was a simple matter for her to turn her back on him and animatedly quiz her neighbour on the other side. Diz eyed the intruder, a bellicose glint appearing through the glaze, but no word was spoken.

Linda heard her own laughter. The players – soldiering on without Sonny Matyola's magical saxophone – had stopped to oil their throats for a few minutes and some of the dancers marked time near their table.

'Say, Stan, look at Diz Dinake,' muttered Ken to Zondeka, who had drawn up a stool on the far side of him. 'He isn't amused when somebody butts in on his preserves. Especially a *moegoe* that nobody's ever seen before. Watch him do a bit of a show-off.'

Diz Dinake had risen to his feet and moved provocatively in front of the stranger.

'What's the betting we'll see some neat knife work before the night is out?' said Ken.

'Is the man a fool, or does he want a fight?' said Zondeka.

'He's green, man. Look at his get-up. Fresh from the country, man. A *moegoe*! Don't you see the grass still sprouting from his ears?'

With an exaggerated air of friendliness Diz Dinake plied the man with questions. What was his name and what village did he come from and who was his father? Perhaps he had come to Goli expecting to make his fortune? This raised a laugh and encouraged Diz in his act.

At first the young man answered in good faith, according to his custom. Linda watched every awkward movement of his body and listened to his slow, polite manner of speech.

So. His name was Simon Manzana. He came from somewhere in the Transkei, some village she had never heard of.

There was something about him that was foreign to her, intriguing to her, because he was different from the men life had hitherto thrown in her path. It was obvious he didn't know his way around. He was a fool, but no coward.

From time to time his glance held hers. She stared through him, but he excited her. She decided she must watch Diz and his antics; he might suddenly become nasty, and she didn't want Simon Manzana to get a bloody head. Or worse.

Diz was drawling on: Was Mr Manzana by any chance looking for someone here in Ma-jaze's place? Man? Or woman? Yes, perhaps it was a woman?

Manzana glanced quickly round the group, catching their varied expressions of amusement and anticipation. His body stiffened, but Diz pressed on.

'What d'you know! That's a natty suit you're wearing. You must introduce me to your tailor sometime.'

Ken Madoda kicked Zondeka's shin hard.

'Hold it, Stan! Look at the fellow's muscles. And he's a good sight taller than Diz Dinake.'

Stan rubbed his bruised shin. 'But he wouldn't stand a chance. He hasn't a knife on him, I'll bet.'

The watching group held its breath. It was a good thing Ma-jaze was busy in the back premises.

'Any more questions?' said Manzana, coming closer to Dinake.

At this point Ken butted in.

'That's right. Tell him to mind his own bloody business.'

He had to dodge a cuff from Dinake.

'Cut the cackle, man!' called another.

'Look out!' whispered Zondeka to Ken. 'Dinake's hackles are up. He'll whip out that knife if you're not careful.'

Diz and Ken stood bristling like two fighting hyenas.

Suddenly Linda put her hand on Diz's arm. With a curse he flung it off.

'You were doing fine, Diz,' she drawled. 'I'm dying of boredom.'

There was a ripple of uneasy laughter.

'That's punctured him,' Ken remarked.

Linda called out to the jazz players: 'Say, there, Stan. What about it? What's the matter with you, Toni? Have you gone to sleep? Come on, folks. Let's dance!'

The players groaned, but fell in with her coaxing and walked over to their instruments.

'What's going on here?' Ma-jaze, who had just come into the room, was sniffing the air like a warhorse.

Her glance fell on Linda, with her hand firmly on Dinake's arm, then moved over to the stranger.

'You were sleeping, Ma-jaze. You nearly missed the show,' teased Ken.

'What show?'

'Ken's pulling your leg, as usual,' answered Linda.

Ma-jaze was not taken in, but reckoned that the young woman had things under control. Only she did look a bit excited.

Stan and Toni manfully made the best of it without Sonny Matyolo and his sax; the dancers clutched their partners and swung into the floor space that was left to them.

'Come on, Diz!' said Linda. Dinake followed her sulkily, too bemused to pursue his objective, but vaguely resentful.

Simon Manzana did not hide his chagrin; making no move to choose a partner, he watched Linda wherever she moved, while she seemed to be completely oblivious of this tense-eyed attention.

'Oh, my poor feet,' moaned Ma-jaze, planting herself on a vacated stool.

'When you count up your takings for the weekend, they won't feel so sore,' was Ken's comment to this.

'Your saucy tongue will get you into trouble one of these days,' she retorted.

'Just watch the *moegoe*. The silly mutt doesn't know he might have been carved up, if Linda hadn't stepped in.'

Ma-jaze followed his glance. 'So that's it? Who is he?'

'He calls himself Simon Manzana. The palooka doesn't know what he's running into. She saved his life. But who knows? Our Linda Malindi is a cunning one.'

'You think she's fallen for him?'

'Why did she bother to stop the show, eh? She isn't squeamish when it comes to a fight.'

'You've said something there.' Ma-jaze removed one of her shoes, massaging her foot tenderly.

'Do you see what I see?' Ken said.

'What now?'

'It's Emily Vermeulen making up to the *moegoe*.'

'That woman again!'

'He's scared of her.'

'That's not how I read the signs. Look where he's still got his eyes skinned.'

'He's too simple for her, Ma-jaze.'

'You mean Linda? I'm not so sure. There's something about him – not so simple as he looks,' she said.

'Take my word for it. He'd bore her in a week.'

'On the other hand, Diz Dinake has had a fairly long innings. She's restless these days. Haven't you noticed?'

'But Diz is useful to her. It's bread and butter. And some more besides.'

'You wouldn't dare say that to her face. She'll look for something better than Diz. God, man, the child deserves something better than that bantam cock.'

'Ma-jaze, you're slipping. Who the devil gets what he deserves in this world? Do you? Do I? We're all left heaving and kicking at the bottom of the pit.'

'You're telling me!'

She rose, grimacing as she struggled into her shoe. 'There'll be trouble if all those glasses aren't filled up.'

'And what about mine?'

'Come and get it for yourself.'

'Lead the way, Ma-jaze.'

Pirouetting after her, Ken winked towards the sweating players.

'Keep it up, Toni! Go it, Stan!'

'Have a heart,' said the guitar player.

'Do me a favour,' shouted Stan, pummelling his xylophone.

'Go and beat up that bastard, Sonny Matyolo.'

'Me, go out into the dark night? Not on your life.'

Thus the night wore on. Other habitués of Ma-jaze's establishment knocked and were admitted through the low doorway by the young stalwart Gudu, who made himself Angels One door-keeper-in-chief on Saturday nights. The fug of smoke thickened. Faster flowed the sweat and the liquor. Suffocating as the atmosphere was, nobody would have thought of opening the window. The closed and curtained window gave the illusion of shutting out the vapours and perils of the night. Simon Manzana wooed Linda with silent importunity. But she evaded him without seeming to do so.

Stan and Toni were having a well-earned breather and a pleasant hum of voices filled the room. Folks were feeling relaxed when suddenly Ken raised an alert head. Those nearest him caught the movement and the hum ceased like a receding wave. Into the silence fell the distant sound of a motor engine stopping, with a screech of brakes; and then sharp and near, the thud of desperately running feet. Whoever it was had stopped outside the Angels One door.

There was an urgent knock, but nobody moved to answer it. At that moment Ma-jaze stood on the threshold of the inner room. The knocking was repeated, even more urgently, and a muffled voice called: 'Open, man! Let me in!'

'Gudu, open!' said Ma-jaze. 'It's Sonny Matyolo.'

Gudu obeyed and Sonny tumbled in as though he'd been winded, clutching his instrument case close to his body with one hand, and his throat with the other.

'Now then, what's happened?' said Ma-jaze.

Sonny collapsed on the nearest chair, gasping for breath. 'The world's gone mad tonight . . . First I nearly ran into a pitched battle . . . between the Cubans and the Tsomi gang . . . There they were . . . right in the middle of the street, stalking one another . . . knives flashing.'

'Is that how they got you?'

'No, no – it was the cops. Just as I reached Luke's corner . . .

I'm damned if I don't bump into the cops – out on a pass raid, busy as hell. Like a bloody fool I'd forgotten my *dompas* at home. Left it in my old coat. Hey! They've bloodied my new one!'

Ma-jaze signalled to Linda who seized a cloth lying among some glasses and knelt to staunch the wound.

'A fellow starts running . . . then another. Now was my chance. So I start running, too . . . But the cops are smart . . . They come after us with the pickup van. They chase us . . . and start shooting – I guess . . .' His strength was ebbing.

'Yes. I heard the van. It must be close by,' said Diz Dinake, looking uneasy.

'It can't . . . come up . . . this road,' said Sonny, fighting for breath.

'You can never tell what the cops are up to. Now do what I say,' snapped Ma-jaze. 'You,' she said to Simon, 'you're tall and strong. Carry Sonny out the back way. Do the best you can for him.'

Mechanically Linda followed Simon as he picked up Sonny and carried him out.

'There mustn't be any sign of blood about the place. Wipe it up,' Ma-jaze ordered Diz Dinake. 'And you, Ken, wipe Sonny's instrument case. Put it out of sight. Carry on as if nothing's happened.'

'Okay, okay, Ma-jaze.'

Gudu remained by the door, while Stan Zondeka stationed himself at the window, trying to see without being seen. He withdrew hastily as a light flashed from outside. Ma-jaze took a seat near the door, drawing a neat shawl about her shoulders. Everyone sat around trying to look indifferent, but their eyes were wary and ill at ease.

'Where has Diz Dinake disappeared to?' asked Ma-jaze.

'Don't ask me,' said Ken with a shrug. 'He's taking no chances where the cops are concerned.'

Several people laughed uneasily.

'He's not the only one,' added Zondeka.

Ma-jaze surveyed her customers quizzically. 'If the cops hear no noise, they'll come nosing around to see what's up. Stan, there, get your drumsticks busy. And you, Toni, pluck our heart strings for all you're worth. Go on, you fools – Dance! Dance! Ken, let's hear what you can do with Sonny's sax.'

Thus prompted, Ken drew from Sonny's instrument some soul-killing sounds.

'Wait! Who says I can't make this baby talk? Just you listen.'

Everyone waited. An excruciating high note burst forth, amid hysterical laughter.

'Try again,' said Ma-jaze.

And Ken did.

'Shh! Shh!' hissed Ma-jaze. 'What's that?'

The revving of a motor engine assailed their ears.

'That's as sweet a sound as Belafonte's latest hit song,' Ken remarked.

'The dogs have packed up and gone,' said Ma-jaze.

'It's a wonder they didn't look in for a swig of the liquor, eh, Ma-jaze? Pass raids must give you a thirst,' said Ken.

He looked round as Simon and Linda entered the room. Linda's step faltered. Simon's arm gently encircled her shoulders.

Silence fell on the group.

'He's dead,' said Simon.

Linda looked stonily in front of her.

Ma-jaze: 'Don't take it like that, child. Come, sit by me.'

Linda did not seem to hear her. Simon, with the same gentle movement, propelled her to a seat beside Ma-jaze, and seated himself on the other side.

'On with the dance,' said Ma-jaze.

She stroked Linda's head. She suspected that some old memory had produced this state of shock, more than the actual death of Sonny Matyolo.

Stan Zondeka struck his drum with a flourish to wake the dead; Toni Ngusa plucked from his guitar all the singing vibration his sensitive fingers could command.

Sonny Matyolo's saxophone lay still.

The first to leap to his feet was Simon Manzana, who seized Linda round the waist and whirled her into a frenzied dance. The two players, like men possessed, gave out one favourite tune after another, answering the cry for 'More! More! More!'

For the rest of the evening Manzana did not leave Linda's side. They saw nobody but each other.

Six

It was the second time Simon Manzana had come to her room. It wasn't easy for them to be alone anywhere. Sophiatown life and privacy don't go together. Linda had fought with the woman from whom she rented the room at a stiff price to get it to herself, and even then she had to put up with two of her raucous kids who usually slept there. Now, when she and Simon arrived, there was a scuffle, punctuated by loud protests from the children. Having successfully pushed them out, she slammed and locked the door. Standing with her back against it, she looked across at Simon shyly.

'That's how it is here. It's fight fight fight all the time, just to be able to breathe.'

'It's worse where I stay,' he said. 'There are fellows sleeping there in the day, and at night – ' he laughed. 'You can just about turn over.'

'I can make you a cup of tea,' she offered.

'Tea would be fine. But I want more than tea.'

Sitting on the bed, he drew her beside him.

'Greedy!' Her fingers touched his face lightly. Then she pulled away and made herself busy with tea-making.

He sat and watched every curve and movement of her body. She decided this was an embarrassing habit of his and surprised herself by feeling self-conscious.

'How long have you been here?' she asked.

'One whole long year.'

'So long? I thought you'd come up from the country only last week.'

'How so?'

'Well . . . how shall I say? You look different; you act different – '

'A *moegoe*, eh? A bit of a country bumpkin?' They laughed together.

'Well, you don't seem to know much about what's what in the city.'

'I have tasted the first miseries of the city.'

'Yes.' Her tone was as laconic as his own. 'And not the last.'

The tinkle of cups filled the silence.

'How did you come to be at Ma-jaze's place? You didn't look exactly at home.'

'Oh, I've tried all sorts. Killing time in the evenings is the worst. It isn't easy to sleep.'

'What kind of job did you get?'

'Several kinds, and none of them fit for a man.'

'You've said it. There's few of them fit for a woman either. Nursing, I don't fancy it. Teaching, I didn't get enough schooling for it.'

'My first job was with the builders,' he said. 'Oh, not making the houses, you understand. Not even throwing up the bricks. Just making daga – mixing the cement and the sand.' He contemplated his outspread hands as he spoke. 'My hands are fit for a better job. A job with skill. The machines! Ah! I like them. I like to touch them, their great strong flanks. They have such power!' He paused. 'That was my second job. A cleaner in a factory, the "boy" sweeping the floors and dusting the machines – when they were idle, but not when they were throbbing with energy.'

'You are bitter,' she said.

'Bitter? Maybe. I'd say – hungry for a man's work. But now it's your turn. Tell me about yourself.'

'Me? Oh, there's nothing to tell. I was born here in Kofifi. I've never been out of it. It's my home. I know it through and through . . .'

'And your parents? Are they here?'

'There's only me. My mother died. My father – ' She shrugged. 'I don't know if he's alive. They took him to a farm-jail.'

He sighed. 'No brothers or sisters?'

She paused. 'None! You are too nosy.' She looked away from him.

'I'm sorry, Linda.' He put his hand over hers but she pulled it away.

'My brother – Joel – was killed in a gang fight. I saw him. They carried him into the house and – ' Then, matter-of-factly: 'Are you still at the factory?'

'No. the foreman kicked me out.'

'Why? What did you do?'

'That's just it. I did nothing. But he said I was cheeky.'

'But how? What did you say?'

'I didn't say: Ja, baas.' They both laughed. 'And he didn't like the way I looked.'

'How did you look?'

'Like myself. I dunno. But now I know better. Now I put on a special face for their benefit.'

'A special face? That's funny. So do I. Let's see your special face.'

'Never! My own's bad enough.'

'It looks all right to me.'

They gazed foolishly into each other's eyes.

'Let me see *your* special face,' he said.

'Never! Mine's bad enough too!'

'It looks beautiful to me.' And he cupped it in his generous hands. With a quick movement she turned away. Simon Manzana didn't behave towards her like the other guys she knew. He didn't talk like them either. His touch excited her, made her feel uneasy.

'And then what was your next job?' She wanted to know more and more.

'Oh, you might call it a step up in the world. I ride a bicycle. I'm a messenger for a grocery firm. Boy come here! Boy go there!'

'A messenger?' Her voice took on a sharp note.

'Yes. Why? What's on your mind?'

'Oh, nothing. Is it a big firm? Probably not big enough.'

'Big enough for what?'

She looked down. 'Oh, it doesn't matter. I wish you could drive a van.'

He seized her hand. 'Shake! That's exactly what I've been wanting to do. Drive a van. How did you know? I *must* drive a van! To feel the power of the machine under my hands! To make it do what I want it to do! Hau! But what's the use of wishing and dreaming? How can I ever get the chance to hold the wheel?'

'Why not? Jo Bula has a posh American car.'

'And who is Jo Bula?'

'A guy I know.'

'Oh, you know him, do you? This Jo Bula and his American car?'

'Well, not really. But if he has a car, why not you?'

'Just show me how! If my guess is right, Jo Bula didn't learn the know-how inside the law.'

'Greenhorn! Simpleton! In the city you have to learn different ideas about how to live, and pretty fast, too. Keeping on the right side of the law isn't one of them. We were born on the wrong side of the law and we'll stay that way.'

'Well, well! Tell me something new, young woman of the city. I'll tell you something we learn in the country, too. Our whole existence is illegal. Even our dead bodies if they lie in the wrong grave.'

'Dead? Hau! That's too serious for me,' she said.

'Too damn serious. My fault. At this moment we are alive.' He bent his head towards her. 'Very much alive, eh, Linda?'

'Mmm.' The sound was distinctly yielding.

'Let's keep it that way, you and me,' he said, and drew her into his arms. She struggled a little. He pushed her gently down on the bed.

But Linda told herself it wasn't that easy. Simon found her provocative, tantalising, yet with an undercurrent of hostility. His senses ached for her, but he knew how to be patient.

Linda, treading strange ground, did not know whether to mock such restraint, or torment him further. She had to admit to herself she had fallen for the stranger from the country in a big way, but she couldn't afford to let him know it. No man, she told herself, would find her a cheap pushover. She behaved testily towards him, finding perverse pleasure in observing his hurt, puzzled look. There was something about him that moved her in a way she hadn't felt since Joel's death. It made her feel exposed, vulnerable. She had tried teasing him for his gaucherie on that first occasion they had met at Ma-jaze's.

'I'll teach you how to live in this city,' she had said. 'I'll show you the ropes.'

He laughed aloud. 'I do not need your teaching.'

'We'll see about that. You, what do you know, dear simpleton?'

For answer he took her in his arms in good earnest. In one respect at least, the simpleton knew her desires better than herself.

In the nights that followed, Simon Manzana gave himself wholeheartedly to the joys and perturbations of being with Linda. If he brought something new and disturbing into her life, she was no less rare to him. She filled his senses with an excitement he had not hitherto experienced. Her unpredictable moods, her subtleties, were strange to him, belonging to a world he did not know. They surprised him with new sensations, fascinated him and sometimes repelled him. She was right when she said he did not yet know that world. Sometimes he perceived a coarseness in her that startled him. Yet she was quick to catch his reserve at such moments and turned on him with fierce resentment. Did he by any chance think he was superior to her? He would have to get that idea out of his head, double quick. She came from Sophiatown, she did. It was hell, but it was her world, her universe. And she was alive because she knew how to look after herself.

What was he? An ignoramus from the country. Let him make no mistake. He'd be lying in a ditch by now, with Diz Dinake's knife stuck in his back, if it wasn't for her. In this world you had to get in first and kill, before the other fellow killed you. That was Sophiatown philosophy.

Half amused, Simon listened to her tirade, then caught her in full tide with an exasperating remark. He seemed to her slow and even dull-witted at times in his reactions to her.

'Now just tell me,' he said. 'What are we quarrelling about?'

'Quarrelling? I'm not quarrelling.'

'No? Then is this the sweet way you usually treat your friends?'

'Sweet, my foot!'

'Exactly. Then why are you putting out your claws at *me*? What have I done to you, Linda? I am all yours. Look. Every pore of me is open to you. Come!'

She stared at him in silence. It was her turn to be amazed at his simplicity. Then she burst into laughter; relief, wonder and sheer joy struggling for expression in it. How she loved this strange man of hers! She flung herself on his breast.

He took her gently. Naked, she felt the supple sinews of the man, unsuspected in the ill-fitting garments he had worn. Like two young foals they played, young foals who gambol for joy of the sunshine after rain, revelling in the sweet-smelling fields. After a time she lay listening to his heartbeat, tasting the sensuous pleasure of the soft, steady rise and fall of his breathing and her own, each rhythmical beat different and distinct in their separate bodies, yet combining in harmony, their secret pulse bound together as one. It was a sound she had never heard before.

The wail of a child crying in the next room shattered this concord. Someone banged on the wall and a harsh voice rumbled in with the child's wail; then silence again. Linda's relaxed body had tightened on his, but he slipped from her grasp. Both knew he could not stay with her throughout the night; before long he would have to leave her and stumble out into the perilous dark to his own lodging. His body began to feel chilled. As he dressed, she lay watching him, loath to stir. She too felt the chill of reality as she watched his face.

'And where is this man you call Diz – what's his name?' he asked suddenly.

He hadn't been unduly perturbed at his rival's menacing attitude towards him in the first week of their acquaintance, being spared perhaps by his ignorance of the nature of the relationship between Dinake and Linda, and her deep involvement in it. And no one had enlightened him. It wasn't worth the risk. Now it dawned on Simon that he hadn't seen the fellow around for some time.

'He isn't dead, is he?'

'Dead?' She laughed, sitting up and pulling her slip over her shoulders. 'That would be too simple. They nabbed him on the job.'

'The police?'

'Who else? It means the Fort for him. Quite a spell, too. He's been in before.'

'What was he doing?'

'Doing? Simpleton! Taking, of course. That's how he lives.'

Manzana made no comment.

'There you go again,' she flashed. 'Being superior.'

'I didn't say anything.'

'Oh, didn't you? You're not above biting his heels, I'll bet.'

Springing away from the bed she glared at him in fury.

'Let me tell you, you know nothing, damn you. A man isn't a man if he doesn't take. That's what I learned from my brother Joel. There was nobody like my brother Joel – and – and they killed him. What do *you* know? If a man goes to jail, whose fault is it? Don't you spit on Diz for that. Jesus, they have robbed us of everything – our homes, our children –' Her voice cracked on the word. Simon put out his hand, drawing her towards the bed. She slipped down at his feet.

'Linda, why fight with me? Why beat *me* to death? Do you

think I don't know the truth of all you've been saying? You seem to have a queer notion of the place where I come from. We have the ways of the people on the land, it's true. We are slow, like the movement of the seasons. We walk on the soil, not on the city pavements of hard white stone. And perhaps we think slowly, too. But we are not stupid. In the country things happen to us, fiendish things, the same as they happen to you in the city. Only there's more din and clamour here. In the country the pangs of hunger grip us too, only there's nothing to steal. And we die too, only nobody hears our death-cry out there, by the huts in the empty fields. Here in the city, as I have found it, there's such a tempest and torment of living, that men here, too, die unheard in the roar and clangour of it.'

Simon bent to look into her face. Was she listening? He was not sure. She had the curiously vacant, almost indifferent expression of one who has emptied herself of emotion long-stored and pressed out of consciousness. He lifted her on to the bed and lay down beside her. Her body did not yield to his nearness. Her eyes were open but unresponsive. He began slowly and softly to stroke her face with his fingers till he felt the rigidity passing out of it. Her lips quivered. A smile lightened her eyes. She flung her arm across his body.

Seven

Like hundreds of thousands of other country folk, Simon Manzana had been sucked into the big city, sucked by the ravenous needs of the gold mines and of industry and no less by the ferocious poverty of the so-called Native Reserves, a land poverty which was the other end of the giant suction pump. The Reserves had been denuded of able-bodied men as much as the soil of its fertility, a chronic lack of land-space having condemned both to exploitation. This monstrous suction pump had moved into action in the eighteen eighties with the discovery of the diamonds and the gold; it had swallowed up man and beast, land and the fruits of the soil, family life and human relationships with satanic impartiality. In the post-war nineteen forties and fifties, with the opening of new gold mines and the leap forward of industrial activity, the suction pump moved into top gear.

In the well-ordered chaos of the city, where in the sacred name of free enterprise a species of cannibalism was of necessity practised at all levels, not all of the African cheap labour force was used up by the mines, the farms and industry. A flotsam and jetsam of humanity supplied the black army of cleaners, messengers and domestic servants, each apartheided in the regimental garments of their menial service. It was to this flotsam and jetsam that Simon Manzana, and Linda too, belonged.

Not that exploitation was simply a one-way traffic as from white to black. Ma-jaze had hit quite near the mark when, in a passion against Jo Bula and his like – guilty of some double-cross at her expense – she had called such men cannibals. But she would have scored a bullseye if she had extended her vision to embrace a whole system in which whites and blacks were locked.

Engrossed as she was in the struggle to keep her head above the murky waters of her own particular pond, she could not pause to conceive the vast and terrible ocean of the city, where monsters large and small devoured one another. In its corruptions and torments Sophiatown was but a microcosm of the City of Gold itself. Small township gangsters like Jo Bula only contrived to imitate their larger white prototypes with a more obviously abominable savagery; in its sum total a puny blow struck at their defenceless brothers, while themselves exposed to violent death in alleys or in jails. But the destructiveness of the so much more powerful monsters of the city was more pitiless in its impersonality, its very indifference to the fate of the individual. It dealt in the mass. As they disported themselves in the heaving waters of the ocean, their iron scales glittered in the sun with a deceptive beauty; masters of opulence and resplendent camouflage, they were able to hide their gaping jaws so insatiable for human flesh.

Simon Manzana, in common with his fellows, considered it preferable to venture into the unknown of the city, with all its hazards, its frantic pleasures and its terrors, to rotting on the land. What he did not reveal to Linda was that he had left behind in the country a young wife and a daughter less than two years old.

Nor had she been straight with him over her relationship with Diz Dinake.

That both of them had to resort to a tacit lie was part of

the pattern of their insecurity, the almost inevitable mores of a brazenly immoral society at every level. Everyone knew that the law forbade an African to bring his family when he was immured in the mine barracks by a system of contract labour. It was almost equally impossible in these days to get permission to bring them into the city townships, a fact that gave countenance to the illicit unions that were a commonplace among them. No doubt Linda suspected that her lover had other ties, but she was careful to say nothing. She lived for the day. It was enough

Out of his meagre wages Manzana tried to send money now and again to his father, with whom lived Simon's wife Boniswa and his daughter Nothanda, as well as his sister Funeka and the girl-wife and child of his younger brother Mvuzo, who worked on a white farm. On the days when a letter arrived from the country, Linda always had to shake him out of his gloom, though he did not confide in her as to the cause of it. It was his wife who penned the letter, but the voice was the stern voice of his father. The money Simon was sending, she wrote, was not enough to put food into their mouths. With their mealie crop long since eaten up, they had to buy from the storekeeper at an exorbitant price. But there was in addition the big debt they owed the storekeeper, which Simon had done nothing to pay off, though he had promised he would do so, once he had a job in the city. Now the storekeeper was threatening not to give them any more credit. Already they had sold him some of their goats, but he did not want any more of their miserable goats. When Funeka and Boniswa went to the store to plead with him, he swore at them and pushed them out. If Manzana's family died of hunger it was none of his business. He, too, had to live and there were bad debts all around. The people seemed to think he toiled in his store just to feed them, and for nothing

Acutely aware of his inability to send the money so badly needed by his family, Simon had come to dread opening a letter from home. How could he explain to them how much more expensive it was to live in the city: the transport, the food, the lodging? He felt frustrated, guilty, and somehow resentful more against his father and his wife than against his circumstances.

Those debts were an incubus round his neck, so that he could only think of home with pain and guilt; the channels of natural feeling were dammed up.

A few days before he had first met Linda at Angels One, he had received another plaintive letter from home, and as soon as he got his month's pay, he sent some money to his father. His heart had felt lighter, but so had his purse. Overcome with a pang of homesickness, he pictured how the letter would travel all the way to his home village; how excited his wife Boniswa and his father would be; and how his sister Funeka would stand by, more excited than any of them, making little sounds that held more of tears than of laughter. He had cursed himself for such daydreaming and jingled the few coins in his pocket. It was then that he had decided to blow them at Angels One. What did it matter?

His plight was different from Linda's. Her parents had been drawn into Sophiatown nearly a quarter of a century earlier, so that while she was bereft of traditions that still provided Simon with a tenuous moral support, she had acquired a protective hide that made survival possible – at a price. Simon had yet to pass through the fire, and anything might happen to him in the process. His hide was still as vulnerable as the tender horns of a young snail. Throughout his childhood and early youth, harsh as its conditions were, he had been blessed with one rare security – affection, that vital soil from which spring human attributes. Through his mother, and perhaps even more his sister Funeka, he had imbibed it as naturally as the fresh morning air when as a boy he took his father's few cattle to the grazing grounds. It was a valuable inheritance, where all other securities were dwindling into chaos

In the city his needs drove him to seek out Linda and the feeling he gave her was warm and spontaneous, natural to one of his character. But his problem was one of divided loyalty.

Where was his home?

In Linda's breast, or with those from whom he had learned his affections?

If the process of acquiring a protective hardening could be

speeded up, Linda was the very one to teach him but, again, at a price. Through her demands a new civilisation – or the township dregs of it which was all the Africans could receive – would all the more powerfully affect him. Here were two young people flung into the maelstrom of the city, where human relationship itself must partake of the general turmoil and confusions of existence. Neither one knew the other. Simon's reticence about his family and his anxieties concerning them left a dangerous territory unmapped between him and Linda.

It would have been better for them both if she had known, and understood, what soil had nourished his affections and loyalties.

His father, an impoverished peasant with a stubborn individuality, had seen his stock seized from him one by one according to the new laws which to him were nothing but legalised robbery. An older brother had died and his sister Funeka had looked after Simon and the two younger boys, Gundani and Mvuzo, while his mother was busy helping her husband in the fields. Funeka was a simple girl, not very robust in health, who lived through the steadfastness of her affections, especially for Simon.

His parents, like Linda's mother, had struggled to give him education. As a boy he had trudged miles every day to one of those single-teacher schools, an oasis in a desert of educational penury. But he was soon hungry for more than it could offer him and, after much painful deliberation, his parents agreed to send him to a bigger mission school in the hope that he might become a teacher and provide his younger brothers with the same opportunity he was receiving.

But Simon never had the chance to finish his schooling.

First there was the drought. To the peasants it seemed that some malign fate had withheld the life-giving rains, and their mealie crop was a failure. As if this was not bad enough, they were thrown into consternation when they found themselves, under the new regulations, compelled to reduce their already meagre stock. At a meeting of the people Simon's father was loud in his protestations. Was it not monstrous to take from those who already had too few cattle for their needs? How, then, could they plough? Where were their children to get milk? His views were strongly supported by other peasants, though there were certain of the wily old headmen – as he reported to the young Simon – who stroked their chins and looked solemn, advising the people to do nothing rash, meaning anything that was likely to offend the white baas. The meeting had broken up in disorder. Then the police had arrived and dragged the agitators – so they were called – off to jail. His father had been lucky to escape arrest. All this meant disruption in the house of Manzana. Struggling beyond his strength to provide food for his family, the old man grew bitter and harsh of tongue.

Eventually, the family began to break up. His second son Gundani was recruited for mine labour, leaving behind his girl-wife who was with child. His third and youngest, Mvuzo, sought work as a farm labourer and his young wife also worked in the house of the white baas on the far distant farm. Neither of them kept in touch with their father, and so far had not sent back any money. Much against his will Simon had to leave the mission school and return home in order to help his father in the fields, relinquishing his ambition to better himself, though he too was sorely tempted to join the hundreds of thousands of work seekers in the city.

Funeka, too, felt there was nothing for her to look forward to and if Simon were to go away also, she would seek employment in the nearest dorp, though she could only work for a pittance as a domestic servant. But her father was ageing rapidly and wouldn't hear of it.

Desperate to hold the family together, Funeka had a plan she was sure would keep Simon from being lured to the City of Gold. She had a friend, Boniswa, a young woman who seemed to her an ideal wife for her favourite brother. She was pretty, and, unlike herself, she was strong and healthy and would bear many children. And as if this was not virtue enough, she was also good natured. So often the pretty ones were vain and selfish, setting too high a price on their physical charms. With the cunning of a devoted matchmaker, Funeka sang in the ears of each the praises of the other, so that when Simon and Boniswa finally met at the wedding feast of a young couple in a neighbouring village, they looked at each other and saw the idealised image that Funeka had so lovingly painted. It was true that Simon should not be entertaining thoughts of marriage in so uncertain a time, especially with the lure of Goli still haunting his dreams. But when did young blood ever stop to measure its actions with the dull wisdom of grey hairs? Besides, if Simon's wife were in the house, Funeka would have someone else to share her labours, especially now that Gundani's wife had lost her baby in childbirth and wanted to seek work in the towns. It was a sad house these days and Boniswa had a gift of laughter. His father, too, oblivious of Simon's secret yearnings, thought marriage would be good for his eldest son; a young man like him needed a woman. If only the good soaking rains would come and he could coax a bigger crop from the soil, then an extra pair of hands, young and strong like Boniswa's, would be an excellent thing.

So Simon and Boniswa were married and the summer rains came, blessing their wedding day and bringing a small measure of life to the weary soil. Simon worked with a will in the fields, glad to see the bitter lines of his father's face relax into a kind of hope.

In course of time the young couple had their firstborn, a daughter, whom they named Nothanda, after his mother. Old Manzana was seen to smile when he bent over his eldest son's child in its mother's arms and spoke the name that had not passed his lips since he had borne his wife's body to the grave at the foot of the hill.

But alas for the hopes of men! The good soaking rains did not fall the following season, and now there were two extra mouths to feed. The young, strong hands of his son's wife were ready to perform their share of work – but where was the harvest? So once more, and now with greater urgency, Simon declared his intention of going to Goli to find work.

In these days it was not an easy thing to get into the city without a permit. Police blocked every channel except where African labour was most needed: the mines and the white farms. Of course he could have entered into a contract to labour in the mines. They were always hunting for cheap black labour. But he hated the idea of working underground as much as he abhorred the slave conditions on the white farms. There was nothing for it but to make his way illegally into the city.

Many others had slipped through the net, so why not he? Strange, wasn't it, how their pass laws, their police, their black spies – not to speak of the white ones – restricted you wherever you went, in the country or in the town? And now – a source of much heartbreak and quarrelling between himself and Boniswa – he could not take her with him to the city townships. For a wife, you needed a permit. Boniswa accused him of not wanting to take her with him. But what could he do? He could not let her and his Nothanda starve in a township, with the threat of police action hanging over her into the bargain. Boniswa must be reasonable. Hau! Was it unreasonable to wish to stay with your husband, a good, hard-working wife? Yes, but what could they do? Always they came back to that question. He had to find some means of helping his father, his sister Funeka and herself, he argued. There were jobs to be had in the big city, if he could escape arrest. And there was money. He was quite sure he could live on next to nothing and send home his earnings.

Funeka agreed with her brother. She added the argument that she and Boniswa together could take Simon's place in helping their father in the fields. She was quite strong enough. And when Boniswa interrupted her, saying Funeka was nothing of the kind, she got a look of reproachful anger for her pains. Old Manzana himself, with bitter but unspoken wrath in his heart, bowed to the inevitable. His wife had been right when she had said they would have to see their sons depart one by one, or else bury them like her firstborn. He was tired of the arguments going on and on. The women talked too much. Let Simon go and prove himself a man.

A final incident clinched the matter. This was the arrival of his brother Mvuzo's young wife. She was with child, and she was unwell. Mvuzo had been allowed to have her with him on the farm because they needed her at the big house, but not now that she was sickly. So here she was, another mouth to feed.

Next day Simon prepared to leave for the city. It was Funeka who insisted that he must set out on his journey decently clad. So she and Boniswa walked to the store some miles off and purchased a new shirt, trousers, a jacket and a blanket. After much pleading, the storekeeper allowed them to have the goods on credit and they came home triumphant, saying he was really a decent man after all.

Linda found that there was an exciting quality to Simon that made him fun to be with. She introduced him to her haunts; she made him part of her way of life and they became more and more dependent on each other.

Ken teased her about her new steady. He was such a well-behaved young man. Too well-behaved. And this was something she had not foreseen: Simon didn't fit in with 'the boys'. He just didn't click. Oh, he was friendly enough, but they didn't trust him. Trust? He seemed honest enough. That was the trouble. He just didn't fit in with their code.

In the inner sanctum of Angels One, burglary jobs and hold-ups were planned. Any alien element was regarded with sharp suspicion and soon removed. In this set-up Jo Bula supplied most of the brains and the unwritten blueprints for those classy jobs with the bait of big money and the casual risk of manslaughter thrown in. Beneath the caricature image his Hollywood gangster get-up gave him, was a cunning and ruthlessness as ready to spill black blood as white. This was something to inspire fear in the district, if not respect. The small fry, tsotsis like Diz Dinake, hovered round this charmed centre but weren't yet ready to make the grade, though Jo Bula kept an eye on them for possible recruits. Hence the enmity that existed between his henchman Nick Noboza and Dinake was not necessarily shared by the boss himself. Jo Bula was not averse to these rivalries, since it kept the youngsters on their toes. In an occupation with a distinctly high accident rate you had to have ready replacements.

One day not long after Simon Manzana's arrival at Ma-jaze's, word was brought to Jo Bula that Dinake, shortly before his arrest, had passed the word around that Manzana did not qualify to be one of 'the boys'. Most decidedly not. Dinake had sounded him on coming in on a small job of taking at the store where Simon was employed as messenger – a quite innocuous affair – and the fellow had shown himself, as Diz had said, to have no liver. In telling his tale Diz had let rip on Manzana's scruples. Bloody fool. Palooka. Serve him right if the police nabbed him for his pass and threw him in the cells. Especially on a Sunday night when they wanted their quota, nabbing them so they could disgorge them up from the cells on Monday morning and fine them as fast as sausages spewing out of a butcher's machine. Who did Manzana think he was?

Jo Bula had shrugged when he heard the tale. Let the small fry manage their own affairs. And if that young woman, Linda Malindi, chose to throw away her talents on this *moegoe*, that was her loss.

But then Diz was arrested. That wasn't so funny. A rumour sprouted as fast as a beanstalk in a muck-heap. Was Simon Manzana a tec? Was he snooping around for information and putting on the country-bumpkin-butter-wouldn't-melt-in-his-mouth act? Christ, if he was so keen to court death, he had better look out. A knife in the back would be too simple. There were other ways.

With her keen nose Linda had at first detected no more than a frost in the air at Ma-jaze's when she appeared with Manzana. In that first week or so she'd had the devil's own job lulling Diz's suspicions as to whither her fancy had strayed. Not exactly a game she disliked, because it served to keep Simon guessing. She had told herself she would have to take his education in hand as far as 'the boys' – and other things – were concerned. He had a thus-far-and-no-further kind of air about him that was, to say the least, tactless. And then there was the small matter of the drinks. He wasn't one to let himself go. That was no damn good if you wanted to be popular. However, she had no doubt she would soon knock him into shape.

But after the arrest of Diz it wasn't a mere frost she detected. It was more like an acid fallout dropping its corrosive on herself as well as her new escort. She was in the dark, a disquieting sensation. Diz hadn't told her about his proposal to Manzana, nor about his repulse. It was only some time after his arrest that Ken gave her the hint. To tell the truth, she had become so caught up in her affair with Simon that she was neglecting her job, her friends, everything, and positively living in a dream. Maybe Diz had wanted to tell her, but she had fought shy of him, and when he did speak to her she had kept a fixed smile turned on to hide the fact that she was practically deaf as far as his dulcet tones were concerned.

So when at last Ken told her about the reported incident between Diz and her Simon, she laughed and said she'd have to put him wise as to what was good for him. Diz's idea hadn't been a bad one. How unnecessarily careful Simon had been to hide the fact from her. But when Ken went on to throw out more sinister hints concerning the rumour going the rounds at Angels One, Linda fixed him with a stare.

'What's the mystery, eh? Diz has been nabbed before. Just what are you getting at, Ken?'

Ken had played dumb and buzzed off. You didn't pick a quarrel with Linda, least of all in her present state. It was fairly obvious that this newcomer, whoever he really was, had knocked her dizzy, at least for the time being. She'd probably come to her senses soon. She'd better, or she'd be messing herself up. Ma-jaze would have to put her straight. There'd be no monkey business when she was around. As for Jo Bula, you could see in that malevolent stare of his when he looked at Manzana that he was up to no good. And his silent henchman Nick had the air of a fellow rubbing his hands in anticipation – or was it his knuckledusters?

Casually sounding Ma-jaze, Ken got the answer that the rumour about Manzana was sheer hot air. To begin with, he should know that Ma-jaze could detect the stink of a cop a mile off and Simon, she averred, smelt as clean as a newly washed infant. Then what about Linda herself? Could she possibly be ratting on them? Never! It was inconceivable. Where, then, could such a crazy rumour have arisen? Nick Noboza was behind it, she wouldn't be a bit surprised. A dirty, vicious troublemaker, consumed with envy. It positively oozed out of him. And Jo Bula abetted him out of devilment. If he'd really thought Manzana was a tec, did Ken think he wouldn't have had him skinned alive long since? Of course they might goad the greenhorn just to see what he was made of. No harm in putting him through his paces so long as they didn't go too far. Nick Noboza would do it, the bastard, just for kicks.

For her part Linda seemed to thrive on threats. If there was to be a showdown, she'd let them see she was ready for it.

It wasn't long in coming.

It was Saturday afternoon at Angels One. Stan and Toni and Sonny Matyolo's replacement, Gus, one of Sophiatown's up-and-coming young saxophone players, hadn't arrived yet to liven things up with their band and let off steam. Folks were moping around. When Linda marched in, with Manzana following at her heels apparently unperturbed, she sniffed the air like a mettlesome young colt that is unused to the bridle and ready to pitch off into the mucky road any rider who dares to mount him. Looking smug, Jo Bula occupied his favourite corner while Nick Noboza and two others of his gang sat with their backs curved towards him, their cigarettes dangling.

'Hi, Jo!' she called. 'How's tricks?'

Jo Bula lifted his clenched hand and gave her an ironic nod without interrupting his conversation.

Smiling hard, she took up a position at another table close to the wall. Simon, tilting his chair against it, called for drinks. Ma-jaze wasn't visible. Now what was the matter with him? He had lit himself a cigarette and was puffing away at it. But he hadn't offered her one. Perhaps he was more nervous than he appeared. Could he fail to catch the hostility in the air? A furious irritation against him simmered inside her. This place was home – and today its face was hostile, and it was all Simon's fault. He'd have to stop putting on airs if he wanted to belong.

'Say, fellows,' said Linda, 'it's freezing cold around here, and it's summer too. Is anybody sick?'

Ma-jaze, at that moment dumping the drinks on the table, shot the shaft back.

'Who's talking about sickness? Folks have been asking: What's come over Linda Malindi these days? Is she sick or something?'

A high-pitched laugh rang out. It was Diz's old flame, Hilda Noyali, sitting beside her boyfriend Nkuku.

'I'm never sick,' said Linda. 'Why should I be sick? And who said it, anyway?'

'Oh, them . . . that wish you safe and well.'

Linda caught the undercurrent of warning in Ma-jaze's tone.

'Tell *them* to mind their own damn business, whoever they are. Tell *them* I can look after myself.'

'It's only that we're missing your old sparkle, our one and only starlet – Linda Malindi!' mocked Ken Madoda.

Hilda's silly laugh rang out again.

'I'll sparkle that mug of yours so's you'll have to keep it shut with sticking plaster for a month.'

Ken bounced out of reach of Linda's flailing fist, and Simon blundered in.

'Come on, Linda, sit down and have your drink. It'll cheer you up.'

'Keep your hands off me, will you!' she shouted. 'All of you.'

'Look at the country bumpkin now,' smirked Nick Noboza, sotto voce.

Jo Bula bared his teeth. 'Somebody will have to skin that saintly look off his face with a razor.'

Suddenly Hilda's piercing voice sang out: 'Has anybody heard what's happened to poor Diz?'

Linda swung round on her.

'When poor Diz comes out, he'll flatten that living corpse of yours so there'll be nothing to pick up. Diz has more guts than the lot of you put together.' Her angry glance included Manzana.

Nick Noboza picked up the game from Hilda. 'Maybe Mister Manzana knows what's happened to Diz – and why! Eh . . . brother?'

Simon measured him coolly. 'I don't know what you're talking about. And don't call me names. I'm not your brother.'

He bent his head carelessly to sip his brandy and Linda was about to whisper a warning. She knew the danger signs better than this simpleton of hers. It had been silly of her to get cross with him.

At that moment a knife whizzed past Manzana's right ear, landing neatly in the wall behind him. Almost simultaneously the two men leapt to their feet. Linda covered her eyes. Oh, no! The scene from her long-forgotten childhood when her father sent the knife into the wall flooded back on her with all its load of remembered anguish.

The room held its breath.

Manzana twisted round and plucked the knife.

'Thank you for the present. It looks clean.'

Nick Noboza grabbed another knife from one of his companions and darted towards Simon.

Jo Bula looked on, saying nothing.

'That's my property. Give here!' shouted Nick.

'Come and take it, then. Not afraid, are you?'

Nick made a snarling lunge for it, which Manzana evaded.

'No knives allowed on my premises!' Ma-jaze's voice startled the onlookers.

Manzana and Nick didn't budge, neither eye nor muscle, each concentrated on his opponent's next move.

'I said – no knives! D'you hear?' thundered Ma-jaze.

'That suits me. I've no wish to go around murdering men,' said Manzana. But he didn't drop his guard.

Jo Bula laughed.

'Jo Bula, what are you up to?' Ma-jaze glared accusingly at him.

'Tell that bastard, Nick Noboza – '

'Nick, put it on the table,' Jo Bula commanded.

Nick scowled defiance.

'Put the knife down, I say!'

Reluctantly Nick obeyed. He did not take his eyes from Manzana, who threw the knife down and then stepped out to face his opponent. Nick went back a pace, casting a furtive glance at his knife on the table.

There was an ominous rustling sound from Jo Bula's other two henchmen. They liked nothing better than watching a good fight.

Linda took in everything. She longed to cry out to Simon, to warn him. What chance had he against Jo Bula's men? Yes, Simon was in better trim, while the youthful Noboza had a frame altogether more slight and undermined by dissipation. On the other hand he was equipped with cunning and a frenzy to maim human flesh.

She watched, fascinated, against her will as the two men closed. At once excited and sickened, she felt the impact of the blows as if with each thud it was her own stomach that was being bombarded. With his tougher physique, Simon made the first headway against the youth, eager to press home his advantage and have done with the business. Too eager, Linda thought. Noboza suddenly landed him one below the belt, causing him to double up. Infuriated, the pain etched into the normally smooth planes of his face, he lunged back. The youth, on prancing toes, dodged him, at the same time edging nearer the table where his own knife still lay. Noboza got in another blow as his opponent again lunged at him, hoping to make use of his superior weight.

Linda suppressed a cry. It wasn't strength that would win this battle. Involuntarily she had a vision of her brother Joel, a pulped, bloody thing they had laid on the bed. If only she could cry out to Simon: The knife! The knife! She pressed her hand to her mouth.

Noboza was playing a retreating game. Nearer and nearer to the table. One more step and the hand could leap out.

She saw it. This time she could not suppress her cry, but in the same instant Simon shot his foot forward, sending table and knife crashing to the ground. Noboza would have lunged for his weapon but Simon, as if galvanised into fury by his opponent's treachery, gave him no respite. With a straight right to the jaw he floored Noboza. Through the room there passed a sound, a sigh like a low wind fluttering at tattered garments stuffed in a broken window pane. Noboza lay moaning and writhing. Kwethuba, one of Jo Bula's companions, sprang up and made a threatening step towards Simon, knife in hand. But it was Bula himself who gripped him so that he staggered back into his seat.

'Enough! Let him be.' He looked slowly around the room,

catching everyone's eye in turn. 'There's another day – and other places.'

'Yes, you want the cops to come down on us, you ruffians!' shouted Ma-jaze. 'A stinking corpse is bad for business.'

'Okay, okay, Ma-jaze. We'll take care of the cops,' said Jo Bula as his two henchmen helped Noboza to his feet.

'And Nick will live to carve other corpses, don't you worry. Eh, Nick?'

Nick's top lip lifted in a hideous grin.

Jo Bula turned to Manzana: 'At least you've proved you aren't a coward.'

Without answering, Simon took Linda by the arm and moved towards the door. Linda could not resist a parting shot.

'At least you've learned something. When I choose a man, I choose a man!'

Back in Linda's room Simon lay on her bed. Having bathed his wounds, she spoke her mind.

'You know you're a bloody fool, don't you?'

'What now?'

Simon could not understand how a woman could have gentle fingers and a spitting tongue all in a moment.

'You deserved what you got,' she continued.

'I gave more than I got.'

'Next time it won't be only Nick Noboza. It'll be half a dozen knives. And don't say I didn't warn you.'

'Just tell me what you're nagging me for.'

'So you don't know why they pitched into you?'

'Maybe they don't like my face. Poor devils. How should I know how they tick?'

'Poor devils, indeed! Simon . . . who brought you up? You're soft, man!'

In view of his proven prowess, this was distinctly unjust. Without looking at her, he stroked his arm muscles tenderly. She caught the reproof and kissed where it was sore.

'Seriously, Simon, let's get this straight. The trouble with the boys is – oh, I'm not thinking of Nick Noboza, he's a dirty stooge anyway – but the rest of them. You make them feel you don't want to belong. You think too much of yourself. And it gets them on the raw.'

'That's a lot of damn nonsense, Linda. I just don't – fit in with the gang. Well, what about it? Give me time.'

'Tell me, why did you turn down Diz's offer of coming in with him?'

'Oh, you've heard about that, have you? I don't know what you mean by "offer". A funny kind of offer. At any rate, it didn't appeal to me. That's all. Let's not talk about it.'

'You can't put me off that way,' she retorted. 'If your precious conscience is bothered about honesty again, forget it. If you're worried about losing your job, forget it. They'll kick you out anyway, whenever it suits them. Just by staying alive we break their laws every day, so what's the odds?'

A banging on the wall interrupted her rough and ready philosophising. Linda banged back. A muffled and irate voice demanded to know when he was going to get some sleep.

'Time for me to be moving,' said Simon. 'No use coddling me and then throwing me out.'

'Who's throwing you out?'

His kisses prevented more words. She clung to him then pushed him out of the room.

Sitting on her haunches in bed, unable to sleep, she pondered over Simon's evasive responses when she had turned the conversation to Diz Dinake's suggestion to come in on the taking racket. For the past few weeks she had been living recklessly, pretty much on air – no, let her face it – on love, without thought for the future. She picked up her purse, poured out a few coins and closed her eyes. The situation was serious – damn serious.

With Diz in jail, she told herself, she needed a new business partner.

Eight

It was a comparatively simple matter for Linda to break Simon into the taking business. His life with her had created new needs, new demands, and there was only one obvious way of solving the expanding problems of living.

One of the first things she contrived was persuading someone to teach him to drive. Here the good-natured Ken Madoda came up to scratch with his old Ford. Simon's pleasure in his newly acquired skill in manipulating a car highly amused Linda. He was ready to burst into a praise-song:

'Behold a plough that has grown itself four magic wheels, a plough that leaps through the stony furrows of Goli. It has sprouted wings, a bird that can fly through the air, making a man lord and master of the ant-like crowds treading the streets on leaden feet . . .'

She smiled at the childlike joy and he opened his arms to receive her embrace.

The next step was procuring a job as driver of a delivery van. That wasn't so easy. But at last a lucky chance turned up. One weekend Linda heard that an acquaintance had gone off sick – heart trouble, somebody said. She knew he was a driver and found out the name of the firm. The job didn't even have time to advertise itself. On Monday morning bright and early Simon presented himself at the warehouse door. He wasn't the only one who'd had the same idea and his heart sank at sight of the queue that had already formed. News of sickness travelled fast. However, by some fluke, the boss ended up choosing him for the job. Maybe he looked sturdier than the rest. And that night he proudly announced his new status to Linda.

For her this meant specifically a step in the right direction. A delivery van was more efficient for their purpose than a bicycle. Simon had already learned how to profit from his black anonymity. To the overseer whose eye is dimmed with the rheum of his racial superiority, one black sheep is the same as another.

Linda was satisfied, too, that since the little fracas at Ma-jaze's place, Simon was more readily accepted by 'the boys'. He had received his baptism. Nick Noboza, taking the cue, had sulkily agreed to a truce, and even Jo Bula condescended to be affable, declaring they'd make something of Manzana one day, but for one small matter. He jibbed at the knife. That was bad. He'd have to cure himself of that unnecessary squeamishness, or he'd never be fit for a real classy job.

Funnily enough, Simon rather fancied handling a gun. His love of machinery blinded him to the real nature of the weapon. One night Kwethuba, one of Jo Bula's gang, produced a small automatic and was showing it around among a few gathered in the inner sanctum at Angels One. It was very late; most of the customers had gone and Ma-jaze herself sat dozing like an unsmiling Buddha. Kwethuba wanted a good price for the gun, so he was giving them plenty of time.

The eyes of the assembled group gleamed as each one in turn handled it, weighed it, stroked it. It gleamed back at them with a single eye of light caught from the table-lamp. Simon's turn hadn't come yet.

Nkuku, Hilda Noyali's friend, looked as if he'd hold on to it for good.

'Give over, man,' said Simon. 'I can't wait all night.'

And Nkuku obeyed.

Simon caressed it, turned it, fondled it. It was the first time he had ever touched such a thing and the smoothness of it, the coldness of it, the hidden power of it gave him a strange feeling.

'Jeessus, isn't she a beaut!'

When Kwethuba proceeded to sound them for offers, it was Simon who coolly bid the highest price, pulling the notes from his hip pocket as careless as you like. The others exchanged glances. The country fellow was earning their respect.

Nkuku teased him.

'You're a sucker, man. I could get one for you at half the price.'

'Aw, to hell, Nkuku! She's worth it and more. Why should I haggle over the cost? Look at her, man!'

The men laughed, some amused, others envious. They weren't all as flush as Manzana seemed to be. Nkuku turned a cynical glance on him.

'And what are you going to do with it now you've got it, eh, Simon? It's jail for you if the police so much as smell it on you.'

The others laughed again. For a moment Simon looked grave, contemplating the small, black shining weapon in his hand. Weapon? To try its power he would have to try his own. To stir it from innocent slumber, impulses in himself would have to be awakened. He looked up at the group to find them all watching him. Then he, too, laughed. It was not a simple laughter. Rather an amazement – or was it incredulity – at this discovery he had made of himself. The others joined in, making a grim crescendo of sound swelling in different keys, then dying down as abruptly as it had burst forth.

In the smoke-fogged lamplight each man remained sunk in his thoughts, and they had little to do with laughter. Ma-jaze woke up with a start.

'What unholy noise is this? What's the joke, you devils?' she said. She observed Simon slip the gun into his hip pocket, but made no comment.

'Get you going, now, all of you, to your lairs. It's late and I need some sleep!'

A few days after he had bought the automatic Simon came back from work to find a letter from his sister Funeka. It was six months since he had sent money to his family, nor had he written in that time. His room happened to be empty, so he sat on his bed and opened the letter with mixed, confused feelings. In the past it had been his wife Boniswa who penned the letters; she had spent longer at school than his sister. Now his heart contracted as he recognised the handwriting as that of Funeka.

The letter had been painfully written and awkwardly penned; as his eyes blurred, the crudely formed letters appeared to be broken symbols of the anguish that had moved her to so painful an effort.

Dear Mta-ka-Bawo, (child of my father)

I hope it is well with you. We have waited many moons for word to come from you.

Boniswa is well. Father works without ceasing as if he was possessed of some demon who drives him on and on. Words seldom pass his lips, but I know that his thoughts carry him far from home. Your little Nothanda had a sickness in the stomach. So had Yiva, one of our brother Mvuzo's children, and sadly he died. But little Nothanda did not die. She is recovered of her sickness, but she cries in the night and keeps her mother awake. Father sold a cow – the black and white one – to the storekeeper to pay for the debt. We take turns to go to the store. Boniswa, Mvuzo's wife Nomonde, and me. We always ask if your letter has come. When Boniswa goes to the store I look after little Nothanda. I wish you could see her. Her features grow like our mother. She is a true child of the Ma-Mtshawe.

It is not well with my legs these last two months. The veins are knotted as if they would burst through the skin. Sometimes

I feel I cannot go any more to the fields. But what can we do? Father is getting so stiff in the joints. He picks at his food, saying his stomach is full. But he does not deceive us.

Why do you not send us a few words to say that you are well? Father watches Boniswa as she returns from the store, sitting in the shade of the hut. He pretends not to be interested. But I know he sees her empty hands. Perhaps it is that your letter is lost or stolen on the road. They do say this happens often to letters sent into the country. The storekeeper is rude, but he would not keep back our letters. No, I cannot believe it to be so.

I hear Boniswa singing a lullaby to little Nothanda. It has a sad sound.

Stay well, my dear brother.
Your loving sister,
Funeka

Simon sat for a long time staring into space. The two cramped pages of the letter slipped from his fingers and fluttered to the floor. Then he took out his pen – it was a Parker, a backdoor job – searched for his writing paper and started to write. He tore up the page, started again, and again tore it up. He felt in his pockets. They were nearly empty. Why had he spent all but his last pound on buying his automatic?

He fetched it from its hiding place under the mattress. Should he resell it? He slid his fingers over its smooth, shining surface, then flung it down at his feet. No, he'd never get his price for it. Even if he did, could he give it up? He picked it up again. Felt the latent power through his fingertips. Wasn't a pistol a man's friend? Didn't it inspire in other people a holy respect for you? Isn't that what he'd seen in the green of those envious eyes? It made you feel equal to two men . . .

Could he ask Linda to lend him some money? He'd pay her back. She wasn't close-fisted with money. He slowly shook his head. No. She'd want to know what he needed the money for. She was a jealous woman. It would mean stirring up a hornet's nest. In a weak moment he'd once spoken about his father and

Funeka. Yes, and then she'd drawn it out of him about Boniswa, too. How old was she? Younger than Linda? And pretty? He had answered evasively, recalling the plump, neat-bosomed girl when he had first met her at a wedding feast. Funeka had looked delicate beside her . . . Now Funeka was not well. She must be worse than she admitted, for she was never one to complain . . .

Linda chose her times for probing into his other life, those other ties that bound him to people she knew nothing of. She could not resist digging the scalpel beneath the skin. She was a strange woman. He could not understand her. At such moments, whether he was silent and forbearing, or replied angrily, or with reserve – whatever his response, she needled him. Nothing satisfied her, nothing pacified her. She was so unlike herself in such moods; she caught him unawares. No, he couldn't ask Linda for the money. He would have to put off writing till he was in funds again. It shouldn't take very long if they had any luck with their backdoor activities. He must think up some better way, better and faster, now more than ever. He must be able to help Funeka to get well. She must have a doctor. There were no doctors where she lived in the country.

Having come to what seemed to him a decision, and relieved himself of the immediate necessity to write a letter, with this evasion he was satisfied. Consulting his wristwatch – another backdoor job – he realised he'd just have time to change into some decent clothes and fetch Linda at her room. She'd kick up a row if he was late.

Pulling a box from under his bed, he took out a clean shirt and a gaudy red and gold tie. After a last glance at his sister's letter he put it away in the box, together with his writing paper. From under his mattress he snatched his best trousers. Then he rushed into the yard to have a wash. There he found Mrs Tsebe, from whom he and three other men rented their room. Though it was so late in the day, she was still bending over her washtub, two of her children grubbing nearby on the muddy ground.

'Good evening, Mrs Tsebe,' he said, pouring some water into the basin set on top of a rusty old petrol drum.

'Good evening, Mr Manzana. You're in a great hurry this

evening.'

'I sure am, Mrs Tsebe.'

Simon splashed and spattered in the basin.

'Go easy with the water. You're not all that dirty,' she admonished him.

'I'll fetch some more for you myself when I get back.'

She laughed. 'That'll be the day! If I know the signs, you're too busy with your lady-love. I guess she keeps you in order.'

'She sure does!'

The two toddlers yelped with delight as Simon scattered soapy bubbles over them. Mouths and hands were open to catch them.

'*Pinda! Pinda!* More! More!' they cried.

Their mother smiled. 'The children like you,' she said. 'You just like a little fun, eh, my chickens?'

Simon was already halfway back to his room.

'Don't you touch that water, now, messing yourselves, you naughty brats,' she said, rescuing the water and adding it to her washtub.

Simon emerged a few minutes later, aware of his landlady's gaze.

'You do look spruce and dandy, Mr Manzana.'

'Thank you, Mrs Tsebe.'

'Go well,' she responded.

'I'll just make it,' he told himself as he sprinted along the alleyways of Sophiatown, avoiding the potholes and dongas and cursing the stray dogs who stopped nosing for scraps to yap at his heels, their ribbed sides panting.

Dusk was falling and the air was chill, for winter was on its way on the High Veld. Simon hunched his shoulders and turned up the collar of his coat. In a number of backyards a garland of smoke hovered in the almost windless air, dimming the harsh contours of the makeshift houses. Women, returned from their day's work in the city, stood over their cooking pots while a brood of younglings plucked at their long skirts, yelping with hunger, faces upturned, mouths open like featherless chicks in a nest. Not all of their menfolk had returned, but here and there sat a few, patiently pulling at their pipes under a crooked corrugated iron canopy jutting from their crude living room. Shabby hats shadowed their faces; in their garments the incongruous mix of two civilisations – ill-shapen trousers and the red-brown blanket slung over their shoulders. A relic of their mountain homelands, thought Simon, then pushed the image from his mind.

Approaching an Indian store he felt the beat of jazz music thrum through his body. Ahead of him he saw a noisy cluster of youths playing dice in the dust and prepared to give them a wide berth. Opposite the store hovered a bevy of stylishly dressed girls apparently oblivious of the catcalls the youths were directing at them. Their dresses made a splash of colour in the twilight; their high heels coquetted in impromptu dance-steps; their giggles belied their innocence.

As Simon came abreast of the youths, one of them, sporting a shiny red shirt, jazzed towards him, then shot out his leg. Simon staggered to regain his balance. A peal of laughter from the girls echoed by the guffaws of the youths rang in his ears. Shaking the gang off was likely to prove troublesome.

But at that moment a welcome distraction was supplied by a fracas at the store entrance, where an exasperated storekeeper, his red fez trampled underfoot and his bald head gleaming like a full moon, was having an argument with a large African woman. In high-pitched rage she was letting the world know that the Indian shark had rooked her of her change. With a gleeful roar the youths eddied towards what promised to be a more profitable source of amusement. In the high-powered tensions of Sophiatown life, hostility between the Indian storekeeper and the mass of impoverished Africans out of whom he had to make a livelihood too often exploded in such scenes. Hostility borne out of the common need to put food on the table.

Simon sped on without stopping to learn the outcome of the altercation. Consulting his watch again, he calculated that he would not be more than five minutes late in arriving at the house where Linda lived. That awful house where she had to live, and his own quarters where he could never bring her . . .

In a trice he fell into daydreaming. If only they could find somewhere to live where they could be together. She had been so difficult of late, her temper exploding out of nothing. She continually spoke about finding a room for just the two of them alone, and at the slightest rumour of a place turning up she went hunting for it. A place of their own, a place they could call home. Home? Supposing he could bring his wife Boniswa to the city and the two women could be as sisters to each other . . . Tixo! He might as well wish for a rocket-flight to the moon . . .

'Hey, you! Why in such a hurry to be a bleeding corpse?'

Simon found himself being violently jerked back out of the way of a large Buick dodging the potholes of the darkening street. As it disappeared in a cloud of dust he turned to thank his rescuer and saw before him a tall man, possibly in his fifties, soberly dressed in a black suit protected by a grey-brown coat, and carrying a leather briefcase. Simon wondered what his occupation might be. A teacher, perhaps.

'That was Jo Bula who nearly caught you napping,' remarked the man.

'Business must be good. Thanks, Mister.'

'It's that young Nick Noboza he had at the wheel.'

'Hau! So it was him having a potshot at me!'

'Live fast. Drive fast. Kill fast,' said the stranger. 'No respect for human life. No more than the whites have. You were nearly a goner that time, my son, if I hadn't grabbed hold of you. Let me tell you, I have a great respect for human life. I see too much of death.'

'Oh, what is your occupation?'

'I'm an agent for a burial society.'

So, not a teacher. He must be one of those insurance agents who combed the townships and shanty towns, touting for the big white firms in the city.

'You must do well in these parts.'

'No complaints from my bosses. I do a good, steady business here in Sophiatown. Would you by any chance like to take out a policy right now? You've had a merciful escape. But if I were you I wouldn't be too free with Providence.'

Simon couldn't help himself. He burst out laughing. He

laughed until his laughter ended in a fit of coughing. The man watched him solemnly.

'I don't see anything to laugh about. In the midst of life we are in death. You saw for yourself. If it hadn't been for me . . . Young man, you shouldn't neglect that cough. It might turn into something serious.'

'Oh, that! I can't help thinking you did the undertakers out of a corpse. Not a bad line of business now that I come to think of it.'

'Don't you be blasphemous, young man. And don't be disrespectful of our trade. Take my advice. What better moment than now to insure yourself against the inevitable fate of all mankind? With the likes of Jo Bula and Nick Noboza to give you a helping hand, it's never far off. Be well advised and give yourself a handsome funeral. You owe it to yourself. You look a nice respectable young man.'

Simon bowed, barely hiding his laughter.

'You wouldn't like to die now, would you, and be thrown into a hole in the ground, without a decent coffin for your bones and proper mourners to say a prayer over your handsome corpse, to speed you on your way? Are you alone in this infamous city?'

Simon stopped laughing. 'Alone?'

'Alone, with no one to bury you. So many people in this city die and have no relatives to perform the last sacred rites.'

'Alone, did you say? When it comes to burying, I guess I am.'

'That's where we come in handy, when you're dead. Be well advised, young man. There's no moment like the present. Take heed. I am at your service.'

'Thanks for your advice. I'll keep it in mind. But at the moment I've barely enough to buy food for my stomach.'

'Oh, don't let that worry you. You need begin payment only at the end of the month. A small monthly fee is all you need to ensure receiving the inestimable benefits of our burial society.'

Before Simon could reply, he had snapped open his briefcase.

'Here is our card. A phone call to this address any hour of the day, or night, we are at your service. Oh, and be sure you give my name – Jeremiah Maoela. Thank you.'

'Sorry, I can't do anything about it now. I'm *very* late for an appointment.'

'I'm sorry, too. May I remind you, you would have been even later if I hadn't . . . Well. Hold on to the card. You may think better of it some day.'

His sales-talk over, Mr Maoela reverted to the speech of his fathers. 'Go well, my son.'

'Stay well,' replied Simon, and departed at a run.

Linda embraced him like a whirlwind. Her scolding was perfunctory and belied by her smiles.

'Oh, why were you so long? I could hardly wait to tell you. Guess what has happened!'

Bad news. Good news. He felt he was having a day of it.

'Go on, Simon! Why aren't you guessing?' She stamped her foot. 'What do you want most of all in the world?'

'Lots of things. I don't know where to begin. A motor car, for one.'

'Oh, of course we'll have a car one day. Guess again, Simon. Guess!'

'What I would like is a thousand pounds. Then I'd send Funeka . . .'

He stopped.

'Silly! I'd fall dead if I got that much. What did you say about your sister Funeka?'

'Never mind. I'm still trying to guess.'

'I give you three guesses. Oh, you're always too slow. I've found a room for us! There!'

'A room?'

'A room for us, silly! For us two. Just us two alone. Nobody else. Isn't that wonderful?'

'Oh, Linda. I can't believe it!'

'Oh, Simon. You'll have to believe it. I found the room and I've paid for it, a month in advance. The landlord asked a lot for it, the shark. Bokomela is his name and I'm afraid his room is just behind ours. But I couldn't let the chance go by. There were lots after it. But I got in first. It's not more than five minutes' walk from here. Let's go and see it straight away. I've got the key. Look. Our key! I haven't had time to tidy up the room. But that doesn't matter.'

'How did all this happen? How did you manage to bring it off?'

'Oh, somebody died. They found three children in the house, crying.'

'Without their mother?'

'They found her dead. Let's not talk about it. Don't look like that. *We* can't help it.'

For some reason Simon suddenly thought of his own wife and his child, Nothanda, without money, without sufficient food to eat. Supposing Boniswa should fall ill and die and his child was left . . . No! In the country you didn't die alone, while inhuman feet tramped up and down past your house, unheeding, callous, indifferent . . . Of course, Boniswa was not ill. And his little Nothanda had got better. It was his sister Funeka . . .

Confused and troubled in his thoughts, he resolved to send money to his family at the earliest possible moment.

'Simon! What on earth's the matter with you?'

'I wonder if they gave the woman a decent funeral,' he said.

'Have you suddenly gone crazy, or what? Here I tell you the most wonderful news, and you talk about funerals.'

Then he explained to her about his meeting with Jeremiah Maoela and how he had pointed out the necessity of taking one's last journey in a manner worthy of a human being.

'Don't be morbid,' she said. 'What have we to do with dying? I find a room for us, for us alone. I expected you to yell with joy. And now just look at you. Funerals indeed!'

'Of course I'm glad. Let's go.'

He shook off his melancholy thoughts and together they hurried along the unlit dusty streets to their new – their first – domain.

'Here's the place,' she said. 'Give me your torch.'

The light raked across two low adjoining structures looking

as if one had grown out of the other like a pack of cards pulled open. 'Ours is the bigger one. I don't know who lives in the other. Hope it's nobody with a bunch of screaming kids.'

'It's all quiet now,' he remarked.

A light from a window across the way showed up in the surrounding darkness as blank as an empty television screen. From behind it came the sounds of a popular jazz tune.

Linda swept her torchlight across a bare window to the door.

'You open it,' she said, giving him the key.

He pressed her hand hard, acknowledging her gesture. The key turned with a screech; the hinges creaked. He drew her across the threshold. Ahead of them the light of the torch ploughed an erratic path across the narrow passageway. The left wall was blank; to the right was another door.

'It isn't locked,' she said. 'Open!'

Side by side they entered, the light darting from floor to ceiling in the empty room.

'There's a candle on the window sill.'

Simon lit the blackened stump; the flame wavered feebly in the draught, staggered and leaned askew as Linda went over and shut the door. Then it righted itself.

'Well, here we are,' she said. 'Kiss me.'

In the light of the candle the room revealed its bareness, already stripped of whatever human belongings the dead woman had possessed. A thin layer of plaster gaped through patches of peeling paint. But at least it was more solid than the room Simon had to put up with at Mrs Tsebe's.

'It looks pretty awful right now. But it's our own – ' Linda's voice broke. 'We'll turn it into something. You'll see, Simon! I've been furnishing it in my head for years. First of all you'll put the walls right. I just can't wait. We'll put the bed there. What do you say? I've got a proper bedcover for it already. Red silk, it is. And I'll match it with the curtain on the window. We'll make the place look gay. We'll put the wardrobe – let me see – there. We'll go and buy it tomorrow. No, we'll have to wait till there's some more money coming in. But at least we can go and choose it. Then there's the dressing table. I simply must have a dressing table, with mirrors at the side. I've always wanted a dressing table with mirrors, so's I can see myself all round. Now where can we put it? It'll be a squeeze, but we can fit it in there, don't you think . . .?'

What on earth was the matter with Simon? 'You're very quiet . . . When we invite Ma-jaze to come and see us, just you watch her face when she spots my dressing table. It'll be much grander than hers. She'll be green . . .'

She pulled him round, dancing wildly. Suddenly she laughed. Then pushed him violently away from her. 'What's up with you?'

'Where's all the money coming from?'

'We'll have to have more than our usual luck. Simon, you'd better put your thinking cap on. Now if only you hadn't spent so much money on that gun of yours. It was crazy of you to buy it anyway. Looking for trouble . . . *Now* what's the matter? Just because I speak about you getting that gun.'

'It isn't that, Linda. I was already regretting I'd spent the money on it.'

'Were you, now?'

'But it was for another reason. I know we need the money – for this . . .'

'Like hell we do,' she said. 'And we're going to get it.'

'Linda, you don't understand. There's something else I must do. I had – I had a letter from home today.'

'Home?' she whispered.

'Funeka – my sister – is ill. And Nothanda . . .'

But she did not allow him to continue.

'So! You cheat! You cheating devil! Here I am, walking myself giddy, looking for a roof to put over our heads. I find it and put down my last penny so that nobody can snatch it from us. And what thanks do I get? You stand there and moan about home. *Home!* This is your home. At least, I thought it was going to be – ' Her lips trembled and she turned away.

'Linda, don't. I have wanted this room as much as you have. You know it. And this very day as I came along to your place, I was wishing we could find it. You must believe me. It's only – the bad news from – from my family – I . . . Linda, what can I do?'

'Right now we need every penny we've got to furnish this room. It's not much of a place . . .' She gazed round the desolate room and his glance followed hers. 'But I'm going to do my damnedest to make it a home – for you and me, Simon. It was you made me feel for the first time that I wanted . . . a home.'

Her manner was no longer imperative, challenging, quarrelsome. This he could have resisted. But now she was expressing something with an emotion she seldom revealed. It carried them both back to that night when she had first lain in his arms, listening to the secret pulse she had never heard before. She leaned her head against him.

'Simon, don't you remember? It's what you've wanted all the time?'

They said no more about his letter from Funeka. Then one day after they had successfully pulled off a backdoor deal, he informed her casually: 'I've sent off five pounds to my father.'

'Oh, you have, have you? You like to keep your secrets, don't you?'

'You can hardly accuse me of that, considering . . .'

'You're a stubborn devil. That's all I can say.'

And they left it at that. Linda was in good humour because she had that day put down a substantial instalment on the bedroom suite she had set her heart on. She was feeling pleased with life.

'The suite will be delivered next week. Thank goodness we can pay it off on the never-never,' she said. 'I'd like to see Majaze's face when she sets eyes on it.'

This was a familiar refrain in Simon's ears.

'She'll have to go and get a bigger, grander suite,' he teased her.

'Good luck to her! Then we'll get a radiogram, grander than hers. And some jazz records!'

'There'll be no space left to eat!'

'Oh, we'll manage. There's always the yard – except for the smells from over the way.'

'Then you'll have our landlord, old Bokomela, ogling you when you're standing over the pots.'

'I'll give him a rotten egg straight in the eye if he does! Now you'll have to get busy on those walls, eh, Simon?'

Nine

One year passed and the second stole stealthily on its way.

Linda and Simon continued to occupy their little room in Sophiatown. The bedroom suite that had to outdo Ma-jaze's monopolised most of the space. But, alas, it had lost its first splendour even before the last payment had been put down. It had seen midnight parties; it had reverberated to jazzing feet and well-oiled throats fervently moaning the latest ditties. The flimsy structures miraculously withstood a weight of bodies they were never meant to carry, but the overcoat of wall-paint was cracking like burnt flesh. The gaudy face of the radiogram winked and leered at its room-mates, as much as to say: Life is hard, eh, you bastards? No use complaining. You've had your day.

In Sophiatown – and the rest of the townships, locations and shanty towns along the Reef – houses were bursting at the seams with tenants who had passes and those who did not. Not only the tsotsis, but work-hungry folk lived on the knife edge of illegality. Frequent police raids were calculated to shake them from their hiding places as a prisoner shakes lice from the folds of his blanket. Men and women swarmed to and fro, toiled in the city by day and at night swarmed back into their houses and shacks, most of them to sleep the sleep of exhaustion; some to watch over a sick bed or a body writhing in child labour; some to dance their barren limbs into a frenzy of life; others to drown themselves in the torpor of drink, or prayer, or debauch in dagga smoking; some to copulate, some to kill and many to die. The movement of men to and fro was as agitated as autumn leaves scattering in their multitudes before a wind heralding a thunderstorm. Laughing, wailing, scolding, cursing, the turbulent human tide flowed on ceaselessly above the gold-bearing reef, while far below in the bowels of the earth, by night and by day, human strength was being poured out in another frenzy of toil.

In the midst of it all, these two young people, Linda Malindi and Simon Manzana, somehow kept alive a feeling for each other. Be it a rare sexual harmony, or a more subtle human quality, they were deeply dependent on each other. Linda, superficially the same shrewd, hard, crude product of the city township, strong through sheer deprivation, had nevertheless tasted through Simon new possibilities of human relationship. Perhaps this made her more vulnerable than she had ever been. He was a good thing to hold and keep, provided she was mistress of the situation. Sometimes, for no apparent reason, she seemed to do her best to destroy what was most precious to her, to drag it nearer the familiar terrain of her harsh adolescence. She quarrelled compulsively. She would taunt Simon over Diz Dinake who, now out of jail had been promoted into Jo Bula's gang. Yet some grains of the new alchemy he had introduced remained, even with the hardening passage of time and precarious living.

Both of them lived for the moment. The demands and pressures of such an existence bore down on Simon Manzana all the more insidiously because they were given flesh and substance through this strange woman of the city. He, too, was made more vulnerable by the bond between them.

He had stopped communicating with his family. When he could not rescue from the greedy demands of their joint set-up enough to meet the needs of his father, his wife, his sister and his brother's wife, a sense of guilt held back his pen. He had not given them his new address.

One day, feeling a compulsion to find out if a letter for him had arrived at Mrs Tsebe's, he had found one from his wife, full of sharp, stinging words of reproof dictated by his father. Then silence. He had evaded the unbearable load of guilt by indulging in resentment against them. Not till some months had passed did he again call on Mrs Tsebe, only to find complete strangers there, who had no idea where Mrs Tsebe had gone and swore they had never received any letters addressed to Mr Manzana. It was a silence, a gulf, too painful to bridge. For how could he explain his behaviour to those he had left behind? How to find words to make them understand his present way of life? He proceeded to live more desperately for the moment.

Now it happened that after a succession of tenants in the room adjoining the one occupied by Linda and Simon, a young man by the name of Abel Sanelo came to live there. Simon was overjoyed to discover in him an old school friend who came from a place close to his home village, though he had never met any of Simon's family. Simon had looked up to him at school – Abel was in the class above him – but of course the school years were all too short and they had lost track of each other. Now here was good luck indeed!

A few years older than Simon, this Sanelo was no ordinary character. Perhaps it is more true to say that his very ordinariness – as it would have appeared in an orderly society – made him appear outstanding in the city jungle. He was a slightly built man in his late twenties, mild, good-natured, gentle, and inordinately fond of books. Whenever he had a few shillings to spare – and even when he hadn't – he would venture into a city bookshop where the whites went, browse along the shelves as long as he dared and, after much weighing of this book and that book, emerge with a precious parcel under his arm. Public libraries were only for whites, so there was no place where he could satisfy his inquisitive mind. Like Simon he had had to cut short his school career and relinquish his ambitions, but unlike Simon he doggedly pursued his thirst for knowledge.

A quiet stubbornness was the essence of his character. He spent his days running errands for a firm of white lawyers in the city. But he was the kind of fellow who never stopped working, as if driven by some perpetual urgency. If he wasn't reading he was making things, small pieces of carpentry and carvings.

'Why do you waste your time making these knick-knacks?' Linda asked him one night. 'You can buy better in the shops – or get them backdoor. Can't he, Simon?'

Sanelo smiled apologetically.

'That's no job for a man,' she continued.

'I agree. They inflict it on us in school, instead of science. They're afraid to teach us science. But I like to keep my hands busy.'

Linda laughed. 'I fancy a better way of keeping my hands busy.'

'It helps me to think,' he answered.

'Helps you to think? He's nuts, Simon.' Her laugh was half amazed, half kindly.

'Don't go on at him,' Simon said, sharply.

'No need to snap my head off,' she retorted. 'Well, I'll leave you to it.'

At the door she turned: 'Coming, Simon?'

'A bit later,' he answered.

'Please yourself,' she snapped.

Simon shut the door after her. Linda heard the sound and wanted to burst it open again. She stood, but controlled the impulse, then tossing her head and her skirts she marched off.

Linda dismissed Sanelo as dull, even more 'soft' and uninitiated than Simon had been before she took him in hand. A *moegoe* if ever she saw one. At night he never left his room and merely shrugged and smiled when she tried to lure him to Angels One.

'My stomach doesn't hold Ma-jaze's concoctions too well. It is a disobedient organ,' he said.

It was ridiculous to be jealous of such an innocuous, mild-tempered man. Nevertheless Linda wasn't at all pleased when

118

her Simon took to slipping next door more frequently. One evening, out of boredom, she joined the two men, and with only half-concealed hostility watched them smoking and chatting, and pottering at some woodwork.

She looked scornfully round the room. Here was one of those peculiar guys who kept a room tidy, though she never so much as smelt a woman about the place. He contrived to keep his clothes remarkably neat, too: brown suit, brown suede shoes, brown fedora – everything brown. She noticed that near his bed he had placed a small bookcase (made by himself) where a few books leaned together, as books do when there is too much space for them. Something like a twinge of jealousy stirred in her when she observed Simon take down a book and open it. He flicked over the pages.

'It looks pretty dry stuff to me,' he said.

'Oh, history isn't so dry, when you can put the pieces together,' said Sanelo. 'The trouble is getting past the lies and the fairy tales they dish out to us.'

'Why bother to read lies?' asked Linda.

'Perhaps to try to get at the truth.'

'There are other ways, besides burying your nose in a book.'

'Ways in which you are the mistress, eh, Miss Malindi?'

She shrugged. 'Maybe. I've had to learn my way about.'

Simon sighed. 'I wish I'd had the opportunity to study more.'

'There's time still. Don't give up,' said Sanelo, smiling. 'I've such an itch myself to get at the bottom of things.'

'What things?' Simon asked.

'Oh, it isn't easy to put it into words, just like that. Take this big city of theirs where all of us work in the day –'

'But where they kick us out at night,' said Simon.

'Exactly. Where so far we suffer the torments but share none of the benefits of civilisation. I hate this city. And yet it fascinates me, all the time. Even if we're only permitted a worm's-eye view of it.'

'Not so much of the worm, Mister Sanelo!' interrupted Linda. 'Speak for yourself!'

'At least that's all we're allowed, officially, Miss Malindi.'

'It's quite another matter what we learn, unofficially,' added Simon.

'And learn pretty fast, too,' said Linda. 'Talking of worms. When I see an African being humble I could kick his backside for him! Patience, humility – these are booby traps for the fools of this world.'

Sanelo laughed. 'Observe the light of battle in her eye. It makes her handsome, eh, Simon? She does some hard thinking, too, but she's so modest, she doesn't know it.'

All three laughed heartily.

'Listen to him, Simon. He's learning the art of flattery.'

'It needs no flattery to speak the truth.'

Linda bowed mockingly.

'Come on, Simon. Time we were going.'

'Wait. Don't be in such a hurry. What exactly were you getting at, Abel, when we got tied up with the worm's-eye view – remember?'

'Oh, now you corner me. How shall I put it? To me, Simon, the city of Goli is a monstrous slaughterhouse. But it is also a great fertile womb where something new is being born. If only we ourselves had the skill and the power to bring a healthy bawling infant into the world!'

'I'm not used to hearing dirty language, Mister Sanelo. We'd better be going.' Linda moved towards the door, chuckling at her own joke.

As Simon rose to follow her, Sanelo called him back. Impatiently, Linda looked over her shoulder at the two men.

'Hey, there! What secrets are you cooking up against me?'

'No secret. At least not between friends. But don't tell the world. I'm smuggling my wife into Sophiatown.'

'Your wife!' Simon felt a curious pang shoot through him.

'So. He's not so dumb as he looks,' said Linda, nodding slowly. 'A love nest, right here! You're a brave man, Mr Sanelo.'

'It's a year ago this month I went home and married Nomasa . . .'

'Nomasa?' There was eager curiosity in Simon's voice.

'Yes. Nomasa, the daughter of Coto.'

'Coto? Then she comes from near my village, too! Was she at the same school? I don't remember . . .'

'She went there after our time. She is still very young, and very shy. At first we agreed she shouldn't come to the city. This is no place for her, but – '

'But we are human,' said Simon.

'That's the trouble, I'm afraid.'

'When does she arrive?'

'Next week.'

'Now I see why you have been so busy,' said Linda. 'A little woodwork, to keep the nest warm. But, if you were sensible, you could line it with an eiderdown – backdoor,' she teased, smiling and rolling her eyes.

'No need! We'll keep each other warm.'

On this happy note they parted.

That night Linda surprised Simon by a passionate softness in her lovemaking that he had long missed. It pained him to feel he was unable to respond to her mood. Sanelo's news had thrown his thoughts into turmoil. Images of his wife, Boniswa, poignant and sharp, tormented him. He had not had a letter from her since – Tixo! Why had he been silent so long? What madness had possessed him? What must be her thoughts of him? He, the father of little Nothanda. And he dared not think of his sister Funeka. What had happened to them all? What misfortune had overtaken them? His father – perhaps . . . perhaps he no longer lived?

He could hardly wait until daylight to send off a telegram. No, that would be too sudden, too ill-advised. What could he say to them in a telegram? From sunrise to sunset would not be long enough for him to pour out all he wanted to tell them. Better, perhaps, to wait and write a long letter. But how would he express himself? Words. Words. It wasn't words that could fill up the great gap of time. If only he could go to Boniswa – see her face to face . . .

It would be impossible. Not just the money. He could get the money together somehow, even if he had to wait. There was

Linda – the ties that bound him to Linda. He looked at her lying beside him. He moved his cramped limbs stealthily so as not to wake her. Involuntarily her hand on his thigh tightened. Was he a monster that he must hurt a woman? And Boniswa, had he not already brought sorrow to her beyond forgiveness?

Suddenly he felt Linda's lips against his neck.

'Simon, what is it? You're so restless. I can't sleep either. Simon – I . . . It has come to me . . . I – you'll never believe it.' She laughed nervously. 'I can hardly believe it myself. Simon, I would like you to give me a child. Funny, isn't it? I think it must be the bad influence of your friend Sanelo, risking his neck and all for his silly love nest. You know, Simon, after I lost my first baby – I haven't told even you – it was stillborn – its father – I can't remember its father – *his* father . . . When it died – when *he* died – I vowed, never again. And now here I am! Wanting your baby – oh Simon! Why don't you say something?'

What could he say to her? Supposing he let the words come out of his mouth? *I do not want to give you a child. I do not want a child by you. Boniswa is my wife . . .*

In a fury of outraged pride she pushed him from her.

'What's come over you?' she said. 'Didn't you hear what I said? *Say* something!'

And then, as though all her energy was spent, she lay still, frozen by his silence; frozen into a paralysis of fear.

Together, yet separated, they outstared the dark, while noises and flickering lights bespoke their inescapable lack of privacy.

The coming of Nomasa, the wife of Abel Sanelo, turned the course of life for three people.

Not that she herself would have dreamed that it would be so. No woman seemed more unlikely to make demands on anyone than this young, gauche, almost timid creature, still less to make Sanelo alter the course of his life. He was devoted to her with a quiet but intense emotion that was part of that stubbornness with which he had resisted the thousand shocks of existence since he was born.

Linda couldn't understand what Sanelo saw in those liquid-gazing cow's eyes, that unprovocative figure in the long shapeless skirt. Ja! Men were fools. Well, at least Simon knew better. She had nothing to fear in that quarter.

She assured Sanelo that she would take his wife under her wing. She would gladly teach her how to walk and talk; initiate the fledgling into the proper ways of Sophiatown dress: short, wide skirts, revealing glimpses of that tender flesh behind the knee, nylon stockings, high-heeled shoes. Before long Nomasa would be demanding all these things from her doting husband and he'd have to pay up with a smile.

Nomasa listened to this flow of words with an expression of some bewilderment and a nervous willing smile, while Abel looked on with tolerant amusement. Simon for his part showed an unexpected irritation.

'Oh, dry up, Linda. Mrs Sanelo is just fine as she is.'

Linda observed his gaze linger on the young woman.

'She doesn't need to doll herself up like – '

'Now what are you getting at, eh Simon?'

'Nothing. Nothing. It's only that everything is new and a bit strange to her,' he added lamely.

'Jeessus, man, I was only trying to make her feel at home.'

'At home! Here, in Sophiatown?' Simon laughed harshly.

'And what's wrong with that?'

'No need to take it that way, Simon,' interrupted Sanelo. 'Nomasa and I understand perfectly. You are very kind, Linda.'

As the year wore on, Linda experienced a profound uneasiness she couldn't give a name to. She told herself Simon couldn't do without her, yet she was unable to throw off the suspicion that he had changed towards her, and this in spite of the fact that there was no evidence of his fancy straying elsewhere. Their quarrels had an edge to them that left her feeling the loser every time.

They quarrelled about such trivial things. She wondered afterwards why she had allowed herself to become so worked up. In the tempest of the moment she said things with a fiendish desire to hurt Simon. But such a bitter aftertaste they had. Their bitterness recoiled on herself. She hoped he would forget them, but her fears told her he could not forget. Words had a dreadful life of their own, and built up a wall between them.

In Nomasa she found herself up against a quiet reserve that baffled her. The woman seemed so passive, a quality Linda despised, and her shyness seemed merely silly. She would have liked to stamp Sanelo's wife out of her mind simply by despising her. But somehow the young woman got under her skin. Two or three times she caught Nomasa staring hard. Damn her eyes! She liked people to talk, not to stare at you.

One evening in Sanelo's room she herself took to staring. Covertly she watched Simon as he spoke to Nomasa. There was no doubt that this was a different Simon from the man she knew. His whole manner changed involuntarily in Nomasa's presence. The words were formal, but his tone was warm and protective. And that face responding so shyly to his attentions. That shy face was sly. You could not read its secrets.

One evening on returning from Ma-jaze's, Linda was furious to discover that Simon was still next door with his two friends. Her blood still tingling with illicit hooch – she would have denied she was under the influence – she knocked noisily and entered. The room had a cosy air and its three occupants looked up, almost startled.

'God's truth! You'd think I wasn't wanted around here.'

Quickly Abel got to his feet.

'Come in, Linda. Simon was just about to leave us when Nomasa said she'd make him a cup of tea.'

'A cup of tea? That would suit me fine, I will say!'

'Please to sit down, Miss Malindi. The tea will quickly make itself.'

Nomasa's smile was friendly.

Linda watched her as she busied herself at the paraffin stove, waiting for the pan of water to boil.

Jesus Christ! Nomasa was pregnant! How hadn't she noticed it before?

In that moment she hated Sanelo's wife. She placed her hands on her own body and a sickening sensation of barrenness gripped her insides.

Simon was speaking: 'I told Nomasa not to bother making tea. She hasn't been feeling well today. Abel wanted her to see a doctor.'

Linda made a long-drawn 'So-o-o!'

What were the two men fussing for? Did a woman never have a baby in Sophiatown before? Ha! Ha! Her own baby. Stillborn. More in her thoughts lately than ever before.

Nomasa broke in hurriedly. 'Nonsense. It was just a passing faintness. I don't want to see a doctor.'

'You are very stubborn in your own way, Nomasa,' said Sanelo.

'But I don't need to see a doctor! I'm all right now. Really I am.'

'Bravo! Stand up for your rights. Don't let them bully you,' Linda applauded with gusto.

'You don't understand,' said Simon. 'Nomasa is – '

'Hell! Since when did you have to teach me what I already know?' she shouted.

She must get out of this room! It was suffocating her. She must get out!

'Oh, aren't you staying to have your tea, Linda?' Sanelo rose to his feet.

'No thanks. It might curdle the gin. Good night, everybody.'

Simon was a long time in coming to their room. When he entered he was not deceived by Linda's rigid stillness, simulating sleep. He began speaking at once: 'Linda, why must you go out of your way to be rude to Abel's wife?'

Linda bounced up, her bare shoulders thrust at him.

'That's a nice way to come into my bed. A fine way to wake me up.'

'You weren't asleep.'

'So I was rude to dear Mrs Sanelo, was I? Dear, simple Nomasa.'

'Why must you do it? She has done you no harm.'

'Oh, hasn't she, the innocent? I like to see the way you stand up for her against me. You always seem to be afraid I'll offend her precious ears. And now that she's going to have a baby . . . The fuss! You make me sick.'

'I don't like to see you being rude to her. That's all.'

'And she is a sweet angel, while I am – you haven't words bad enough to describe me. Damn you, you seem to think I'm not good enough for your Mister and Missus Sanelo.'

'That's just being silly, Linda. Why have you got your knife into her? I'm sure she never harmed anybody in her life.'

'All the worse for her. I don't like your milk and water virtues.'

'This bickering won't get us anywhere. Why can't you be a sister to Nomasa? She's younger than you, Linda. What are you making faces for? And especially now, she's lonely with none of her people near her.'

'Lonely! Ha! I like that. Nobody's lonely in this hell – except little Nomasa. Nobody's lonely except her!'

'Why do you go on like this? What's got into you? I don't understand you.'

'Like hell, you don't. And you never will. I'm going out, if you'd like to know.'

'Linda, it isn't safe.'

'A lot you care.'

Frenziedly she grabbed her clothing and dressed, while Simon watched her in unhappy silence.

'What are you staring at, eh? Have you never seen my body before?'

There was a curious mixture of rage and desperate allurement in her voice. Simon turned away. With a wild laugh she went out, banging the door behind her.

Linda had no key to curing the estrangement between herself and Simon. Jealousy sharpened her senses, but her situation had none of the clear-cut outlines where she could follow her natural instinct – to kick the obstacle out of her path. She was beyond her depth. Her increasing attitude of possessiveness towards him merely alienated him the more. Tormented by her jealousy of Nomasa, she began to be haunted by a hatred that could find no outlet.

To strike at an opponent – that made sense. You got a kick out of a good fight. But here the object she sought to strike vanished before she could touch it. How gladly she would have rid herself of her anguish with a blow. But at what? Simon showed none of the obvious marks of the unfaithful lover. These she could have given fight to. Both he and Nomasa had the maddening aspect of innocence. The young woman apparently adored her husband; she had eyes for none but him. Could such an innocent-seeming creature be possessed of some devilish cunning that she could deceive both her husband and a woman like herself? If only she knew what kind of thoughts went on in Nomasa's head. A sense of helplessness in the situation, her inability to break through, added fuel to the fire of Linda's resentment.

With Simon she quarrelled more than ever. He was moody. He no longer played and laughed with her. Oh, God, how happy they had been! Gone were the jolly evenings at Ma-jaze's. He was becoming more and more tied to Abel Sanelo and his wife. Yes, that was the strange thing. Sanelo was uncommonly attached to Simon. If Simon had his eyes on his wife, his friend was completely trusting. Simon was a man who hid his thoughts. She didn't understand him any more.

Simon had cause to hide his thoughts. Linda's jealousy aimed blind when it spent its venom on Nomasa. Sharp as it was, it consumed itself with the shadow instead of the substance. Nomasa, yes, Nomasa was constantly before Simon's eyes, but she was an innocent substitute, a blameless ghost in place of a woman of warm flesh and blood – his wife Boniswa.

Caught in the toils of his conflict between his wife and Linda, he had been unable to come to any decision about returning to his family, unable therefore even to communicate with them. The impulse some time ago to send a telegram or write, that had seemed possible in the dead of night, in the cold light of dawn had lost itself in shame and hesitation. But these outraged bonds revenged themselves in his ever-growing feelings of remorse. With the coming of Abel Sanelo, a living link with his youth, his home, his past and his traditions, his old affections had taken on new shoots, like a tree whose sap has been dormant in the chill blasts, the storms and frosts of winter. Then with the coming of Sanelo's young wife, the frosts had thawed into a flood; the pangs of remorse were sharpened into the torments of longing.

Yet the ties binding him to Linda were not easily to be broken.

Simon felt there was nobody to whom he could confide his dilemma. To speak to Abel Sanelo was to expose his own shortcomings to a man whose opinion he valued. More than this, he felt it would be an act of disloyalty to Linda. But from her, least of all, could he expect understanding. Even if he had tried to give expression, however painful, to the remorse that gnawed at him, she was not the one to give it sympathy. The turbulence of life in Sophiatown leaves no time for the backward glance. Still less dared he reveal the heart and core of his longing.

What he did not realise was her total incomprehension of the relationship between himself and Nomasa – a tradition accepted quite simply by Nomasa herself and her husband. That special warmth and respect he would naturally bestow on the wife of his closest friend. The purity of that feeling was something outside Linda's ken. The very word would have excited a shout of derision from her. Yet it was this very feeling that released in Simon the flood of longing for his home, his wife and his child, his sister and his father.

Where words of mutual understanding might have bridged the estrangement between Linda and Simon, bitter and trivial discord could only widen it, the more so as the petty squabbling was no true expression of the profound unhappiness on both sides. The very intensity of the conflicting emotions that each inspired in the other was a measure of their strength. He could not lightly forsake the woman to whom he had given and with whom he had shared so much in this new, hazardous life in the city. The thought of wounding her paralysed his will. And she, who wanted to hate, could only feel more strongly her need for him, her dependence on him. Her frustrated desire to bear him a son focused her jealousy on the wife of Sanelo, so abundantly heavy with child.

Preoccupied with his own worries and conflicts, Simon was

at first unaware that a shadow had descended on the house of his neighbour. Abel Sanelo and his wife had to face up to a new problem. After much heart-searching Sanelo had decided that he would have to let Nomasa return to their home village to have her baby. He knew there was a hospital in the city where non-whites could be delivered of a child probably more safely than in the country. Reason told him this and he put it to her. But this gentle being who had braved the terrors of the city to be with her husband, showed a passionate determination to bear her child at home and nowhere else.

'I must go home! I must go home!' she repeated, rocking herself to and fro, as if the words had some magic power to transport her there, an incantation to carry her to the place of her husband's people. His heart smote him as he looked at her. He realised that no argument would move her.

'Your mother will not forgive you,' she said, 'if you do not let her deliver her son's child.'

'Dear wife, you do not know what you ask of me.'

'I do. I do know. But think of your mother – her first grandchild and she has waited so long for it.'

'You are a cunning one, Nomasa. It is what *you* wish. That is all that matters to me. But have you thought – the long journey? I will not be able to come with you.'

'I faced the journey before. I can endure it again.'

'But not as you are now. The trains are cattle-trucks. And your time is already far gone.'

'Do not frighten me. I must go. I have waited too long already. I must go at once. Oh, father of my child, please let me go home!'

'Nomasa, you do not need to beg anything of me. Heaven forbid that you should suffer more.'

'Forgive me, father of my child, forgive me.'

'There is nothing to forgive. I'll find a way to get you home.'

Neither of them dared to voice the thought: how long would they be parted?

As Simon knocked and entered he realised something serious was in the air.

'Nomasa is going home to my people. We have decided,' said Sanelo, matter-of-factly.

Simon knew what this decision meant for both of them.

'I am sure it is for the best,' he said.

He was rewarded with a grateful look from Nomasa.

'We must act at once,' continued her husband. 'Tomorrow I shall get your railway ticket.'

Simon judged it best to cut his visit short and for the next few moments they took refuge in discussing the practical details of Nomasa's departure.

Simon could not bring himself to mention his friend's problem and their drastic decision to Linda. It was never easy to mention their names, and now least of all.

Meanwhile, driven to exasperation by his increasing taciturnity and what appeared to be his secretiveness, Linda was churning up for an outburst. On the night following Sanelo's decision, Simon, on his return from work, was eager to run next door and lend him a hand if necessary. He was in too great a hurry even to touch his supper.

'Oh, so now you won't even eat the food I prepare for you,' cried Linda.

'Nonsense. I'm sorry, Linda. But I have to see Abel.'

'As if you aren't always going to see Abel and his wife. That's fine! Of course it doesn't matter what happens to me.'

'I'm sorry, I tell you. But I absolutely must see them tonight. There's no need to look like a tragedy queen about it.'

'Tragedy queen! Better and better! Carry on, my dear. Say some more.'

'Oh, to hell with it. You're making a big mistake if you think I'm going to be tied for good and all to your bedpost.'

'You ungrateful dog! You'll take back those words. You think I don't know what's eating you? A fine thing, smelling after a woman and she fat with another man's child!'

For the first time in their life together, Simon struck her. Not hard, thank goodness, for she ducked away from him in time to soften the blow. As he made for the door she leapt at him, her face contorted with a mixture of hate, shock and humiliation.

'I'll pay you back for this!' she screamed. 'You'll see. You – you – '

Hating himself, he flung her off.

The door slammed behind him, knocking a glass figurine of a dancer he'd given her off the dressing table. The delicate ornament was shattered. With an exclamation of dismay she knelt down and with tears coursing down her cheeks she began picking up the pieces. Then suddenly she hurled them at the closed door.

As if to mock the ineffectual tinkle of her rage against the wood, a thunderous knocking arrested her outstretched hand. Hau! That must be at Sanelo's door.

At that moment Simon burst back into the room.

'Oh, so you thought better of it?' she said.

'It's the police. Cover yourself up.'

A sound of shouting and banging interrupted him and, sobered by his look, she obeyed.

'What's up? Is it a raid?'

'They're on the hunt for somebody. Heaven knows, it can't be Abel Sanelo. But two whites and one black dog are in there now. The pickup van's outside.'

Through the flimsy walls dividing their room from Sanelo's they could hear the loud-mouthed demands of the police and Abel's muffled replies, punctuated by thumps, bangs and curses.

A sickening thud shook the room.

'I can't stand it! They're beating him up!' cried Simon, making for the door.

'You fool!' she shouted. 'Keep out of it. What can you do but get a bloody head and land yourself in jail?'

'Have you no heart?'

'Heart! These thugs with guns have come to kick our guts out, and you talk about a heart!'

They glared at each other like enemies.

'If looks could kill, I'm dead. That's all the thanks I get for trying to save you. Why blame me?'

She stopped abruptly as a woman's wailing cry penetrated

the room.

'Think of Nomasa!' he said and rushed out, leaving the door open behind him.

'Simon, don't take your gun with you. They'll kill you for that!'

But he was gone. She dared not follow him. She ran into the passageway, she ran to the window, but by this time it was too dark to see what was happening. Only her ears told her they must be dragging something heavy across the room . . .

A woman's piercing scream split the air. Linda took a step towards the door and halted as a shot rang out.

'My God! Simon!'

Rushing outside, she was in time to see the black policeman push violently past Simon and out through the door of Sanelo's room. In the same instant one of the white policemen ordered the black: 'Lug the carcass into the van, eh? Hurry up, man!'

In the light of their torches she saw a body sprawled beside the van, the sightless eyes facing the room.

Tixo! It was Abel Sanelo.

One said to the other: 'That's one more of the bastards.'

'Ja. Wasn't it crazy the way the kaffir tried to run back into the house?'

'Get a move on there. We've got more work to do.'

The door of the pickup van clanged shut and the vehicle zoomed off with a roar.

Shuddering, Linda went up to Simon. Without a word he entered Sanelo's room and she followed.

The place was in a shambles; the bed disarranged, Sanelo's books scattered about the floor, wooden ornaments in splinters. In a corner of the room Nomasa sat huddled on the floor like one bereft of all emotion.

Linda went up to her, pity driving out every other thought.

'Nomasa, Nomasa. Let the tears come, Nomasa.'

The young woman made no response.

'I'll make up your bed,' said Linda. To Simon she whispered: 'They didn't touch her, did they? Why did they shoot?'

'That black dog must have laid hands on her. Abel was like a madman. He tried to rush back.'

Quietly they restored the room to some semblance of order. Nomasa made no sound. From time to time her body trembled.

'They even kicked his books around,' murmured Linda.

'The books would make them more mad than anything,' he said.

'Come, Nomasa.' Linda spoke gently. 'I'll help you to bed and you'll try to get some rest.'

But Nomasa pulled her hand away. Linda tried again.

'Nomasa, would you like to come to our room?'

She shook her head.

Simon went over to Nomasa and gently but firmly led her to the bed, where he sat down beside her.

'Nomasa, we are here. I shall take care of you.'

At last she spoke. 'I must go home. The father of my child – he said I must go home. I have the ticket here. Today he bought it.'

'You cannot travel alone,' said Simon. 'Nomasa, I will take you home to your husband's people.'

'What? What did you say, Simon? What?' Startled, Linda looked from one to the other.

Having at last persuaded Nomasa to go to bed, Simon and Linda retired to their room, but not to rest. The tragedy of Abel Sanelo's death, which had lifted them out of themselves, now served to renew their battle with redoubled force.

Simon's decision to accompany the bereaved woman to her husband's home was a perfectly natural one, indeed a duty, according to tradition. He did not analyse the sense of well-being that came to him as soon as he had made up his mind. If he had done so, he would have recognised not only the satisfaction of acting in the spirit of his fathers, as well as finding in action some relief from that sense of impotence that overwhelms a man in face of another's grief, but also – and most of all – because in so doing he resolved his own problem.

His longing to see his family again could now be fulfilled. Doubts, hesitations, scruples – all vanished. He had been more than glad to see how Linda had acted towards Nomasa as a sister should, revealing a side of her nature she seldom gave expression to. So now when she turned on him in fury he was taken completely unawares.

With a strong effort at self-control she had waited till they were in their own room. She had been sufficiently shaken by the events of the evening to be carried into Nomasa's grief. But when Simon without hesitation stated his purpose, one look at Nomasa's face then back to his convinced her that he meant it. Instantly, she experienced such a revulsion of feeling that she caught her breath. She felt she had been deliberately betrayed into the emotions of sympathy she had bestowed on Sanelo's wife. She had been tricked, mocked, cheated, to make the way easy for Simon to desert her.

In her obsession with this thought she didn't allow reason to question whether Nomasa was an accomplice in this act of treachery. She assumed it. It was enough that Simon was taking her with him to the country. She knew that Nomasa lived somewhere near his home village. She began speaking quietly enough.

'So you've made all your plans, have you, for taking the woman to the country with you?'

'I don't know what you mean by plans. I'll have to arrange things pretty fast tomorrow, if we are going to get on that train in the afternoon.'

This cool matter of factness infuriated her.

'You think you're clever, very clever, eh?'

'What do you mean?'

'You spring this plan on me suddenly, thinking that way I can't do a damn thing about it?'

'I don't see what you can do about it. I have to go. That's all.'

'Awu! That's what you calculated on, you cheat.'

'Mrs Sanelo's plight is desperate. Have you no pity?'

'Pity!' She spat the word.

'Look, Linda, I don't know what it is that's bothering you. You're all worked up, and no wonder. Haven't we been through enough for one night? Let be, now. Come. We're both tired. Come, Linda.'

'None of that! None of that! It's only another of your tricks.'

'What's come over you? Surely I don't need to explain to you I *have* to take Sanelo's wife home to his people.'

'Tell me another! And why must it be you? Can't somebody else take her?'

'It could be somebody belonging to his clan. But who? With time so short. Tixo! I'm his nearest friend. What are we arguing about? Have you no feeling after all that's happened to his wife tonight. Nomasa – '

'Nomasa! Nomasa! Whoever cared whether *I* lived or died? Since childhood, till now! Now! Now! Who ever had pity on me? Or my brother Joel?'

'Linda!' That last cry exposed her to the very core.

They stood face to face. Yet Simon was uneasily aware that, while he could avow his innocence where the wife of Sanelo was concerned, to answer Linda was nevertheless to deceive her. How in her present passion could he speak of what was in his mind? In making his decision to go into the country, he had not looked beyond the journey he was taking, neither backwards nor forwards. It had become as simple as that. For him it was enough that he was going home. Enough that he would see Boniswa face to face. Was this to be exonerated of treachery?

Misreading his unhappy expression, Linda sought to take advantage of it.

'Simon, don't go away. Don't leave me. I feel – I'm afraid, afraid I'll never see you again. Simon . . .'

At this he took a sudden resolve.

'Linda, there's something I want to tell you. There's something you must know. It's true. I'm going home – to see my family. Would you deny me that? I want to see my wife and child again.'

She stared at him, unable to speak. Then she burst into laughter. Laughter that even to her ears sounded more like the yelp of a hyena.

'Did you say I hadn't a heart? I almost believed you. And a minute ago I laid it – there, right there. And do you know what you did? You kicked it hard, harder than ever happened to me before. I'll not forget it. I'll remember that. By God, I will!'

'Linda, don't. Let me speak.'

'Save your breath. I'll not trust a word you're saying. Never again. Serves me right. But don't worry, I won't lose a night's sleep over it. I forget bad dreams easy. Go! Go! Run back home. And I wish you luck of it! But you'll never see my face again.'

'Linda . . .'

'Tixo! You think I'll let you rot inside me, like the child they ripped out of me? I was seventeen. It near killed me. Touch and go. Never again! Go. Take your things. You better hurry. That woman's baby, it might die on the way. Die! Die!'

Without speaking Simon left her with the wild word on her lips. The door closed quietly. He was gone.

Linda stood silent, numbed by her own passion.

Ten

In spite of the responsibility of his sad mission, it was with a secret sense of exhilaration and excitement that Simon boarded the south-bound train with the wife of Sanelo the following afternoon. In the crowded, noisy, uncomfortable carriage they spoke little, each one wrapped in a separate world of thought. A mingled expression of resignation and relief gave Nomasa's features unexpected repose; her hands rested without tension on the handle of her basket. In Simon she had complete trust.

For himself, with an effort he pushed out of his mind the memory of Linda as he had last seen her, and let his thoughts dwell on the moment of his arrival home. He pictured the surprise and the sudden joy of reunion, without allowing himself to figure out what the gap of time might have done. There was no clear image in his mind of Boniswa, his father or of Funeka. They floated vaguely in a mist of memory and anticipated pleasure. A sense of euphoria enveloped him, wiping out every sharp contour of remorse for the past or apprehension of what the future might hold.

A day and a night brought the travellers to Iamata and from there they travelled by bus to Engcobo. The next part of the journey was on foot, where Nomasa had to be the guide. She wanted first to go to the house of her father Coto, where Simon would leave her. In due time they would take her to the home of her husband's people, where his child would be born.

While they were yet far off, Nomasa's mother and father, working in the fields, looked in wonder, dropping their tools as the two figures appeared over the rise of the hill. They recognised their daughter and marvelled at what had brought her home. For they had received no news either of the impending return or the tragedy that had forerun it.

Nomasa fled to her mother's arms and it was Simon's unhappy task to break the news. A little later grief gave way to gratitude and Coto thanked Simon as a true friend of the murdered Sanelo in bringing their daughter safely home. The mother and father sang his praises as a worthy son of the old peasant, Manzana. They were not acquainted with him, but they were sure he would be proud of such a son. There would be much rejoicing in the house of his father at his return.

Simon was eager to be on his way. However, the day was by this time so far advanced that he judged it wise to curb his impatience and accept the hospitality offered him by Nomasa's parents.

As he shared their simple meal, Coto spoke of worsening conditions on the land. Simon must know how it was everywhere, but of late things had come to such a pass that there were signs of restlessness among the peasants. Their patience was at an end. There had been a number of incidents involving death and the burning of huts; for there were traitors amongst their own people, and some of them were known to be police. Always, the people must suffer. No doubt old Manzana would unpack his heart on his son's return. There were tales to tell such as men feared to speak of. At such a moment as this he would say no more. His child Nomasa needed all their care.

By sunrise next morning Simon was up and ready to set out

for home. He bade his kind hosts goodbye and was surprised to see Nomasa slip out of the hut to stand by her mother's side, a warm smile of gratitude momentarily lighting her sad young face.

Following Coto's directions, Simon picked up his bag and retraced his steps to the main road, then struck out briskly in the opposite direction. It would take some hours of good hard walking but with luck he would reach home well before sunset.

It was a warm October day with some cloud heralding the rains that every man hopes will fall in early summer. It is on such days that the peasant ploughs his fields and sows his mealies that provide his staple food for the winter months. Enjoying the exhilaration of the open road after so many years spent amid the smells and alleyways of Sophiatown, Simon slipped imperceptibly into a daydream of youthful memories. It was the haunts of his childhood that he traversed in his thoughts, scenes that were part of his being long before the droughts and tribulations that first drove him to the City of Goli. He is the barefoot boy taking his father's cattle to the grazing ground on the hillside. He whistles and calls in the morning air; his stick cut from the willow tree by the stream smacks the rump of the leader as he clambers up the green slope; his feet scatter the dewdrops, drinking their coolness before the greedy sun should quench its thirst . . . Now the unseen cicadas sing the shrill song of high noon while he and the other herdboys laze in the shade of the oldest willow and the cattle chew the cud in dignified contentment. A lizard darts shadow-swift across a sun-baked stone. Or is it the stone that breathes? . . . Shouts and the crack-crack of sticks break the magic stillness of the late afternoon, for the boys are having their puppy-fights, playing at the battles of men . . . Evensong is the lowing of the cattle leisurely trekking homewards; the setting sun – red-gold bull of the skies – draws them back to the kraals . . . Now his mother has called him to go and gather firewood. Stick in hand, the youngling steps lithely through the woods, stalking the hares. There goes a bobbing tail – there it goes! The young hunter slithers forward on his belly like a snake. There it goes! . . . It is gone. So down into the stream with a leap and a lusty shout. Like the swathes of the lush-green mealie leaves, the waters refresh his sweating body . . . From the nostrils of the night fires blue smoke spirals the still air, and after the evening meal young feet stamp and prance in the triumph of old battles refought, battles before the coming of the white man. Then plaintive voices tell the tale of two royal lovers who had fled, seeking a new home on the other side of the mountains, lest the wrath of their chief should slay them and all those who had received their initiation on the selfsame day . . .

Lulled by such memories, Simon lost track of time and place. But long before midday his limbs began to ache; his breathing became laboured and sweat trickled down his back in clammy runlets. The townsman was no longer able to take the miles in his stride.

Looking round for a shady place where he could rest and eat – Coto's wife had insisted on him taking something for the journey – he became aware of a landscape familiar and yet bare, peculiarly lacking in the spirit of welcome he expected the familiar to possess.

The shade was hard to find. Now it struck him he had met no man on the way within hailing distance. Some huts he had passed, far from the road, showed no signs of life; distant figures in the fields were those of womenfolk, their backs to the sun, their faces to the soil. One woman had waved to him and shouted, but she had been too far off and he had passed on. He experienced the unpleasant sensation of being wrenched back from his daydreams into harsh reality.

Where exactly was he? How far had he still to go? Not so far as he had thought after all. There on the horizon was the very hill where he and the other herdboys used to take the cattle to the grazing grounds, and there on its left flank the spreading forests. Out of sight at this angle was the cluster of huts where his father Manzana and a few other poor peasants lived, and beyond these their plots where they eked out their meagre harvests. At the foot of the hill before turning right to reach his home, there would be the little cemetery where slept their forefathers. Here it was that

Simon and his father had carried his mother to her last resting place.

In the heat of the midday sun the landscape had an ashen look. If it had opened its bosom to the spring, its flowers must have quickly faded; the stricken grasslands undulating towards the distant hills were charred and brown, hungry for the rains. Here and there the hooves of the patient cattle, lean as a winter's tree, stirred up wisps of powdery earth. His ravenous eyes searched for some scrap of green, some leaf with the sap and sheen of young life. Growing by the roadside the prickly pear had defied the drought; its coarse, thick leaves jutted their clumsy thorned hands as if to guard their succulence. Amid bushes like unkempt hair the spiky aloe had wrested its one red bloom from among the stones.

A group of women drew abreast of him, empty bowl or bucket perched on their heads, one of them with a baby strapped on her back; bare feet and long skirts red-brown with dust, and the head-doek too carrying slivers of fine dust in its folds. They exchanged greetings with him, telling him they had come far to find water for their cooking pots. When they had passed he turned to look at them, slow and heavy of motion. It struck him that none of them were young, none of them were comely. Hau! He had become too much of the townsman!

The journey on foot had tired him out. Why must his chest have this feeling of tightness, of bursting for lack of air? These were his homelands; how often had he traversed these roads on his way to school? Soon he would reach home. He blessed the familiar woods visible on the hillside, dark, sturdy pines that took on shape and colour as he drew nearer his journey's end.

There to the right the huts had come into view. The image of Boniswa suddenly became startlingly real in his mind and he quickened his steps. Would she be at home looking after their baby? But of course Nothanda was a baby no longer. What had he been thinking of? Most likely his wife would be working in the fields with his father. It was Funeka he'd find at home.

Funeka. How like their mother Funeka was – a woman with a large heart though she lacked her strong body. And he had to go away from home to discover what a woman Funeka was. Ah, well, they would soon be seeing each other. The years between would fall away as if they had never been.

Strange, how you had to go away to get a proper idea of the people you lived with . . . How would his father receive him? He wasn't a hard man, really. Those bitter words he had made Boniswa write in the letters – well, he deserved them, all of them – didn't he? Would he be able to talk to his father, tell him some of the things he had been through in the city? Simon smiled as he felt the automatic in his pocket. What would his father say if he knew he had a gun?

Another mile at most and he would be there. The little cemetery itself wasn't half a mile away. There was a stone over the family grave. It had been put up when his elder brother died. His father was able to afford such things then. It was his mother who had insisted on it, and she used to go regularly to the graveside, though his father refused to go. Simon had not thought about it at the time. What does a youngster know about death? He could not even remember his brother . . .

Saddened by the barrenness of the countryside, stretching bleak and bare as far as the eye could see, he increased his pace. He reached the cemetery and stopped to locate the exact spot where his mother lay. Here and there headstones with their pathetically brief memorials of the dead leaned awry over mounds of earth, or only the mounds themselves marked the place where the living hand had laid the dead to rest. Somehow the stones leaning this way and that suggested desolation and neglect more than the unmarked graves. It should be easy to discover his mother's grave because there was an old oak tree hard by.

As he looked about him, he became aware of a group of people, huddled together, heads bent away from him. They were near the tree. There was an eerie stillness in the air that carried neither voice nor movement. He had not meant to intrude on the mourners at a funeral. He would slip out silently and visit his mother's grave some other time.

He was turning away when the sight of a familiar figure sent a shock through his body.

'Father!' he cried and leapt towards the group.

The old man looked up, startled.

'My son! Oh, my son!'

Grief gave place to a great wonder to see his son restored to him at such a moment; joy succeeded grief and grief succeeded joy again – emotions that could find no expression in words. But for Simon one terrible question was uppermost.

'Father, who . . .?'

'Your sister. Funeka,' he said, and closed his eyes.

Simon gave a loud cry and stepped to the edge of the gaping hole. The grave was still open, the funeral rites not yet completed. No earth had been cast over the coffin.

Could it be that his sister's body lay under that thin plank of wood? Was that face to be hidden from him for ever? The words of farewell – and of forgiveness – for ever unspoken?

No!

Something like madness possessed him. He looked wildly round at the mourners, without perceiving who they were. Could someone not assist him to lift the body from the grave? Oh, God, to be too late for the greeting that had to be spoken between them! That *must* be spoken! She had waited for him to come back; so long she had waited – in vain. But he would explain everything to her and she would understand. Funeka always understood, more than anyone else –

A man took Simon by the arm. It was the minister who was officiating at the burial.

'My son, your heart is rebellious. Accept God's will. It is the only way.'

Shaking off the restraining hand, Simon took a step nearer the brink of the grave.

'Father of Nothanda!' a woman cried. He turned. It was his wife Boniswa.

The pitiful look, the tear-stained face drew him from the grave. He took her in his arms, comforting and being comforted. Then father, son and wife stood side by side in stillness while the ceremony was completed.

Simon heard and saw as if in a dream. What hollow sound was

that, of the clod of earth striking the coffin lid? The irrevocable closing of the grave. No human being lay beneath that clod of earth. It could not breathe. It could not hear. It could not see.

The first thing he did on entering the house was to look round for Funeka. Here he had always found her when he came back from school; how often had he seen her standing over the cooking pots when he and his father returned from the fields? Then he remembered.

He looked towards Boniswa, only to find a peculiar expression of constraint in her face. A common grief had united them at the graveside, spanning the gulf of absence, recrimination, reproach. But now other feelings were reasserting themselves. How else explain this reserve so chilling in its silence?

He was seeing her for the first time since his return and his heart broke at what he saw. Her good looks were blunted, the lines of her face had been etched by penury and patience beyond measure. Here was something more harsh than the grief that had united them at their sister's grave.

Stirred by a new disquiet, he glanced across at his father. He, too, was different from what he remembered. His wrinkled flesh had been carved with the anguish of more than hunger. His brows were furrowed like a bare field.

With yearning intentness Simon continued to watch Boniswa as she prepared a meal, assisted by a girl of about twenty who, his father explained, was Nomonde, the wife of his youngest brother, Mvuzo. What had become of Mvuzo? Oh, he had run away from the white farm. The farmer had set the dogs on him but he had the swift foot of a deer and escaped. Then, like his brother Gundani, he had only last month joined a batch of recruits to work in the gold mines. He was on a two-year contract and lived in the mine barracks, so his young wife wouldn't be able to see him for a long time. Yes, Gundani was still working in the mines and had occasionally sent them some money. His wife had never showed up again after her miscarriage, when she went to the town to find work.

Father and son sat in the shade of the hut. Simon ached to

speak of Funeka but it seemed that his father needed the solitude of his own thoughts to quell his grief.

At their feet three children were playing in the sand. Simon barely noticed the two younger, one of them a boy about three years old, the other a baby girl at the crawling stage, both of whom he assumed were his brother Mvuzo's children, his first son Yiva having died of a stomach sickness.

He had eyes only for the eldest, a girl who looked about seven years of age, he was sure. There was no doubt about her likeness to his mother. She was – oh yes – yes – she was his daughter.

Nothanda.

He took her on his knee. He felt her muscles tense as her lithe body yielded to his touch. With his fingertips he traced the contours of her face, then cupped her chin in his palm as he gazed into her frightened eyes, tasting the painful joy of fatherhood. The child began to cry at this strange man and kicked and pushed hard against him. Simon willingly released her, vowing that he would soon overcome this strangeness. A feeling of tenderness came over him, thinking of the child's mother, to whom Nothanda now ran, hiding her face in Boniswa's skirts.

In spite of his overriding sorrow, Simon began to enjoy a sense of domestic peace conveyed by the scene. Time enough to talk; time enough to do something to melt away the barriers the years had erected. No need to rush things. Just to be home was enough. If only Funeka were here. If only he had come sooner. Oh, if only . . .

Boniswa and his brother's wife Nomonde drew near and gave the men something to eat and drink. Simon was hungry after his long walk, and he was still hungry at the end of the meal. But far be it for him to make any comment. It would have pleased him to have Boniswa come and sit beside him. Why should she avoid his glances so persistently? The children kept her inordinately busy. Could she not leave them to Nomonde's care? Once he put out a hand to catch the hem of her dress, but she evaded him. Her reserve made him all the more eager for the moment when they would be alone together.

Becoming aware of his father's scrutiny, he wondered uneasily what it might portend. Could he and Boniswa not find it in their hearts to forgive him? If he could only find words to tell them about life in the city.

He jumped up, remembering that he had brought a brightly coloured scarf for his wife. Now was the moment to produce it from his pocket. He went up to her and, before she could protest, laid the scarlet scarf about her shoulders. She gave a little cry, but not of pleasure, and snatched off the scarf, keeping it in her hand and looking from Simon to his father as if about to burst into tears. Then, covering her face with her hands, she ran inside her hut.

His father said nothing.

Concealing his chagrin, Simon fumbled in the small suitcase he had brought and produced a doll for Nothanda. He had the pleasure of luring her back to his knee with this pretty bait. This time she was too enraptured with her toy to try to run away. The other two children also gathered close and there was an angry yell from Nothanda as the baby girl snatched at the doll, which was in danger of being torn to pieces between them. However, Nomonde saved the situation by carrying off the two younger children. Simon laughed at this domestic storm. It was not unpleasant. He still had Nothanda on his knee.

'Are you coming with me to the fields?' asked his father a little later. 'There is still enough light.'

Simon nodded. With the women and children withdrawn to their huts, what better opportunity to ask his father's forgiveness?

The two men walked side by side and Simon experienced a rare glow of satisfaction in this simple fact of proximity to his father. Looking out across the fields he perceived the same denuded soil he had observed along the way. Yet he was pleased to see how his father had contrived to grow two or three small patches of vegetables. He had already started ploughing in preparation for planting his mealies.

'You must take it easy, father,' said Simon. 'I'll finish the ploughing.'

His father gave a harsh cackle of laughter.

'If these clouds were not misers and would drop their cargo on our fields, it would be worth your labour. Every day I'm expecting the rains. But that's not all our troubles. Such things have been happening, my son, it pains me here to tell you.'

His emaciated hands gripped the whole front of his body. 'Such things you would hardly believe.'

'What things, father?'

'Men have become wolves. They devour us. Forcing us to cull our cattle. That was only the beginning. Let me tell you, for my ploughing I had to borrow two oxen from our neighbour Sigebenga. I have only one ox left, and some goats.'

'Tixo! What happened to the rest? And our sheep?'

'See that length of barbed wire fence. Over there. It's quite a story.'

'Barbed wire!'

'No less – that's how they stole our grazing land from us. I've cut the wire down but those white dogs bring men to set it up again. That's what their regulations have come to – for the good of the land, they call it. While we die for lack of land! Whichever way we turn – whether it's our grazing lands, or what we must plough, or the number of cattle we may keep – they put up barbed wire restrictions to impale us. Our cattle, our goats can't tread inside that barbed wire. Then officials come along and point out certain beasts they don't like. They have the impudence to order us to get rid of them. Isn't it a strange thing, my son, that we who have lived all our lives on this land and have bred cattle long before the white man came – isn't it strange that we should not know which beast does well in these parts and which does not?'

The old man laughed mirthlessly.

'Go on, father. I want to hear more,' said Simon, relieved that the time had not yet come for the old man to admonish him for his own sins.

'Oh, first they took some of our sheep and castrated them. We suffered them to do it. Then they bade us sell our scrub cattle, and we did it. I needn't tell you scrub cattle sell for a song. They said it was all for our good. We looked at our kraals that were nearly empty and we were even more hungry than before. Then one day they came and wanted to seize our bulls and castrate them, too. This we refused! Now the womenfolk were up in arms, raging and threatening to do something drastic, I can tell you! And the officials ran for their lives. Castrate our bulls? That was the last straw. But listen to what happened next, my son. Gwaza, the headman – you remember him? A creature with a stuffed paunch, so – came strutting into the village with his neck thrust out, as if he thought he was a white man. But before he could even open his mouth, we shouted at him: "Give us back the balls of our sheep!" You should have seen him scurrying away with his tail between his legs. But that wasn't the end of it. The Chief himself called us together. Our Chief – and he spoke with a white man's voice. Yes, that's what it has come to. "If you do not do as the law commands," he threatened us, "you shall be punished for it." And we said one to another: "Our chiefs are chiefs no longer. They go to the little window for their pay from the white hand. A faceless white hand." So we refused to listen to the words of the Chief. But alas, my son, that is not yet the end of the story. The officials give us no peace. When we refuse to carry out their vicious orders they drag us to the courts, ordering us to pay fines. Having devoured our sole means of staying alive, they fine us for it! Believe me, there is no end to their greed. They would bleed us to death. We feel and we suffer.'

'But, father, I don't understand. Is there no way of resisting these sharks?'

'How? They send their police, with arms. They spread terror in our villages. They burn our crops. They arrest those who would speak for us. We never see our men again – '

'What is it all for?'

'They are madmen. They know only one language – violence. Simon, it is a silent war – to destroy us. It seems to me they are determined to squeeze us off the land altogether.'

'Father! We must find a way to resist them. We cannot lie down and die.'

'When we starve – then the vultures come – recruiting agents come and herd our youth together – '

'So we are a human sacrifice – to their god – the mines! From the land to the bowels of the earth – '

'You have said it, son. From this grave, this dying land, to their pits of gold. But, my son, we are not alone. What is happening here is happening all over, let me tell you. We have had spokesmen from other parts of the country who have travelled a long way to confer with us. Men with the same rage burning in their hearts. What is to be done? Our patience has a limit. What is to be done?'

As they turned back towards the huts, a youth appeared some way off driving a few cattle before him.

'That is Sigebenga's youngest son Xolile,' said old Manzana.

Simon looked and saw a barefoot youth who might have been himself – how many years back? He was afraid to think how long.

'He is a good lad,' his father continued. 'He tends his father's cattle along with those of some few of us who still have cattle left.'

Simon knew what it cost the old man to admit this degree of his poverty.'You remember his other son, Andile Sigebenga?' asked his father.

'Of course. We used to hunt hares together in the woods. What of him?'

'He has come home from the mines – a very sick man, I'm afraid.'

'Sickness of the lungs?'

'I fear it. His days are numbered.'

'That is sad news, father. I must go and see him.'

'He is so changed, you will hardly know him.'

'I must go as soon as I can.'

Old Manzana hailed the youth Xolile, who gave greeting and passed on, a halo of red-brown dust about his feet and enveloping his cattle.

The setting sun had turned the clouds from a miser's silver to a miser's gold; their bellies were heavy with unfallen rain. By the time father and son returned to the huts, the children were asleep and only Nomonde was busy among the pots.

'Where is Boniswa?' asked Simon.

'She is with the children,' answered Nomonde.

Simon made to go into his wife's hut.

'Stay,' said his father. 'The time is not yet. I have to hear *your* story. Why were you so long silent? You knew something of our plight. And' – speaking with deliberation – 'of Boniswa. Your wife.'

Simon had been wondering when the old man would ask these questions. He knew they were poised on his lips.

'Father, I admit my wrong.'

His father waited, reproof in his silence.

'It is hard to tell you what life is like in the city. There, too, are vultures. But it is different. I . . .'

Simon began first by describing the events that led up to his bringing Nomasa home.

'You did well,' said his father, waiting.

'Father – ' Simon hesitated, dropping his eyes away from his father's gaze. 'Let me tell you another day – all that has befallen me. It is not to be said in a few words – '

'I can guess some of it.' His father's voice was heavy with condemnation. 'Others have returned and I know more than you might think. Your clothes. You did not pick up that coat without money in your pocket . . .'

'Tomorrow, father. I would speak with Boniswa now.'

His father watched him as he entered the hut, his face inscrutable.

On waking next morning, Simon found himself alone, the rest of the family already astir. Boniswa was gone from the hut. It disturbed him to realise that his wife's constraint in his presence had in no way abated. He told himself that his second wooing of her would be far more difficult than the first. If only Funeka were alive, he thought, she would have played the part of the devoted go-between. She would have found the words to melt Boniswa's obdurate heart. Funeka . . .

Watching his wife as she set out with Nomonde, each carrying on her head the earthen water pot, he observed the fullness of her breasts. Her body was thin, too thin, yet she still moved with unconscious grace. But the face – something about its expression deeply troubled him. As he remembered her, her glance had always been free and open. She had not been a shy girl, like Abel Sanelo's young wife. This constrained, averted look, almost shrinking, was wholly out of keeping with her character. Did she hate him so much? Or did she fear all that the city had done to him? In that moment at Funeka's graveside, her voice, her touch, her eyes had spoken her affection like a drowning body drawing its first liberated breath of air. But since then, nothing but constraint.

His father did not leave him long in doubt.

The three children were playing at their feet, Nothanda busy washing her doll with a liberal application of sand and the girl-baby beside her happily assisting in these dusty ablutions. A little way apart the boy was unmaking his own sandcastles. The two women had disappeared to carry water and continue with their chores.

'It is time to speak,' said old Manzana slowly. He turned on his stool to face his son.

Simon looked at him in surprise.

'You have come home and you have learned only a part of all that has happened in your long absence.'

'I realise that much has happened in my absence,' replied Simon.

'What I have to speak about, my son, is part of all these things that weigh upon us. But this more closely concerns yourself and your home.'

'I do not understand you, father. What have you to tell me?'

'You see the child,' began Manzana. 'No, not your Nothanda. The other girl-child.'

'I confess I had hardly noticed her. She must be Mvuzo's little one.'

'No, my son. Look closely.' He paused, his eyes not on the child but straight at Simon's face. 'She is Boniswa's child.'

'Boniswa, my wife!'

'Your wife, whom you had forsaken.'

'Boniswa's child? I do not believe you.'

'You will have to believe me.'

'Tixo! But who . . .? No, father. No! No! Not Boniswa! Not my wife! I'll not believe such a thing of her.'

'Would any man believe what *you* have done, my son. Were you blameless in the big city? You look moved.'

Simon stood up, walked three paces from his father, stopped, then walked three paces back, as if by this simple ritual it would banish the hurt coursing through his body.

'Tell me, what villain was it? Where is he? Let me find him. I'll – I'll – only tell me his name!'

'That I will not do.'

'You must tell me! Is he in these parts? I'll seek him out . . .'

'He is gone. Like you, he is a sojourner in the city. He returned here but he could not stay.'

'Tell me his name and I will search him out in the city – with this!'

Simon pulled out his gun.

'So. That is what you find in the city, and you would resolve your problems with violence?'

'Violence has been done to me!'

'Violence is being done daily to us all, my son. You are not alone. And there are men here, too, in our homelands, who are asking for guns. We are learning to think differently and to act differently.'

Simon did not hear his father.

'Father, I entreat you, tell me who is this man? It is my right to know.'

'You would be revenged, would you? And what would vengeance serve you? How would it help Boniswa, or the child? Do you want to bring more sorrow on her head than she already suffers?'

'But, father, the dog – whoever he is – has brought dishonour to me, and to this house.'

'Simon, sit down. I have thought much about this dishonour. There was a time when I, too, would have shouted and cried aloud for vengeance, if a man should dare to outrage my honour.

But the vultures of our affliction in these times have not pecked out the eyes of my wisdom. In truth, my son, I have found a new wisdom, such as our fathers knew not of; for life did not demand it of them. I ask, what is this honour? Have you, Simon, kept that shield of your honour bright and untarnished in the city? Have you the right to shout "Villain" – when you left that honour all unprotected in the weak hands of your young wife? Since when must a man leave his honour in his wife's keeping, while he himself is far away on the devil knows what game of his own?'

'Father, I know only one thing – Boniswa is my wife!'

'Since when have you known it? Did you remember it all these long years – these days, months, weeks, hours, when your wife was alone, caring for your child, toiling for it, and not a word of tenderness from its father? Not a penny sent to feed the hungry mouths. How did you keep full the cup of her affection? Was it not empty as the udders of a famished cow? For all we knew, your silence meant death; the death of a son, the death of a husband. The death of a father. It is common enough when a man is swallowed up in the city.'

Simon covered his face with his hands.

'My son, the bitter gall of your silence, your indifference, was your wife's only portion.'

'Not indifference, father! I swear. You are unjust to me. You don't know what life in the city is like. You don't know what torments I – '

'I have a shrewd suspicion what the city does to a man. I see the evidence before me.'

'What do you know? You do not know, father. You cannot know!'

'My son, consider well what I have said. At this moment you can think only of your wounded pride. It seeks the satisfaction of revenge. Do not add evil to what you have already committed. You have seen how it is with her. She is overcome with shame, poor child. Remember, in forgiving her, you will thereby forgive yourself – and there is much to forgive. To punish her is to punish yourself. This you cannot escape.'

Simon had one desire and that was to be alone. His promise

to help his father with the ploughing was forgotten, and the old man knew better than to remind him.

He took the path up the hill towards the old grazing lands. Plunged in thought, he did not remember what his father had told him – that they were now forcibly fenced in. It was only when he stumbled against the barbed wire that he drew back with a curse and knew that these boyhood haunts were closed to him for ever. Holding to the left of the hill, he made for the woods.

His father had put his finger on the raw wound of his son's grievance. Hurt pride rendered him deaf to the old man's words of wisdom; it blinded him to the unreason of his own attitude. Paradoxically it was left to his father, wrestling to survive in his destitute homeland, to grope towards a new morality. Perhaps if Simon had not been tormented by the bitter memory of his parting from Linda, the unresolved conflict in his feeling for the two women, he would not have been so much at the mercy of impotent rage, disgust and disillusionment. His father had spoken of forgiveness. The word had no meaning. He felt he had returned home, only to be cast out. His father's castigation rankled in his mind; he felt it to be unjust. What did they know of the ceaseless war to survive in the city? He would not permit himself to examine the old man's stern defence of Boniswa. No, no, no! He would not –

A voice broke into his unhappy reverie.

'Young man, it is forbidden to trespass in these woods. If you seek firewood, you must go elsewhere.'

Simon made a sound that might have been called a laugh. A black man in uniform barred his way.

'In these woods I seek my lost youth,' he said.

'That's as may be. But to trespass here is to be subject to a fine of two pounds.'

Simon looked the fellow up and down.

'You are an officious individual. I am not acquainted with your rules and regulations.'

'They are not my rules and regulations. But ignorance of the law is no excuse.'

154

'You are a stranger in these parts, no doubt?' said Simon rudely.

'No stranger neither. I know my duties.'

'Ah, then that makes you a stranger. A man born in these parts knows loyalties, not duties. However, I'll leave you to your duties.'

Descending the hill, Simon could not bring himself to return to his father's house. To confront so soon those cold eyes of accusation would open anew the rawness of his wounds. It was then he bethought him of Andile Sigebenga, who his father had told him had come back from working in the mines. He had been fond of Andile, a venturesome youngster always ready to land himself in scrapes. He had been good company, but he had gone off to the city long before himself.

Simon found Andile sitting outside his father's main hut.

Or was it he? This man with bent back, sitting like a stone in the sun? Why, he and Andile were nearly of an age!

The man spoke. '*Sakubona*, Simon.'

'Andile! It is you!'

'Yes, you are looking at the shadow of a man. Eight years in the mines . . .'

'My father didn't tell me. He did, but . . .'

'The eyes tell more than the tongue,' said Andile. 'You don't need to explain. Sit down next to me. It's been a long time.'

'Oh, Andile, I would have come sooner!'

'I could wait, Simon. The days and the nights are my own here, all my own. I'm sure you were tasting the joys of your homecoming.'

'You mock me, Andile.'

'Forgive me. Funeka, your sister. She always said you would come home.'

Simon could only clasp Andile's hand.

A young woman appeared from inside the hut.

'Simon, meet my wife. Nosisi, this is an old friend of mine, Simon Manzana.'

As they greeted each other, Simon felt the thin hand limp

in his. But Nosisi's smile was all that he had missed since his homecoming.

He wanted to refuse her offer of food, but Andile would not take no for an answer.

'Allow me to play the tyrant,' he said. 'I'll take it ill if you do not share the cup of friendship with us.'

Simon knew it would be churlish to refuse. The young woman left them and for a few moments the two men sat without speaking.

'A visitor like you is a rare pleasure for my wife,' began Andile. 'She hankers after the city, I'm afraid. You see . . .' He paused, as if not sure how to continue. 'We are childless – ' He paused again. 'And her hands are not as full as she would like them to be. Of course, I'm her big baby, but she often scolds me.'

He chuckled and coughed together. Simon said nothing. He waited for Andile's breath to return to his lungs.

'Yes, my friend, they have thrown back on the ash heap the cracked vessel they have no more use for. But I've cheated them. I've cheated them! Do you remember, Simon, I was always too fond of the girls. There was one – I'll not say who, though you knew her – I should have married her. She went home to stay with her own people in the Cala district. She's there still – with my son . . .'

'Your son?'

'My son. Do you know, he's a fine lad, though he's the image of that rascal, his father – at least as he used to be.'

The chuckling cough interrupted him again.

'How old is he?' said Simon.

'Ah, now you're talking. Let me see. Tixo! He must be eleven years old. A strapping lad he is, with a bit of the devil in him, if you ask me. And he says he wants to go to high school! What do you think of that? That's more than I ever did. His grandfather – that's his mother's father – has agreed to let him carry on with his education. In fact he's keen to help the boy. But tell me, Simon, how is it with yourself?'

Simon shrugged. 'Oh, it's the usual tale. I have been five years in the city.'

'Five years? Long enough to learn the ways of the city, eh, Simon?'

'Long enough for a man to lose his home. The centre post of the hut is gone.'

'Ah, there you have spoken. Everywhere we see the centre posts being broken up and the huts collapsing. Has your father told you all that has been happening in our homelands?'

'Some of it he has told me. I walked by the old grazing lands, and cut my shins on the barbed wire fences. I went into the woods – *our* woods, Andile. Do you remember?'

'I remember.'

'And there an officious fool ordered me off, saying I was trespassing. Trespassing, mark you, in our own woods. He threatened me with a fine of two pounds. Two pounds! Tixo!'

'One of their stooges, that's what he is. If I weren't tied to one spot with these foolish lungs of mine, I'd defy the devil himself. The hares must be having it all their own way. Time we shook them out of their burrows, eh, Simon? What do you say?'

But Simon was not responding to his sad humour.

'What ails you, Simon?'

'Nothing. Nothing. These tales my father had to tell – they left my spirits low.'

'Yes, we feel and we suffer.'

'Those are my father's very words.'

'You know, Simon, as I sit here, I turn over many things in my mind. I see things as I have never seen them before, as I never had time to see them. Pity that understanding comes to a man so late . . . Look at these homelands of ours. A place for starvelings, the old and the very young – and the likes of me. Why, Simon? Have you asked yourself why? Look there, right to the horizon, our homes are nests desolated by plundering hands. Our able-bodied men go out into the cities and return – as I am, a discarded worn-out tool that has served its purpose. Or else our young men do not return at all, devoured by a thousand deaths in the cities. Look at these spectral valleys, as if a plague of locusts had descended into them. Stone and dust.

'As I sit here, I see the ghosts of all the cattle that used to go out in the dawn to our grazing grounds, treading the dew, coming home at sunset with heavy udders. Today, where are they, our cattle? Our kraals are empty. Our calabashes are empty of milk. Sitting here day after day, Simon, I ask myself: What monster is it that has stripped these homelands bare to the bone? And a strange thought comes to me. Our land – has it not been turned into a vast cemetery? Is it not a land of the dead? . . . My thoughts give me no rest. I lift up my eyes and see the land stretching beyond the horizon, beyond these regions that we have been penned into, regions that are no longer ours. I look – and it is as if our cattle that had died had all risen again. In the thick green pasture I see such fine beasts with their proud necks glinting in the sun. But, alas, they are no longer our cattle. I do not dream these things, Simon. Ask your brother, Mvuzo, he who went to work on the white farms; he will tell you how the fields he toiled in from dawn to dusk are bursting with heavy-eared corn, how the ripe grain sings in the wind a song that is not for him and his children . . .'

'You have spoken, Andile. All these things I have seen, too, on my homeward journey . . . Did I say "home"?'

'Yes, it is a pity, Simon, that understanding comes to a man so late. Now if I were not so helpless, what would I not do? But there are others. Many others. And they are learning fast. It is well that people see and know what is happening to them, and begin to understand. It is not enough to suffer.'

'Do you think they are beginning to understand?'

'I am sure of it. Men come to me here from other regions, where they have the same tale to tell, of lands taken from them, of violence when the police vans roll into their villages. We talk and discuss things together. We want to know what to do.'

'Talking will not help us.'

'Ah, there you are mistaken. Such talk is a way to clear the mind of its confusions, of all the things whereby it has been deceived. It clears the mind for action.'

'Andile, I am going back to the city.'

'When?'

'Today. Tomorrow. As soon as I can make some arrangement . . .'

'Tixo! You cannot go so soon. You are not yet here!'

'I have already been here too long.'

'Simon, you have something to tell me. What is on your mind?'

'It is nothing. How should I add my troubles to yours? You have more than your share.'

'That's no way to talk. It doesn't make sense between friends. I have my wife, Nosisi, here . . . She'll tell you what an ill-natured fellow I am. With her I can share my burdens. A man must, or there is no saying what will happen to him. Speak, Simon.'

But this only made Simon avert his gaze.

'Simon, don't you trust me?'

'It is not a question of trust between us. The problem does not concern myself alone.'

'As you will. But it is not the act of a friend.'

'Forgive me, Andile.'

'What is a friend for, if in a time of trouble – '

'I confess, at the moment I don't know where I stand. If I can be alone, I'll try to work things out.'

'That's where you make your mistake, Simon, thinking your problems are yours alone. Ah, here comes Nosisi with some food.'

'Andile, can you and your wife forgive me? I am grateful for your kindness, but at this moment . . .' Simon was already on his feet.

'Nosisi will forgive you, Simon. I think I know how it is with you. I understand. Go well, my friend.'

'Stay well, Andile. Stay well, Nosisi.'

'Perhaps,' said Andile, 'I shall – see you again?'

Simon clasped his friend's hand as if he could not let it go. Then he hastened away.

Andile watched him without moving, lifting his hand when Simon looked back once before he disappeared along the sandy path between the huts.

Simon had now one compulsive desire, to leave the home that he felt no longer had a place for him. Speaking to Andile had not solved anything, yet the interview had brought about a subtle change in the tumult of his emotions since his father had told him the truth about his wife. Simon had caught something of the dying man's urgency to comprehend – what was it? – the turmoil in their lives? Yes, but how did it happen? What was the root of it all? Whether in the city or in their barren homelands, it affected them all. He himself simply hadn't found words to explain away what to his father was simply his guilt. But that was only partly true. He had wanted to open his father's eyes to what his life in the city was like – and failed. And his father, and Boniswa, what of their existence? They had all changed from what they used to be.

As Simon walked back home, seeing nothing around him, the memory of his talk with Andile had something of a calming effect on him. Not exactly calm, but digging deeper than his first explosive reaction. The shock of Boniswa's infidelity, his feeling of betrayal, the impulse of revenge had lost their sharp edge. They gave way not so much to an admission of his own part in the situation, as to a growing sense that his father, his wife and himself were all impelled by powerful forces, forces which he was far from understanding. Andile was a dying man but he had this burning desire to search for an answer. He, Simon, would never find it here. Here was nothing but stagnation, dust and decay. His strongest impulse, for every reason, was to return at once to the city.

Uppermost in his mind was a sense of personal estrangement from his family, something he could not heal. Of course, never again would he fail to send them whatever money he could spare. That was the least he could do. All the more reason why he must return to Goli.

What Simon could not realise was that the chasm separating him from his past traditions, and more especially his own act of cutting himself off from that core of affection which had bound him most of all since early childhood to his sister Funeka, now dead and buried, wrenched from under him a prop that had hitherto sustained him, though unconsciously, through all the tempestuous rages of life in Sophiatown. Finding no outlet in a burst of anger, a clean blow or any overt action to give his personal hurt relief, he hardened within. It was an effort of self-control that brought him perhaps nearer to Linda's outlook, her rough and ready philosophy, than he had ever been.

By this time a sensation of physical exhaustion had come over him, but he forced himself to go in search of his father. He found him in the field. The old man did not demur when he took the plough from his hands. There was a question in his glance, though no word was spoken between them. Strangely enough, Simon discovered relief in physical effort, almost an exhilaration in recapturing a skill so long neglected.

'I feel sure the rains are not far off,' said old Manzana. 'My nose tells me. There is a certain smell in the wind. This week we shall sow the seed.'

That embracing 'we' deprived Simon of his courage to reveal his decision. Tomorrow he would speak.

The evening meal passed off in a pretence of normality, made possible by the presence of the children. Nothanda, her shyness completely evaporated, clung to this kind stranger, this giver of the lovely doll.

Next morning father and son set off for the fields and spent the day together. But still Simon could not bring himself to speak.

Arrived at the huts, the two men sat at their ease while the women were busy preparing the evening meal. In spite of himself, Simon stole a glance at Boniswa as she bent over the pots. Pleasantly tired from the day's work, he watched her. The drooping posture of her body and the sad, resigned face smote him sharply. Would his resolution hold? A new conflict arose. Her living presence, his very need of her did something to cajole him out of his bitterness.

After the meal little Nothanda refused to be parted from her father, demanding that he carry her to bed. Here was a dilemma. Boniswa had already taken the younger child into her hut. He realised that he would be brought face to face with his wife. Nothanda plucked at his sleeve, still calling for a ride on her daddy's back. Bending low, he did as she requested and in this way they made their entrance. Laughingly he toppled her on to her sleeping-mat, stopping for a moment while the soft little feet pummelled his head. Only then he straightened up and allowed himself to look at his wife.

She was suckling her baby. His body stiffened at the sight. Observing it, she made a gesture with her shawl, as if to protect the child, and got to her feet. There was no fear and no longer any shame in her glance. This woman was a stranger to him.

'Father of Nothanda, the child is innocent,' she said.

'You love your child?'

'Both my children are dear to me,' she answered.

'You have chosen,' he said.

She bowed her head over the baby, hiding her face. She knew what his answer meant. She made no plea, no protest. There was no more to be said.

He turned and went out.

His father still sat in the half-light. To him, he said: 'Father, I am going away, back to the city.'

'So that is your decision?'

'What choice have I? Sooner or later I would have to go, as I did before. I shall find work in the city and send you money, I promise you.'

'That is a dishonest answer, my son. You cannot find it in your heart to forgive. It's your pride that will not let you be a man.'

'Believe me, father, I forgive her. I feel no bitterness towards her.'

'Words, words, my son. You deceive yourself. Forgiveness speaks in action. I see none in yours.'

'Father, I have tried. But my feelings . . . It chokes me here!'

'Feelings of self-love are irresistible. You have much to learn, my son.'

'I am leaving this money with you, as much as I can spare,' said Simon. 'I will send more for her, and my child Nothanda. This I promise you. I shall not fail.'

'Self-righteousness is not forgiveness – though your money will buy food. Consider well. It is you who will suffer most from this.'

'Father, I must go. I feel that this is no longer my home.'

'No longer your home! And whose fault is that?'

'Oh, father, to speak of blame – it no longer serves us. Circumstances are stronger than us. I cannot help you by staying on here. You know it.'

'And where do you intend to go?'

'I know my way about the city by now.'

For the first time the old man's eyes glowed black with anger.

'You can think only of yourself! I tell you, you cannot go while your heart is hardened against your wife Boniswa. There is one, who, if she were alive, would weep to hear you. It is well she cannot hear you. You have closed your heart to the dead as well as to the living!'

'Father! It is not so! I go because I must.'

Still trembling with anger, the old man rose and disappeared inside the hut, leaving his son alone in the gathering darkness.

Next morning, before anyone was astir, Simon slipped away from his father's house. His first steps led him to the cemetery, to where his mother lay. Standing with bowed head, he silently spoke his farewells, telling her he would be back, though he knew not when. And then, with lips trembling he moved to the freshly turned soil of his sister's grave.

'Funeka,' he said, 'forgive me,' and did not wait for her reply.

Blindly he struck northwards to the road that led back to the city. It would mean a long and devious trek to escape the vigilance of the police, since he had no official permit to re-enter Goli.

But there was one more thing he wanted to do before leaving his homelands and that was to find out how it fared with Sanelo's wife, Nomasa.

After a day's journey on foot he reached the house of Coto, who received him gladly, though with some surprise at his quick return. Simon informed Coto and his wife of the death of his sister Funeka, and in answer to their questions assured them that he had found his father in good health. But as to the rest, they respected his reserve, while observing that all was not well with their young guest. Recounting their news of Nomasa brought smiles to all their faces. Her journey to the house of her husband's people could not have been better timed. It was as if the unborn could not wait to bring joy to the hearts of those who mourned and to fill the place of the murdered husband and son. Abel Sanelo's mother, who was a widow, had had her wish fulfilled. With her own hands she had delivered her first grandchild to Nomasa, a son. Wonderful to relate, he was already one day old!

It was agreed that on the following day Simon, accompanied by Nomasa's mother, would take the short journey to Sanelo's home. Arrived there, he was greeted warmly by Sanelo's mother and had to listen once more to the tale of the miraculous event, with all the embellishments that a proud grandmother could invent. She brought the baby from the hut where Nomasa was lying, so that Abel's good friend might see and judge for himself. He had to swear how marvellous was the likeness between its dewy-soft features and those of the dead father. Aware that Nomasa must be listening, he could not resist speaking to her from the open doorway.

'For your sake, Nomasa, I am happy. In the child you will find consolation. What will you call him?'

She herself appeared before him, steadying herself with a hand on the strong wooden post. In a clear voice she answered: 'His name is Loyiso.'

'Loyiso? A brave name for the son of the finest man I have known.'

'There is no better son,' said Sanelo's mother. 'May Loyiso live to be as good to his mother as my son to me.'

Simon was moved at the sight of Nomasa and her fatherless child. He thought of Abel Sanelo, who had never seen his son. He thought of Boniswa, his wife. She, too, would lie alone, uncomforted in the dead of night. Oh, God, should he return home? How different his mood had been on his homeward journey.

He became aware that Sanelo's mother was thanking him for all he had done to carry out her dead son's intentions, and somewhat abruptly disclaimed any right to her praises.

'Is all well at your home?' she asked, looking up into his face with shrewd eyes and observing his constraint. Briefly he repeated the story of his sister's death and indicated that the needs of his family required his return to the city. The two older women agreed that it was dire necessity that denuded their homelands of their young able-bodied men.

It happened that Nomasa's mother, before returning home, intended taking the opportunity of going to East London to make some purchases for her daughter. It was a rare thing for her to undertake such a journey and she was only too glad when Simon offered to accompany her. For him it was a matter of expediency. East London could be the first lap of his journey back to Goli. Back to Linda.

As soon as he allowed himself to think of her a feeling of anticipation and excitement overcame him. He looked at the miserable sum in the palm of his hand. He would first have to find work in order to continue his journey. To get into any town without a proper pass was a hazardous business. With luck it would be easier to slip into the smaller township where Nomasa's mother had a relation who would squeeze a place for him in his two-roomed house.

Alas for his hopes of saving money quickly. Unable to procure a job as a van driver, he had to fall back on what came to hand. As handyman in a store, he had a desperately small margin for saving after paying for his food and rent for his share of a room. He wasn't even able to send money to his father, as he had promised. What he had already handed over to him would have to suffice for the time being.

It was three months before he scraped together enough to enable him to board the train for Goli, armed with a false pass – for which he had paid dearly.

Eleven

Linda, left alone, plunged into a nightlife of bitter gaiety.

Ma-jaze, who thought she had become inured to the spectacle of men and women wrecking themselves, could not stand by with indifference while Linda Malindi in her opinion made a fool of herself. She was a young woman, she thought, made in her own likeness; one who could take knocks and retain a steady core, in spite of them all. But the way Linda was going on was about as good as a cork bobbing about in a stormy sea. One big wave and she'd be out – finished. And that wasn't good enough. Not by a long way. Ma-jaze had been mighty pleased when Linda and Simon made a go of it. You didn't meet that kind of young man every day. And the way Linda had ripened under his influence had almost shattered her conviction that two young people could never stick together in this jungle of a city, where no human relationship could easily survive.

When Simon Manzana had disappeared, Linda was tight as a clam about it, and went around as if something had gouged the soul right out of her. And now, of all the scum floating about in Sophiatown – and there was a damn sight too much of it – she must needs take up with Nick Noboza, who had a sleek smirk on his face these days. Linda must be aiming higher – heaven help her. Love me, love my dog, as they said. For Nick was as much Jo Bula's stooge as ever. The amount of feeling he could give a woman wouldn't keep a rat's litter alive. It could only be vanity, of which he had a frightening amount, that kept him on the string. And a weird sense of revenge against the missing Simon Manzana.

On principle Ma-jaze didn't interfere in people's lives if she could help it. She knew it could be a costly business. To involve yourself in the life of another was to lay yourself open to hazards and sorrows in an already hazardous life. It was wisest to leave them to choose their own length of rope for hanging themselves. However, in this instance, Ma-jaze allowed feeling to prevail over judgement and decided to speak to Linda.

It wasn't easy to get an opportunity to do so. She seemed to barricade herself from communication by surrounding herself with acquaintances of the minute; noisy, hilarious, loose of tongue, empty-headed. Linda and laughter went together, laughter that crackled in the throat but never got as far as the eyes. Ma-jaze hated the sound of it.

Ken Madoda was another who had a soft spot for her, considering himself to have been in at the birth, so to speak, almost as much as Ma-jaze.

Late one night, guessing what was bothering Ma-jaze, and exchanging a wise-guy look with her, he cornered Linda. It was convenient that Nick Noboza was absent on very important business with Jo Bula. By this time most of the customers avid for their desperate pleasures had given up the unequal struggle and slunk off to bed, all except Linda and a handful of hangers-on. Ken made short shrift of these, shooing them off like so many bluebottle flies from a cherry cake. He observed that she had had about as much liquor as she could decently carry.

'Now just tell me, Linda Malindi,' he breezed, 'why you are giving the cold shoulder to the oldest friend you've got?'

'Don't come over on me with that bullshit. Oldest friend, my foot.'

'Spit away. An old friend can take it. But confess, now. We never have fun like we used to. We never have jolly chats like we used to – '

'You mean I don't give you a chance to talk your head off? You bore me to death.'

'Okay. So I can talk the hindleg off a donkey.'

'Like hell you can. But tonight I'm deaf, Kenny boy. Stone deaf.' She stood up. 'I'm going.'

'What's the hurry? Here comes Ma-jaze.'

Linda protested, but observing the look of steel in Ma-jaze's eyes and the urgency in the huge body as it beelined towards her, she sat down again, while Ken did a discreet fade-out.

Ma-jaze sat herself down squarely opposite the young woman, put down her glass of ginger ale in front of her, then looked over her shoulder to where a few remaining stragglers were still singing, their voices harmonising and their feet tapping to the beat of the latest jitterbug record. Jumping to her feet she shooed them out of the place, locking the door after them and switching off the radiogram before returning to Linda.

'You're all bristles, my girl. Come off the porcupine act,' she said. 'What are you afraid of?'

'Me? Afraid? That's a good one.'

'Who are you afraid of?'

'Now what are you getting at? I'm afraid of nobody.'

'You don't behave like it. You're scared stiff of something. You're shivering inside.'

'My insides are my own and I'll be obliged if you'll stop prying into them.'

'If you ask me, you're afraid of yourself.'

'I didn't ask you, and will you mind your own bloody business!'

'I don't like to see you going about making a fool of yourself.'

'Your insults break no bones.'

'I could break your neck right this minute, seeing you messing yourself up. Now don't waste your time sparring with me, Linda. You ought to know better. You're itching for a fight. Good! Fight tooth and nail and I'll back you up. But for God's sake, do you know what you're fighting, or whom you're fighting? Right now you're standing in the boxing ring, all set under the floodlights. The crowd's watching out there in the dark. Everybody's keyed up. The gong's about to go. And you? The great boxer? Star of the show? You start shadow-boxing all on your own in an empty ring. Don't blame them out there in the dark if they think you've gone off your rocker.'

Linda took her time in answering, keeping Ma-jaze in the direct beam of her unwavering gaze.

'Thank you for the sermon. Now will you make yourself scarce? All I ask is to be left to go to the devil in my own way.'

'Not if I know it. Come on. Get it off your chest, whatever it is. You used to be the sanest bit of female flesh around here – '

'Can anybody remain sane in this world?'

'You have one on me there. It's a mad world and there's not one of us who hasn't a taint of that madness – or we wouldn't be able to stay alive. Tell me, what possesses you to take up with Nick Noboza?'

'Oh, he has his uses.'

'I thought you knew your own worth better than to throw yourself away on that scum.'

'Mind your language, if you please. If I threw myself away on anybody, it was – Oh, what the hell does it matter? Anyway, I got a good kick for my pains.'

'You mean Simon Manzana, don't you? What happened to him? Not in jail, is he?'

'If it was only jail, I'd have waited for him. For years I would. No, he did the dirty on me. Went running back to the country. Home, he called it. Home! As much as to say I was scum and the home I made for him here meant nothing to him. Ha! Ha! You remember the bedroom suite I bought, that you were so green about?'

'Me, green about a bedroom suite of yours? You're raving, my girl.'

'You were green all right! That bed we had! There wasn't another like it in Africa.'

'What happened to it?'

'I sold it. To guess who?'

'Who?'

'To Mrs Pakati, the storekeeper's wife.'

'That sanctimonious hypocrite? What could she do with your bed? It ought to give her nightmares.'

'That was the idea.'

'But, Linda – oh, you're a strange woman. Whatever he did, Simon Manzana was a man, while Nick Noboza . . . How could you?'

'You'd like to know, would you? I'll tell you. You once said: "Linda," you said, "never let them drink your blood. These men!" But that's what's happened. It was your nice, good man, your saint Simon who did just that. Now with Nick Noboza I know where I am. I can kick him out tomorrow.'

'Don't you be so sure of that. There's one thing I know about Nick Noboza and that is, he's mean. He's full of spite, as dangerous as a spitting cobra. Linda, you must know it. He hates Simon Manzana ever since that fight they had. He must think he's Jesus Christ now, at last getting one up on Manzana – '

'Leave me alone! You don't know what Simon Manzana did to me – in here!'

She beat her breast until her eyes seemed to bulge from her head.

'I'd say it's what you're doing to yourself,' Ma-jaze said softly. 'What, after all, is Simon guilty of? Could he help himself? Isn't it the same for him as for all the others, when they have to leave their families in the country?'

'Simon was different.'

'How was he different?'

'He loved me. And I loved him – fool that I was.'

'Then you were mighty lucky, Linda. He loved you! How many people in this lousy world ever get the love you had? Then what happened?'

'I don't know. I don't know. That's what I keep asking

myself.'

'Could he help what happened to him? Did you ever try to find out?'

'He walked out on me, that's what he did and don't you try making excuses for him – '

'Linda, I'll tell you something. If you were to ask Simon Manzana, you'd find him just as mixed up as you are. Love isn't something you clutch in your hand like a foul penny-piece. You don't grab it and never let go. You might as well try to grab the rainwater falling out of the clouds on to your face, as expect what you're calling love to stay the same. Life on this filthy slag heap is shaking us to bits all the time. So where does love come in? Where does it get the chance to survive?'

'I don't know what you're talking about. Love's a dirty word as far as I'm concerned. I've been cured of it. Don't you worry.'

Ma-jaze shifted in her chair, arranged her skirt and brushed away a fly that had settled on the rim of her glass. 'And when Simon Manzana comes back from the country?' she said slowly.

'Comes back? Comes back! Don't make me die of laughter!'

Yet was there a wild hope in Linda's voice?

'Of course he'll come back. What else can he do? What else can any of them do? I've seen them come and I've seen them go, longer than I like to think of. A whole army of go-homers – who have no home any more. I don't need to be told what they find when they get there. Their homelands? Don't make *me* laugh. You're a town brat, born and bred so you know nothing about that. They find death in their homelands. And dust. And starvation. You – you know nothing yet, my girl.'

'Oh, ho! Listen to her. I know nothing, says she. I'll tell you this much, Ma-jaze. If Simon Manzana comes back it's not Linda Malindi he'll find sitting waiting for him.'

'So you want to throw him to the wolves – out of spite? Sheer spite. Stop trying to save face, my child. Who are you trying to convince? I thought you knew your own interests better than that.'

'I've got my pride.'

'Oh. We've got our pride, have we? That's fine – to be sure

of one thing in this world at least. You're lucky. But if I know anything about Simon and what he must be feeling – '

'Don't talk to me about *his* feelings. I know all about that. I've had enough of feelings. Finish! And it was he who killed them. Let me tell you that. Finish!'

'All I can say is – you're making the mistake of your life.' Ma-jaze leaned across the table and took Linda's hand in hers. Linda jerked it away.

'So what! Leave me alone, will you?'

'You don't know anything about yourself. You're walking on quicksand, my girl.'

'Thanks. And I've had enough of your talk.' Scraping her chair backwards so that it toppled over behind her, Linda threw herself away from Ma-jaze.

Ma-jaze lumbered to her feet and followed Linda to the door. 'Linda, I don't know why I waste my words on you. Go home and get some sleep. You're losing your good looks – fast.'

'Thanks again. Same to you!'

'Oh, you can go to the devil in your own way then. Get going!'

She unlocked the door and Linda sailed out into the night.

'Okay, Ma-jaze,' she shouted over her shoulder. 'Same to you!'

Ma-jaze locked the door after her.

Still consumed with thoughts of Linda, Ma-jaze went through the nightly ritual of bringing order to the disarray left by her clients. Linda did not know herself, but neither did Ma-jaze know her, shrewd as she was, and moved by concern for her welfare. Being an old hand she thought she had the measure of the character she was dealing with. And so she had, up to a point. However, her own phrase: 'life on this filthy slag heap is shaking us all to bits', was more accurate than she realised. The rage of existence left little that was permanently in its place; nothing in the way of material security or any other kind. It was like a tornado that uproots giant trees, tearing them from the solid earth, hurling them in grotesque flight to crash in violent abasement, their proud tops tasting the dust. Under such conditions what could happen to a human being was incalculable.

Linda lay on her empty bed as on a rack, a prey to wild emotions, outraged pride, tied to a maddening sense of helplessness to prove its worth; hate that was an inseparable part of her desire. Carried headlong from a state of blind jealousy of Sanelo's wife to the shock of what could only appear as Simon's desertion of her, she had been shaken with a passion outside her knowledge of the human psyche. Thwarted of her dearest possession, she brooded in secret on her fate. She was consumed with a compulsion to pay Simon back in some way – but he was out of her reach. She would never forgive him.

Never.

Journeying back to Goli meant one thing for Simon Manzana – he was going to seek out Linda. True, he remembered uneasily the night of Abel Sanelo's murder, which for him and Linda had ended in such bitter parting. Like a time bomb with delayed action, his own experience impelled him to have some idea of her feelings when he left her, though he was far from guessing their magnitude. She was a proud woman. Yet he saw no reason why they could not come together again. They had quarrelled because they misunderstood each other. She simply had no idea of what had driven him to take his dead friend's widow to her people, and still less what his family had meant to him.

But now he knew he belonged with her as he had never done before.

It was the middle of a thundery summer's afternoon when the East London train disgorged from its segregated compartments its various loads of whites and non-whites on to the platform of the main train station in Goli, where they rapidly separated again according to the apartheid signs that controlled their exits and their entrances.

Keeping a wary eye on the police since his pass was a false one, Simon promptly deposited his suitcase in the left-luggage office. The less he looked like a new arrival from the country the safer he would be from the lynx eye of white officialdom.

This was Goli.

Simon had already experienced that peculiar mixture of excitement and apprehensiveness that this city inspires more than any other. The approaches to the city seen from his compartment window had all the symbols of a high-powered industrial system. The forest of pylons and shining high tension cables; the steel and concrete mine headgear, its wheels, its rigging and runways sprouting out of the flat veld; the double phalanx of huge concrete storage towers and the city's man-made mountains, now golden-yellow in the pale shafts of late afternoon sun – the monstrous refuse of a plundered earth in the gouging out of the gold, sepulchres of the strength of countless black men like himself.

With a wry sense of recognition he had perceived the houses of the newer black townships furthest removed from the city, row upon regular row scarring the bare veld and packed tightly as the mounds in an overcrowded cemetery. In contrast to them the older shanty towns and locations showed up as a raggedy grey smudge of refuse on the parched landscape. These were the outlying neighbours of the oldest township of them all – Sophiatown.

Then came the serried ranks of streets, skyscrapers, factories, shops, flats, the outlying flank of the white city itself, battlements of stone that shut him out, him and all his people. He recalled what Abel Sanelo had once said: 'I hate this city, and yet there's something about it that excites me.' What had Abel called it? A great slaughterhouse . . . He had always been the one who could use words. Yes, that was Goli all right.

Emerging from the station, but without looking at the white people in the crowded streets, he made his way to the bus queue for Sophiatown. He couldn't hang about the city. He'd be nabbed by the police without a valid work pass. He must find Linda. Tomorrow he would look for a job. And collect his suitcase.

But first – Linda.

The bus queue was already long, mostly women going home from work, many laden with large bundles of clothes that they would launder at home. How familiar all this hustling and pushing for a place. The oppressive heat of summer, the hot stone pavements and the sun beating down out of a metallic sky didn't improve anybody's temper. Above the city skyscrapers and the now ashen mine-hills the leaden-edged clouds piled high, massing themselves for the storm that would burst with a crack of thunder in an hour or two. Or the clouds might withhold their lightning and unload themselves another day.

Throwing off the vague feeling of apprehension that had hung over him since walking the white streets, Simon fixed his thoughts on Linda. He wondered if he should go straight to her room – their room – or look for her at Angels One. The trouble was it was too early to be sure of finding her in either place. Perhaps, considering all things, it would be better to wait and surprise her at Angels One, where they had first met. It would be jolly there, and Ma-jaze herself would be pleased to see him.

Someone hailed him. It was Hilda Noyali, Diz Dinake's one-time girlfriend, looking very smart. They exchanged a hearty time of day with the forced jollity of people who mean nothing to each other.

'We wondered when we didn't see you around,' she said.

To this he murmured something about family business taking him unexpectedly into the country.

'Linda Malindi certainly doesn't let the grass grow under her feet,' continued Hilda with a smirk. 'She's sporting her new boyfriend, Nick Noboza. He's gone up in the world.'

Simon kept an answering smirk frozen on his face.

'They're as thick as thieves,' she giggled. 'Linda's hitting a new high at the poshest nightspots. Jitterbugging the nights away. We hardly see her these days. Too bad, she and Ma-jaze had a falling-out. Don't ask me what it's all about.'

Simon didn't hear the rest of Hilda's venomous chatter. Muttering a pretext about some forgotten luggage, he hurriedly left her and his place in the queue, and someone else was only too glad to push into his vacant place.

Linda and Nick Noboza? His Linda? It wasn't possible! Could he believe Hilda Noyali's gossip? There was certainly no love lost between the two women. Now supposing he didn't find Linda at Ma-jaze's? But he must see her. He must. He couldn't wait. He'd catch the next bus and go straight – home. The word came to him involuntarily, in a surge of hope and fear. Home.

The first time he walked past the familiar window of their room it had a shuttered, empty look. Not a sound, not a footstep answered his knocking. Of course it was too early for Linda to be home. There was nobody next door either, where he had gone so often to see Abel Sanelo. The people, whoever they were, must still be at work. A ragged bit of curtain hung over the window. Simon had a desolate shut-out feeling, thinking of the dead.

He wandered round the streets, aimlessly, deciding it was too far to go to Ma-jaze's first, then retraced his steps, searching the streets in case she should be on her way home.

Darkness was falling when he approached the house the second – or was it the third time? Turning the corner of the street, in a minute now, he told himself, he would be on the doorstep –

He stopped. There was a car outside. Jo Bula's car. Did that mean Nick Noboza was with her? He knew Nick was allowed to make free with the car when Jo Bula was in the mood. He couldn't make out if there was a light inside or not. The curtain on Linda's window ensured as much privacy as it was possible to have in this crowded area.

He stared at the blank window. What kind of a fool was he, spying on her? A nice way to arrive back! He hovered in the street, disconsolately, uncertain what to do. There was a dim light like a half-lidded eye coming from Abel Sanelo's room. Should he knock? But what could he say to strangers? How explain to them what he wanted to know? Should he try the door to Linda's room? Fool! It would be locked anyway. He had no key. He had given it back to her – that night. Best go to Ma-jaze's after all. He'd find out from her.

Ma-jaze, though friendly, was reserved. But she said enough. So it was true. And Linda didn't even put in an appearance at her place.

Simon did not allow himself to explore the anguish of his new experience. He had difficulty in finding another job, and he had no money left. To appease his loneliness he fell in with Hilda Noyali, who for some reason set her sights on him. The association was a convenient one, enabling him to slip back all the more easily into the backdoor business. Hilda was an expert hand at the game and knew how to be careful. After all, she had served an honourable sentence in jail and had every intention of keeping out of it. Hilda was well pleased. Her new boyfriend was considered quite a catch. And she experienced a feline satisfaction in getting her own back on Linda Malindi.

It was a few days before Linda discovered what had happened.

She had sauntered one night into Angels One. The trio was in full swing and she sat tapping her foot to the beat, a look of studied nonchalance on her face that belied her thoughts.

'You're a rare bird,' remarked Ken. 'You don't recognise your old pals any more.'

'Nonsense,' retorted Linda. 'I'd love a drink.'

A little later Ken slipped into a seat beside her. He handed her the drink.

'Guess who turned up here the other night,' he said, with an exaggeratedly casual air.

'How should I know? Or care?'

'I don't suppose you remember him – Simon Manzana.'

'Simon!'

For a moment her defences were down. The carefully blasé manner she affected disappeared.

'Is that true?'

'S'help me! I saw him with my own eyes. And there was somebody hanging on to him as if she'd eat him up.'

'Who?'

'An old chum of yours.'

'Stop baiting me. Who was it?'

'You know, Linda, I wouldn't let her get away with it.'

'Who? Who?'

'Seriously, I wouldn't.'

'Ken, for pity's sake!'

'Hilda Noyali.'

'You devil!'

'What now? What have I done?'

'It's not true.'

'I wish to God it wasn't, Linda Malindi. It's your own fault.'

Violently she flung the liquor in her glass full in his face and fled through the door while he was still wiping his eyes.

The night Linda and Simon did meet at Ma-jaze's, everybody was keyed up, greedy for something to happen. After receiving Ken's information she had insisted on showing up several nights in succession, Nick Noboza in attendance. And Nick was sulky. Whether or not someone had tipped him off about Simon Manzana's return, he didn't hide the fact that he was bored at Ma-jaze's. Angels One was no longer good enough for him. But Linda was adamant.

Then on the third night Simon walked in with Hilda Noyali.

Ken swore afterwards that there was a lightning flash when Linda Malindi caught sight of Simon Manzana, and there was a second flash when Nick Noboza looked up and saw the two of them locked in an embrace – at least their eyes were. Of course Ken was known shamelessly to embellish any tale he told and no doubt his romantic hopes were guilty of hallucinations. Though Simon stood there as if he'd stay rooted until Linda came and took her proper place beside him, she on the other hand quickly recovered her equanimity and acted up with Nick as if he were Jo Bula himself.

Simon might as well have been a mummified white cop, for all the notice she took of him. Hilda Noyali, looking petulant and pretty, had plucked at his sleeve to put him into motion again, and they'd weaved their way across the room to another table.

As soon as the trio – Stan, Toni and Gus, the lively new saxophonist – got under way and the dancing started, Linda was the sprightliest on the floor. Simon wouldn't dance and Hilda had to find other partners. He just wandered around watching Linda as on that night – how many centuries ago? – when they first met.

When Nick and Linda returned to their table, Simon being close by, Nick fixed him with such a look that Ken almost expected to see the knife blade sticking in Simon's back. And, to be sure, Simon gave as good as he got. But nothing further happened, so folks forgot them after a time.

Something about that night galvanised Simon with a new ambition: to get in with the Jo Bula gang. He had always known that Jo Bula held a great fascination for Linda Malindi, a fascination he himself couldn't understand; Jo Bula seemed pretty much of a beast to him, though possessed of a cynical daring attractive to youth.

Jo Bula himself had had his eye on Simon as a possible recruit ever since he'd witnessed Nick Noboza lick the dust the night they fought each other. Conscious of Noboza's dependence on himself, and well aware of his envious hatred of Manzana, the gangster found a sadistic pleasure in provoking him by showing some favour towards the newcomer, so long as he considered the young man could be useful to him.

Jo Bula tried Simon out on some minor jobs, such things as a small shop robbery, and helping 'the boys' – as he called them – to empty a railway delivery trailer in record time. His immediate associates included Diz Dinake, who now fancied himself as a small stick of dynamite; Ben Kwethuba, from whom Simon had bought his gun; Ted Nompu, a new recruit, a tough-muscled tyke whose favourite c expression was: 'Ha! Ha! I'd like to put Goli into a bloody sweat of fear!'

When they were all drinking together Simon was reasonably popular among them, except with Nick Noboza. Between these two there was an uneasy truce.

'So I'm your pal,' said Nick, standing in front of him with a fiendish grin on his face and holding up his glass as if for a toast.

'To hell with you!' retorted Simon, turning his back and not troubling to hide his contempt.

On one occasion Jo Bula snarled at Simon when one of the gang again commented on his stubborn avoidance of knife-work under any circumstances. It was then that 'the boys' took it on themselves to give him some sound advice, for his health's sake, as they expressed it.

'If you want your rake-off, just do what you're told,' said Ben Kwethuba.

'Damn it, I'm not going to lick his ass!' protested Simon.

'If you don't do a thing exactly as Jo likes it done, he'll rub you out!' said Nick, with a crude gesture, enjoying this game of baiting Simon.

'He'll rub you out – finish! Without pity,' added Diz Dinake.

'Ha! Ha! Without pity,' echoed Ted Nompu.

'I'm warning you. Don't get on the wrong side of Jo Bula,' said Ben.

'Remember what happened to Slim Qala?' said Nick, directing a smirk at Simon.

'Poor Slim!' they chorused, with sadistic glee.

Simon thought it healthiest not to pursue the matter of Slim's fate.

'He'll put you through the meat grinder,' went on Ted Nompu.

Dinake took up the cue. 'Ha! Ha! The meat grinder.'

'But you're doing fine, Simon, man,' Kwethuba reassured him. 'Before long you'll get into the big time. You'll see. You have the guts for it.'

'He's only praising the palooka to make him feel big,' muttered Nick to Dinake.

'You ought at least to have done a spell in the Fort,' said Ted Nompu. 'You come out with just the right amount of hate for the bastards.'

'All in good time. What are you moaning about? All in good time,' said Dinake with a snigger.

'So far you've been damned lucky. Not a scratch on you.' Nick looked at Simon's tall unblemished body with undisguised avidity.

Ben laughed. 'Oh, that's just beginner's luck.'

'Live fast. Drive fast. Kill fast!' chanted Ted Nompu.

'And make money fast,' added Nick.

'That's the way to win your dame,' mocked Dinake, straight at Simon's face.

Nick snickered.

Simon scowled.

'Live fast. Drive fast. Kill fast!' sang the others.

Linda Malindi surprised everybody by suddenly throwing over Nick Noboza. Speculation was rife at Angels One. Was this the first step in a new campaign to win back Simon Manzana?

If so, she had better look out – if she wanted her man alive.

Simon Manzana had better look out, too, if he wanted his woman. His life hung by a hair. For Nick Noboza, they said, would never forgive an insult.

But Linda showed no sign of wanting to win back Simon. She never went near him. In fact people were puzzled by the behaviour of Linda Malindi. She wasn't being seen around with anybody. It wasn't natural. Could she be playing a waiting game, of a very unusual kind? Yet anybody could see Simon was dying to have her back.

Ken Madoda was arguing out loud to Ma-jaze. He was mighty worried, he said. It wasn't any scruple about Hilda Noyali's feelings that was putting the curb on Linda, he said. She could walk over her and not notice the bump. Linda must have something on her mind. What was it? Could she possibly be afraid of what Nick Noboza might do? When she took up with that scum to spite Manzana, she didn't reckon on the cost. With Simon walking out on her she had been in a fine simmer. In fact she had gone plumb mad. She couldn't have foreseen what her own mixed-up feelings would lead her into when she came face to face with Simon on his return. Only now her crazy actions had caught up with her. Yeah. Like hell, they had. She was in a spot and didn't know which way to turn. It wasn't like her to be so dead quiet . . .

Ma-jaze listened but said nothing. She did not look happy.

'Do you know,' said Ken, 'Linda and Nick Noboza are playing a life and death game, and for very high stakes – no less than Simon Manzana. She daren't make a move because she's afraid of what Noboza will do. That must be it. It's a queer thing that Simon is now in with the Jo Bula gang. Something must be driving him hard.'

'They're both mad,' said Ma-jaze.

'Is it love?' said Ken. 'Or hate?'

Ma-jaze replied, 'Or both?'

'But to be in with Jo Bula is to be rubbing shoulders with Nick Noboza,' said Ken. 'It doesn't make sense.'

'It's a black business,' said Ma-jaze, hooding her eyebrows.

Ken wondered if his overactive imagination wasn't running away with him. He must be going nuts. He didn't want any disaster to befall Linda Malindi and he could swear Ma-jaze didn't either. But he couldn't get another word out of her. He found her formidably silent and aloof; her expression closed and stern; her wary eyes sunk deep in their sockets.

Darkness means danger in the city streets. It stalks even more grimly in the unlit townships spawned around the city. Darkness has no distance. In the dark a man cannot measure how near or how far his enemy is and his senses revert to the animal. Substance and shadow are confused. A shape has the nameless terror of being bodiless and a shadow has the shuddering menace of a breathing thing, without form. Houses are thickened shadows, lurking places for the assassin's knife.

For the first time Simon found moral support in the possession of his gun. Night and day he kept it on him wherever he went. Its cold, hard body took warmth from his living body. To be discovered with it by the police – this he considered to be the least of his dangers. He had acquired a compulsive necessity to look behind him when he went out alone.

Not that he was a coward. He felt he could tackle anything head-on, in the open. But not this nameless dread that was continually dogging his footsteps. He told himself it couldn't be Nick Noboza he was afraid of. Hadn't he proved himself to be the stronger? Noboza feared him, for all his bravado. And now they were members of the same gang. Whatever their private feelings were, they were both Jo Bula's men. What was it, then? Why was he so jumpy?

Walking back from Jo Bula's place late one night, he had the sensation that he was being followed. An impenetrable darkness lay around him. The houses were asleep, masking their secrets. The moonless night air was oppressive, heavy with the threat of a summer storm.

He stopped sharply. But he heard not a sound, no echo of stealthy footsteps drawing nearer. He told himself his fears were absurd and resumed his journey, hurrying a little.

Again the prickling sensation assailed his skin: his ears strained to detect the sound of footsteps distinct from his own but the blood thumping in his head made it impossible to listen.

This only heightened his apprehension.

Who could be taking such an unhealthy interest in him? It couldn't be a cop. The cowards never risked their necks by going about alone. And besides, they had no need for stealth; Abel Sanelo's murder had been shouted through the street. Was it perhaps a casual night thief lurking in wait for the unwary straggler returning from the gambling den that Ma-jaze's rival, Ma Rosie, was now running? If it was, the thief would find his victim a dead loss, for his pockets were nearly empty.

Could it be one of the Tsomi gang? They had it in for Jo Bula in a big way, ever since he'd abandoned them, which meant that any of his lot was fair game for foul play. Then Simon remembered there had been a raid on the Tsomi gang only two nights before, when some had been captured and others had scuttled for their burrows. Not likely they'd be bothering their heads about small fry like him. They'd have their hands full looking after their own skins.

Once more taking refuge in the absurdity of his fears, he kept on at a steady pace. At a corner he stopped.

This time he was certain.

Whoever was on his trail had ventured closer. Putting on a spurt, he shot up a side street. But his pursuer, running now, was after him, his feet padding in the darkness. He was getting nearer and nearer.

Simon turned, aiming his gun wildly at what he thought was

his enemy, though he made out no more than a shadow. Then he fled.

Whether or not his bullet had struck the target, the sound of pursuit no longer invaded his ears. At last he slackened his pace, breathing hard. Maybe he had killed a man. It would be the first time. Who had his pursuer been?

Or had he imagined it all?

Jo Bula decided that it was time for a major project. Among his small elite gang he had the monopoly for audacity in planning and his hangers-on paid him homage accordingly. Audacity crowned with success sends a gangster rocketing into a dangerous eminence. He must repeat the performance. Audacity falling on failure is damned as imbecile recklessness and sends him plumb out of favour, down at the bottom of the heap. Between these two poles a gang leader's position swings in precarious balance.

The job Jo Bula wanted to pull off presented a challenge. It was a big warehouse in the city, where a wholesale firm kept bales of much coveted cloth for the burgeoning fashion trade. So far it had not been successfully entered. It was well guarded at night, with two watchmen outside as well as one inside. Members of the Tsomi gang had had a go at it and been foiled in their attempt. It would be a feather in Jo Bula's cap if some of his new gang managed to pull it off. He hissed at the mention of the faithful African watchmen, those stooges guarding their master's goods with their lives.

He calculated it would require five men for the job, a biggish bunch when you considered that each one would expect his rake-off, leaving so much less of the lion's share for Jo Bula. However, the haul should be a good one, worth thousands with luck. Once in their hands, the bales would vanish with lightning speed through Sophiatown and the various townships. Speed in distribution was essential, otherwise the damn stuff could burn your fingers.

Jo Bula was jealous of his reputation for attention to detail in his planning. 'Attend to the details,' he would say, 'and the job will run on its own like clockwork.' As much as to say his henchmen were mere automatons, while the great Jo Bula pulled the strings. Of course it was all a matter of distant control. He'd never risk his own neck on the actual job.

Preparations involved casing the joint, finding out the lie of the land, timing the movements and habits of the victims, the conscientious watchmen who had to be eliminated one way or another. This part of the business fell to Ben Kwethuba, who had a nondescript, respectable appearance when in the city, but not too respectable to attract the attention of the white cops.

Then each of the chosen men had to be allocated his particular role: Nick Noboza was in charge of the outfit and would superintend the business of breaking in and handling the bales at top speed. Ben Kwethuba would be on the spot to help him. The special problem of looking after the watchmen fell to Ted Nompu and Diz Dinake, both experienced hands without scruple, if nightwatchmen should be so foolish as to put their master's filthy lucre first and their own skins second. With time to spare they'd also speed up the bale-shifting.

Finally, Simon Manzana would have the task of ensuring a safe getaway for the four men and the loot. Of course he would operate with a stolen delivery van. That part of it should be a walkover, since the required vehicle would be cased beforehand. When they were through with the job they'd abandon the van out of town and transfer to Jo Bula's spacious Buick.

They were all set for the assignment. It just wanted Jo Bula to name the night. He hit on a Friday, reckoning it was a busy night anyway, with plenty of other jobs to keep the cops busy.

Thursday.

Simon felt restless. One more night to go. He thought of Linda. He told himself she wouldn't know about the Jo Bula job and his part in it. Nor would she care. Yet somehow the thought of the hazard of the job impelled him to find her. He must find her. It wouldn't matter what they would say to each other. If he could just see her it would be enough. Words would not be necessary.

He went out into the streets, drawn irresistibly to Linda's room, but was out of luck; the room was in darkness. Empty.

Where else could he look for her?

Dejected, he walked on.

That evening Linda was restless too. She didn't know what to do with herself. Ken hadn't been far wrong when he said she was scared of what Nick Noboza might do to Simon. Her instinct warned her to play a waiting game. But there was more to her waiting than that. In spite of herself, her pride, her hate, her sense of folly at having given her heart away, she had come to realise Simon was the only man for her. Yet she could not give in readily to what she most wanted. She wasn't love's fool, she told herself. Simon had taunted her for what he called her hardness of heart. Well, then, it was true. But why was she afraid of Nick Noboza and what he might do to Simon?

Linda blamed part of her restlessness on the weather. It made her feel even worse than she'd been feeling already. A thunderstorm had been brooding for days over the city. Why it didn't explode and be done with it – as it usually did at this time of the year – nobody could understand. The leaden yellow-crested clouds piled up each day, dark and ominous as the deadly mushroom pall from an atomic blast. People looked up at them with exasperated hope. They longed for relief from the brazen eye of the sun. The heat came at you from the skies and hit you from the hot earth below, like sjambok blows out of sizzling stone pavements in the city, or the baked sandy earth in Sophiatown's streets. The heat blared at you like Sonny Matyolo's saxophone used to do, swelling to a strident peak of sound; it shrivelled your brain; it pressed on you like the walls of a prison cell.

On an impulse Linda went early that Thursday evening to Angels One, hoping and yet fearing to find Simon there. She saw Ma-jaze eyeing her from the doorway of her den, but she deliberately avoided talking to her. Simon was nowhere to be seen. In a short time she found the stifling heat of the place unbearable. Racking her brains to think whom she could go and see, she remembered her old friend Miriam Ndisele, whom she had already been in contact with to ease her loneliness after Simon's departure. Older than Linda, she had one important thing in her favour – she had known her brother Joel well. Linda found comfort in listening to the one person she knew who remembered her brother – her only link with her lost family.

Miriam worked for an English-speaking white family and occupied a room in the backyard of her employer's house. It wasn't safe travelling at night to the edge of a city suburb where the white people lived, and it certainly wouldn't be any cooler there. But with a perverse determination Linda decided to make the journey. It would be better than sitting still while this desperate feeling went on churning inside her.

Downing her drink at a gulp, Linda called to nobody in particular: 'Well, I'm off.'

The few clients around gave her a careless 'Cheerio.'

The ever-inquisitive Ken Madoda tried to hold her back.

'Where are you off to now, Linda Malindi?'

'To Miriam Ndisele, to the place where she works, if you'd like to know. Any objection?'

Ken answered her in a serious tone. 'Your brother's friend is a true friend. I can understand. But why on such a night as this? And can't you wait until she gets her night off? Her white missus may – well – you know – '

Linda shrugged. 'To hell with her white missus.'

'Agreed. But all the same – '

'I'm suffocating to death here in this heat and that's a fact.'

'You're going in the wrong direction,' he quipped knowingly, well aware of what was driving her.

'And what might that mean?' she snapped, throwing off his friendly hand on her arm.

In a totally different but still serious tone he answered her.

'The cops will nab you in the city streets for trespassing. But don't let me keep you.' He shrugged in turn.

There were no buses for non-whites to take her to the suburb where Miriam worked as cook to the affluent white family, but Linda reckoned she could make it by taking several short cuts. She didn't need to hurry. After all, she was out to kill time – and whatever else it was that was eating her.

Her limbs felt leaden in the sultry air. From time to time a distant flicker of lightning shook the dark of the sky, soundless, like the muscles of a cheetah rippling his body as he leaps for his prey.

Traversing the pavements of this alien, hostile region she began mechanically counting the street lights; there were none in the black townships. Behind high, well-trimmed hedges she caught glimpses of spacious mansions. Through the locked gates she could see wide lighted windows barricaded with iron burglar proofing, the fancy design failing to disguise its prison-like function. She started when two watchdogs snarled and barked as they bounded the whole length of a garden railing. She snatched the hem of her dress out of their reach as they scrabbled to push their snouts through the bars to bite at her legs. Their barking set up a chorus of dogs near and far; a hysterical sound, the very voice of the angst of this City of Gold.

For it was not only Linda who was frightened. Fear stalked the streets of the City of Gold at night. Fear of the black man, to whom after sunset it was a forbidden city. Of the hundreds of thousands who worked there by day, only a few were allowed to remain legally by night. These were the maidservants – like Linda's friend Miriam Ndisele – who occupied a boxroom in the backyards of big houses; or menservants, workers in blocks of flats, who occupied kennels at the very top of the buildings.

It could not be said that the streets of suburbia belonged at night either to the whites or the blacks. Within their own closed circuits, the blacks would visit a fellow servant in a nearby backyard, or climb to a kennel-in-the-sky for a game of cards, a drink and some fun.

Linda hurried past a nightwatchman who stood like a shadow inside a gate.

He did not greet Linda.

Further on she shrank into the hedge while the gates of a house were opened as if by invisible hands. A long, gleaming car emerged, headlights full on. She caught a glimpse of a black chauffeur in uniform and an elderly white woman in sparkling evening dress sitting in the back seat. A watchman closed the gates after them. No doubt he would be standing there and would open the gates again when his employer returned. The chauffeur would deposit her on the doorstep and the watchman would once more close the gates.

Two men in starched white uniforms stood chatting outside a gate. They greeted Linda as she passed. 'You better look out,' called one of the men to Linda.

'Have you your *dompas* on you?'

'Me! Carry a *dompas*?' She laughed and carried on.

A few moments later she heard the familiar sound of a pickup van drive at speed out of a side street making straight for the gate where the two men still stood chatting and smoking. Glancing swiftly back she saw the van stop. Two policemen leapt out. The men were trying to shut the gate in their faces but they were yanked out on to the pavement. Then started an altercation about their passes. 'I work here!' shouted one of the men. My pass is inside. And this is my friend – '

Linda saw the police seize the two men, yelling at them and dragging them into the van. In terror she fled blindly into another street, not knowing where she was going.

Suddenly a hand shot out and seized her arm. Her heart lurched. Another hand clamped over her mouth, stifling her scream as she fought madly to escape. Then an all too familiar voice spoke: 'Gently on, Linda. It's me. I won't let them touch you.'

She could hardly believe her senses.

'You – Simon!' She clung to him as if she would never again let him go. For a moment they forgot where they were, in alien territory.

'How? How did you know where to find me?'

'You silly one. We missed each other at Ma-jaze's. Oh, just by a few minutes. But thanks to Ken – '

'He always was a nosy-parker,' she said, unable to stop her smile.

'Let's get out of here,' he said, gripping her arm and forcing her on at a steady pace. 'I saw the pickup van. What possessed you to venture into these parts at this time of night?'

'What do you think? I was looking for you,' she jibed, knowing that in essence she was speaking the truth.

'Come on. We're going home,' he said. There was no doubt as to who was master of the situation.

Their bodies close together they hurried silently along, looking over their shoulders, cutting through side streets, taking no chances. They were leaving behind them the region of dogs on guard, barred gates and lamps.

Above them the dark canopy of the sky grew ever blacker, the ominous clouds occasionally lit by a tumbling succession of distant lightning. This was followed by a boom of thunder, though still distant. Simon stopped for a second to look at his wristwatch.

'Let's make for Marsh's Corner,' he said. 'With luck we'll just be in time to catch the last bus.'

Their luck was in. And they were no sooner seated when, peering through the muddy windows at the eerie landscape a shaft of lightning zigzagged the darkness. A salvo of deafening sound split the atmosphere. Simon and Linda clasped hands and their smiling faces were jaggedly reflected in the glass. Seconds later heavy raindrops exploded on the dusty window panes.

'They look just like bullet holes,' said Linda, pressing her head against Simon's shoulder.

Arrived at the terminus, the bus load tumbled and scattered into the already muddy alleyways. Small dongas gored by the rushing rains of other storms only made the going more hazardous. Still holding hands, Simon and Linda hurried along, heedless as the artillery of the heavens let loose a barrage of sound as if to make up for the unnatural calm of these last smouldering days. The skies reverberated; the summer rain pounded down, and the usual gloom of Sophiatown alleys was shot with a lurid glow that fitfully illuminated the craggy dongas now turned into torrents of mud and sand. With a sense of exultation the lovers ran stumbling and laughing and at last reached home – their home.

Soaked to the skin they peeled off their clinging clothes, fought laughingly over the towel Linda had seized to dry herself. Tossing it at Simon she leapt away and on to the bed.

She lay still a moment, then slowly held out her hand to him. Her expression had a gentleness he had never seen in her before. Hardly breathing he approached the bed and sank into her arms.

Not a word had been spoken. The great gap of time needed only the silent passion of their loving.

The storm had outspent itself. The morning light filtered past the curtains and unwillingly Simon opened his eyes. He gazed with contentment and peace and wonderment at the sleeping woman beside him. Nothing would part them now, he told himself. Gently he touched her. She stirred, snuggled closer into his arm but did not open her eyes.

Glancing at his watch he sat up with a jerk. He had a bus to catch and the queue would already be forming. It would be all right for Linda, who hadn't a job at the moment. Out of bed and scrambling for his clothes, he was struck with a new thought: 'Good God. It's Friday! Tonight's the night.'

Linda's voice from the bed made him spin round. He hadn't realised he'd spoken aloud.

'Friday. So – what's on tonight?'

She was sitting up, wide awake.

'I –'

'Oh, so you don't want to tell me.'

'It's – kind of a secret, Linda.'

'Not for me, it isn't. No more secrets between you and me, Simon. Ever again. Come,' she said, smiling and holding out her hand to him with that come-hither look of hers he knew so well.

He went on with his hurried dressing. 'I'm late,' he said.

'So what?'

She watched him from the bed.

Her intent look disturbed him. If only he didn't have to go to work.

'Come on, Simon. Out with it.'

So he told her, briefly. But his casual air did not deceive her.

'So, you're a big guy, in with the gang now. You know what Jo Bula's like?'

'How do you mean?'

'He'll eat you up and spit the pips out. Is Noboza in on this business?'

'Of course.'

'You know that guy hates your guts.'

'I can't do anything about that. We're on a job.'

'I don't like it.'

Naked, Linda stood close to him, but she did not touch him.

'Linda, what's come over you? This'll mean a good haul for us. You and me, Linda.' He drew her into his arms. 'You and me, at last!'

For a moment she clung to him. Then she pushed him away, went to the bed and carelessly pulled a garment round her shoulders, preoccupied with her fears.

He knew too well that stubborn lip of hers, the battle in her eyes.

'I'm late as hell now,' he said.

'*Simon!*'

'What? I'm late.'

'Don't go tonight.'

'In heaven's name, Linda. I must. What would the rest of the bunch think of me – a skunk?'

'Let them think what they like. Somebody else will be glad to jump into your place.'

'You know it's not possible. Linda . . .' He looked at her, lying huddled on the bed. He moved towards her, stopped, then moved again. 'I want you to be proud of me.'

'You fool. You don't need to prove yourself to anybody. You are Simon. *My* Simon. We are together.'

Her hands were about his neck.

He freed himself but still held her wrists.

'What's come over you today? My brave warrior, that's what I call you.'

'Then you should be strapping on my armour – '

'I'm not laughing. Simon – for my sake – don't go with them tonight.'

'But it's for your sake I want to be in on this business.'

'So much for your protestations last night!' She jerked her wrists away. 'You've had me. Now go to hell.'

'Linda! God, will you and I ever be at peace with each other?'

'Never. Go on, you're late.'

She turned her back on him.

'I promise you I'll be careful as hell.'

She ignored him.

'I'll come straight back here. See you wait up for me, eh?'

With a gesture of blind appeal, he hesitated. Then quickly he opened the door, shutting it quietly behind him.

Linda heard the click. She swung round.

'Simon!'

She was alone in an empty room. She sat on the untidy bed, staring at her thoughts.

It was past midnight in the City of Gold. They were all set for the job. Every move had been calculated. There had been just one small hitch, a short, sharp exchange of words between Noboza and Jo Bula over choosing Simon Manzana as one of the outfit. After all, he was a novice – a *moegoe* – who hadn't even done time .

'You fool, harping on that again,' snapped Jo Bula. 'Manzana's no *moegoe*. Manzana's okay. Trust me to know that. And what I say goes! And let me tell you, Noboza, I've had just about enough of your grousing. Understand?'

Noboza gazed back at the man he loved.

Jo Bula dismissed him with a gesture. 'Snap out of it!' he said.

The altercation was over before the others had time to notice it.

Well-primed in their respective roles, and armed with the necessary tools, the five men left Jo Bula at his place at exactly one o'clock in the morning. He himself, according to his usual custom, remained behind – the mastermind in his den. The group assumed a casual air and Simon did his best to imitate them, but there was a burning ball of excitement in his chest. He fingered his automatic to make sure it was there. He knew Ben Kwethuba also had a gun. The others favoured knife practice and no doubt blades had been sharpened.

They drove off in Jo Bula's Buick, Noboza at the wheel. The plan was to drop Simon near the site of his van-removing trick, proceed to an out-of-the-way spot outside the city and wait for Simon to catch up. Then they would all transfer to the van, depositing themselves inside and leaving the Buick well hidden till their return. They had no intention of letting the cops nose around, interfering with their little game – not if they could help it.

The preliminary stages went off without a hitch. Simon headed the stolen van for the industrial heart of the forbidden city. It had enough petrol for the job, thank God! Sitting alone in the front, his live cargo safely hidden inside, Simon kept a sharp lookout for the roaming police vans always hungry for their prey. He was in charge.

As he drove along the empty streets, still with their lamps blazing, they seemed to him to have a ghostly air, as if the white crowds had fled in terror from some aerial visitation. Gaudily illuminated shop-windows, laden with merchandise, looked as if they too had been precipitately deserted by their infatuated devotees, fleeing from their doomed city. But for him, too, with his precious human cargo, there was peril in this light that assaulted the eyes.

The glare was mercifully lessened as he swiftly approached the site of their objective. Here was the region of factories and warehouses, storehouses full of costly goods, but emptied of their legion of workers. At this dread hour of night only a pale, secretive light here and there marked where a nightwatchman kept his lonely vigil.

Here it was! The old three-storey building he had already familiarised himself with.

Switching off his headlamps, Simon slowed down, quietly sliding the van forward over the last few hundred yards. The four men tumbled out of the back of the van almost before he had stopped.

'Here we go!' whispered Nick Noboza. And to Simon: 'When I signal, bring the van as close as you can for loading. You know the spot. Then be ready for the take-off.'

Simon felt that these injunctions were superfluous. Noboza liked to play the little boss.

The four men disappeared into the grounds of the building and Simon was left alone in the darkness. He switched off the engine.

For the first few minutes his ears were at the stretch to catch the slightest hint of danger. Diz Dinake and Ted Nompu had their work cut out tackling the two outside watchmen, the more brutally swift and silent the better. If there was another watchman inside, one clumsy move and he would set off the alarm – then the cops would be on them like a hundred devils.

So far so good. He thought he heard a thud and a smothered groan, but that was only because he was listening for it. When, after another minute or two nothing happened, he assumed that the second watchman must have been successfully gagged.

Now Noboza and Ben must be at the windows on the side of the building. Straining to listen and hearing no further sound he assumed that if they'd encountered anyone inside, they'd been able to silence him. As he waited, Simon had the sensation of being marooned in a dark, shoreless no-man's-land, out of sight and hearing of anything human. Those men inside the building – he could not feel they had any sense of comradeship with him, though they all faced a common danger. He pictured what they were doing. But what was the use? His part of the job came later. Nick Noboza . . . He did not want to think about Nick Noboza.

Unbidden, the image of Linda rose up in his mind; confused images of their passion and then their quarrel that morning. He had not been able to return to her place, as he had half hoped he might. They had all gone straight to Jo Bula's after work. He could understand Linda's anxiety for his safety. Yet he would have expected her to be as full of the excitement of the game as he was. Oh, he'd make it up to her when he got back. Then they'd laugh together at her silly fears. Tixo! His companions were taking too long over the job. It was time for the next stage. Waiting was the worst part of it –

Ah, there was Dinake running up to the van.

'Nick Noboza is cursing. He says to bring the van to the side. Quick, you bastard!'

That hadn't been the arrangement but Simon obeyed without a word.

For the next space of immeasurable time neither thought nor feeling existed for Simon. All his attention was concentrated on the job in hand, cool, controlled, yet with a sensation of being at the centre of a whirling vortex. Along with Noboza, Ben and Dinake, he worked with demonic energy to load the van. They had left Ted Nompu as the lookout man.

They had nearly finished when an ear-splitting police whistle speared the darkness.

Simultaneously Ted Nompu rushed up. His speech was almost incomprehensible. One of the watchmen left lying in the grounds had sufficiently recovered from their blows to start up an unholy squawking. This had brought two policemen sprinting from out of nowhere. There'd been no time to cosh the watchman into silence. Hell was let loose. Any minute now the flying squad would be on the spot –

Simon leapt into the driver's seat, Noboza beside him, while the other three dived into the van among the bulging bales. Would they get away ahead of the flying squad? Simon swung the van, jerking the wheel, skidding round the corner of the building and almost knocking over one of the policemen who had responded to the watchman's cry.

A shot rang out, narrowly missing Simon's head. The windscreen was shattered, drenching his face and neck with a shower of glass.

Noboza shouted that the back doors of the van had swung open; another shot must have found its mark, for there was a screaming howl from inside. Which one of them had been hit?

Answering shots volleyed back at the policeman who was running after them for all he was worth. That must be Ben's gun. The frenzied speed of the car sent the shots wide. Then Noboza leaned out from his side and fired. The policeman let out a mighty bellow and fell squirming to the ground.

'That's got the bastard!' yelled Noboza.

'It was unnecessary to have more blood on our hands,' Simon remarked involuntarily.

'Keep your bloody mouth shut.'

Simon did not see the expression on Noboza's face, but dodged as the man made as if to strike him.

The car raced on. Simon was relieved that they seemed to have got a good start on the flying squad.

'Faster, faster!' shouted Noboza. 'Step on the gas! The police van will eat us up on this hill.'

But their stolen van was an up-to-the-minute model and responded like a bird to Simon's touch on the accelerator. Twisting, turning and hugging the byways, he piloted the van out of the city. He was reasonably certain they had shaken off their pursuers, though they weren't out of the woods yet. The pack would be hunting them through the night.

Would Jo Bula's Buick be where they had left it hidden? Warily Simon approached the spot and, with a shout of relief, Nick Noboza was the first to catch sight of it. At desperate speed they transferred the stuff to the Buick and abandoned the stolen van. Ted Nompu had received a glancing shot in the shoulder and was bleeding profusely. Noboza cursed at the damage to one or two of the bales from the shots and Ted's superfluous blood, as well as his clumsy efforts to help with the loading. This trail of blood would do them no good.

With Noboza at the wheel, the Buick sped back into Sophiatown, into those streets where the police seldom ventured at night unless in force, with Saracens and Sten guns. Here township gangsterdom could pursue its violent course with impunity.

Relieved of his strenuous responsibility, Simon slumped back among the bales, oblivious of where he was. His companions had relaxed and were giving expression to their gleeful sense of achievement. Curiously enough Nick Noboza was uncommonly taciturn; on such occasions it had been his habit to lead the chorus of self-congratulation.

Simon felt nothing but enormous lassitude, a sense not of achievement but of having emptied himself out to the last drop of his substance both of body and spirit. He longed to lie down and sleep. If he could only sleep! And he knew exactly where he wanted to lay his head. There was only one bosom that could give him rest.

The deeds of night and darkness had still to be completed. None of them would take long. Such deeds never do.

Having dumped the bales of cloth at different prearranged hideouts, the group reported back to Jo Bula, who was waiting for them. Not much was said, but what was said was to the point. There was the problem of quick distribution. As a matter of urgency, arrangements for meeting contacts next morning were forthwith discussed and settled.

'How do we split?' asked Noboza.

Jo Bula was as stingy as he dared. They haggled a bit and finally agreed with some grumbling to their respective shares.

'You've done a good job, fellows,' said Jo Bula. 'Pity about all that shooting. You're a bit quick on the trigger, you know, Noboza.'

Noboza growled. 'I wasn't the only one shooting.'

'I hope there isn't a dead man on our hands, eh? Then we'll have to lie low a bit longer.'

They heartily agreed and without more ado the group broke up.

'Going my way?' asked Ted of Diz Dinake, whereupon they set off together. Ben Kwethuba accompanied Simon only a short distance. His room was not far off.

'Stay well, Ben,' said Simon.

'Go well,' said Ben.

Simon continued his way alone, his thoughts travelling ahead of him. She would be asleep. He would creep in quietly. Press up close to her and tomorrow . . . tomorrow . . .

Nick Noboza was the last to leave Jo Bula's. The two men had a drink together and Noboza helped himself to a stiff one. Then he, too, set off on foot in the same direction as Simon Manzana.

He seemed to be in a hurry.

A few hours later, in the grey light of dawn, a woman on her way to work stumbled over the body of a young man lying face down in a Sophiatown alleyway. He had been stabbed in the back.

His name was Simon Manzana, and his pass book was not in order. The police took charge of the body. They confiscated the gun, an illegal weapon.

'A useful little thing,' they said.

The body was taken to the police mortuary, where Ma-jaze traced it late that day. She and Ken Madoda brought the news to Linda.

It was a few weeks later that Jo Bula was having a small celebration at Ma-jaze's. That night he danced only with Linda Malindi. She sat at his table and her laughter was the gayest of any in the room.

'I like you because you know how to laugh,' he said.

And she laughed again, right in his face. But that night she did not let him take her home.

In her present mood all the world seemed foul and treacherous, a bawdy house for laughter. When she entered her empty room she stared about her. This room, filled with the ghosts of all their happy hours together. The ghosts of every sound of that voice, every movement, every turn of his body towards her.

A deadly stillness came over her limbs and numbed her mind. Treading slowly, like a sleepwalker, she went over to her dressing table, sank on to the stool and sat staring at her face in the mirror, searching for an answer.

A long time she sat, adjusting the side mirrors, studying her face from every angle, unable to stir herself to lie down in her bed – her empty bed.

The face looking back at her she did not know. It was the mask of a face.

That was all.

It said nothing and gave no answer to her staring.

ACKNOWLEDGEMENTS

I am grateful to Alison Lowry and everyone at Penguin South Africa for bringing to reality my mother's dream to have her fiction published by Penguin.

A special thank you to Dr Pallo Jordan and The Department of Arts and Culture for their recognition of Dora Taylor's contribution to South African literature, in awarding her the South African Literary Posthumous Award 2008.

I would also like to thank my husband Colin for his patience, forbearance and cooperation during the editing and preparation of the manuscript.

And most importantly my love and devotion to my mother, especially for completing the final chapter while in a state of despair at never being able to return to her beloved South Africa.

Dora Taylor, Aberdeen University, 1922

Dora & Sheila, Zambia, 1962

Dora Taylor

Dora Taylor was born in Scotland in 1899. Orphaned at an early age, she suffered physical abuse and neglect by a succession of indifferent relatives, until eventually she was adopted by the headmistress of the local Aberdeen school. Though this straight-laced Victorian spinster gave her neither love nor affection, she nevertheless gave her the opportunity to develop her intellectual abilities. After graduating with an MA Honours degree in English Literature at Aberdeen University, where she met her future husband, James Garden Taylor, she became a teacher, inspiring new generations with her passionate love of literature. In 1924 Jim, as James Taylor was known to all, accepted a post as lecturer in psychology at the University of Cape Town, where later his pioneering research into perception led to major advances in that science. After their marriage in 1926, Dora joined him in Cape Town, a city that would change her forever and inspire her life's work.

With seeming inevitability Dora was drawn into intellectual discussion in a politically motivated climate where with her pen she was moved to contribute to the struggle for a non-racial democracy in South Africa, collaborating with the African leader, I.B. Tabata. Always careful to keep a low profile, she used a variety of pseudonyms. Her *Role of the Missionaries in Conquest* in particular was greatly valued, a radical history of missionary activity and colonial conquest in South Africa, first published in 1952 under the pseudonym *Nosipho Majeke*. This historical work was reprinted in 1986 and distributed in universities and colleges, devoured by those seeking to unravel the truth, and although now out of print is still sought after.

But ultimately, while in Boston, Massachusetts where Jim had been invited in the early sixties to lecture at Harvard University, Dora was advised against returning home because of a spate of arrests by the S.A. Government. She never recovered from being torn from her beloved South Africa and the friends and colleagues she had left behind, and died in exile in England in 1976.

She was a poet, playwright, short story writer, essayist and novelist; a philosopher, a literary critic, a teacher and a lecturer. As a devotee of all the arts, and hungry for knowledge in every sphere, she was an avid theatre goer, film buff, music and ballet lover, and made frequent trips to museums and art galleries in Europe and America. She imparted this passion to her three daughters, and to all those friends, young and old, with whom she loved to talk away the night.

She was for many years Literary Adviser to the Junior Literary Society, during which time she was responsible for compiling *The Treasure Casket*, eight volumes of selected literature for children. For this publication she wrote the introductions and chose and edited all the works included in the volumes; she also responded to hundreds of young readers' and their parents' query letters on subjects ranging from birth control to the origin of the universe.

To her sorrow none of her prose fiction was published in her lifetime, though in 1928 four of her early poems were included in *Some Scottish Verse - an Anthology of Contemporary Scottish Poetry*, published in London. Although some of her plays were performed by an amateur group in Cape Town, none was commercially published, and the long, hauntingly beautiful dramatic poem, *Tristan and Iseult*, was never submitted for publication.

However, the bulk of her work was non-fiction, and in the 1940s and 50s more than a hundred literary and political critiques were published in the progressive magazine *Trek*, using several pen names. Among her works of literary criticism is a 148-page piece on Gorky, and an almost complete study of Nadine Gordimer, which she was working on when she died. Other South African writers covered are Pauline Smith, Sarah Gertrude Millin, Olive Schreiner and Alan Paton, to name but a few. In her literary criticisms she always looked at the authors' fundamental beliefs, including their racial attitudes, in the context of the socio-economic backgrounds. This gave her work a wider significance within the political climate of the time, making her a unique figure in the recent history of South Africa.

Dora was a small, graceful woman, nimble in her movements and nimble in thought. A person of intense emotion, exceptionally sensitive to mood and expression in others, she gave the appearance of being shy and reserved, but had great hidden strengths. Her deep concern, her pity and her empathy for all disadvantaged people, no matter who they were or where in the world they lived, or how they came to be in a state of desperation, was the stimulus for all her writing.

Sheila Belshaw, 2007

BY THE SAME AUTHOR

Kathie   Dora Taylor

Kathie was born as dark as her Cape Coloured father. This was a social disaster in the eyes of her mother and near-white grandmother, who rejoice when Kathie's new baby sister Stella is fair skinned. Nothing is going to stop them propelling Stella into Cape Town's privileged white world. Kathie adores her little sister, but only when Stella is sent to a white school does Kathie learn, with a terrible sense of shock, that she is 'different' from her sister. While Stella strives to join the white world, Kathie throws herself into her studies, though she never abandons her sister, whose painfully convoluted life is finally intertwined with her own in a most astonishing way.

Cruelly opposed by the unyielding forces of the times, Kathie remains undaunted. Even as the final cataclysmic event overwhelms her, she declares, 'The future is ours!'

'Kathie is absorbing. Dora Taylor's novel is thoroughly alert to the social geography and complex snobberies of 1950s Cape Town. As such, *Kathie* is interesting to read as a lively account of place and period. What makes it still a fresh and enjoyable read is Taylor's crisp prose and sharply drawn characters wrapped within a compelling narrative. In other words Taylor's sense of humanity's foibles is combined with good storytelling.'

– Professor Vivian Bickford-Smith, Head of Department of Historical Studies, University of Cape Town

BY THE SAME AUTHOR

Don't Tread On My Dreams Dora Taylor

Whether set in Cape Town, Johannesburg or the remoteness of lonely farms, these stories present an acute and heartfelt sensitivity for the troubles of ordinary people during apartheid. They provide a rare historical record of the times, revealing the hopes and dreams of people of all races, that are only now becoming a reality

Dora Taylor's powers of observation enable her to conjure up the vibrancy of a city, the squalor of a shanty town or the peace of the veld. Although the stories are often heart-rendingly tragic, there is always an underlying quality of hope, springing from the author's intense desire that things should improve, an objective to which she devoted her life.

Although forced to leave in 1963, Dora Taylor never gave up her struggle to bring about change in South Africa. She was unable to return to her beloved Cape Town and died in exile in 1976. These stories, written in the 1950s and 60s, were safely kept amongst Taylor's papers for many years after her death. They are published here for the first time, in the climate of today's new South Africa, and are all the more remarkable in the context of the recent past.

'The publication of these works by the late Dora Taylor is a moment of profound significance in South African literary history.'

– Professor Ciraj Rassool, University of the Western Cape